Books in the Parabaloni Series:

The Parabaloni

The Slingshot Effect

As the Eagle Flies

Solitaire

Adèlie Angst

Blind Leader

The Parabaloni

Parabaloni 1

Catherine Gruben Smtih

Be brave, for the Lord your God is with you.

Catherine Gruben Smith

Sola Deo Gloria

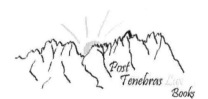

"In the beginning God created... and man became a living soul."
-*Genesis 1:1, 2:7*

To my spectacular parents; thanks for being bold enough to be peculiar people. (1 Peter 2:9, Deuteronomy 6:6-7)

Contents

PROLOGUE

The freight elevator seemed to drop forever, its hums and groans sounding remarkably like an achy troll to the reporter standing nervously on its metal floor. Jenny Rhen was trembling like a leaf, but it was from excitement, not fear. Or that's what she told herself as she readjusted the stolen black hood covering her head. Jenny had been an investigative reporter for thirty years, and yet this felt like her first real story. She had found a group of hooded murderers working inside America. A strange, nefarious gang had been spotted at two different murder scenes she was working, in two different states. It was like a resurgence of the Klu Klux Klan, or something equally as strange and frightening. They all wore hoods covering their entire face and head, and even called each other by coded names; and this bizarre story was all hers. But right now she didn't have much of a story besides their mysterious headwear. She needed to know what they were doing before she could write it up, and get some proof. Which meant a few risks were necessary. It had taken a lot of guts to steal a hood and follow these crazies underground into what she assumed would be their headquarters, but Jenny Rhen had always had plenty of guts.

The elevator finally drew to a shuddering, jerky stop, and the door slid open. An enormous, domed, white cavity filled the reporter's vision, with a vast silver picture of a healthy oak tree growing out of a dying tree. White plaster spread over the natural Vermont rocks and gave the underground hideaway a surprising modernity. It was as large as a Philadelphian shopping mall, with two levels liberally pocked with doors, four different escalators, and people moving everywhere despite the fact it was ten at night on a weekday. Jenny stepped briskly into the crowd, moving confidently with her notebook in full view. Someone who looked confident and

11

busy was hardly ever noticed, she knew from hard-won experience. Inside, her mind whirled and her stomach flipped in fear. There were hundreds of people down here. All of them wore the black hoods of this strange murderous group, the ends draping elegantly over their shoulders, the almond shaped eyeholes the only thing to show it was a human underneath the black fabric. Jenny had no idea this group was so large. If there were this many of them just down here, there must be thousands of these scary hooded people wandering over America. She thought of how slowly that elevator moved and the single, long concrete hallway it opened to at the top, and suddenly realized she had no real escape route. And judging from the little she did know of these hooded weirdoes, there would be no mercy either. For just a moment she inwardly cursed her editor, Daniel Yates, for setting her on this trail in the first place. Then her eye caught something and her fiery reporter's curiosity burned away her fear.

Jenny Rhen passed a hallway and saw someone in a white lab coat turn a sharp corner five yards from her. He wore a white hood instead of a black one. She spun into the hallway without a second thought, her worn sneakers making hardly a sound as she padded over the tile floor in cautious pursuit of the white figure, and moved on around a sharp corner with the same confident ease that had carried her through the crowded main room. A white-walled hallway stretched on for some thirty feet in front of her, and it was starkly empty. But a smooth metal door rested at her left elbow and a large picture window spanned half the length of the hall. Inside the window was a very large lab, gleaming in its spotlessness. The multitude of metal tables and counters were packed with test tubes, some empty, some filled with a thick red liquid that almost glowed. The white figure moved past the window on the inside of the lab, toward a large silver machine at the back of the room. Jenny squinted, trying to get a closer look. For a wild instant the gadget made her think of the cold morgues she had been in during the course of her career. There was a section with a rounded bottom and a square, thick lid with a shape and size that could fit a small person inside. It was rocking back and forth in a gentle motion, with wires of white, yellow, and red attached at the thick base of the machine. Jenny pursed her lips trying to remember where she had seen something like this before. The lab worker moved toward a touch screen mounted in a blocky fashion on the top left of the silver machine, and Jenny suddenly knew. It was during her story on the flu vaccine; she had gone into the lab where various people were using different tests in their research, and seen one of these immense gadgets. It was a WAVE Bioreactor 200, designed to create a safe place for cultures of viruses to grow. They were making something nasty here.

The lab worker tapped a button with his white gloved hand and the touch screen blinked to life. Jenny stared through her glasses, unconsciously stepping closer to the window as she tried to get the right focus through her gradual lenses, and cursing old age's affect on her vision. Her stolen hood's skinny eyeholes were not helping and she whipped the black fabric off, managing to focus in time to read the words that flicked to life at the top of the screen and see what was in that bioreactor. "Adenovirus Cultures Batch 104" it said, as clear as Richard Harding Davis had described the German's march into Brussels. Jenny stifled an ecstatic squeak as she realized she had confirmed her deepest fear with this group, and gained her reporter's gleeful hope of a world-changing story[1]. These hooded crazies were making a live virus, a ton of it judging by all the test

---

[1] Some argue that Jenny Rhen had already written a world-changing story when she uncovered the gumbo smugglers some eight years ago, but Jenny has always held it only exposed the gang in the mid-west and left the rest of the world unchanged.

tubes scattered around, for some nefarious purpose of their own. This was the evidence she needed to write her story.

Jenny pulled her miniature camera out of her pocket and began to snap pictures. She was ecstatic with her find. But her excitement and the knowledge she was getting the proof she needed distracted her. And her hearing was beginning to go the way of her eyesight, though only her husband admitted it yet, and Jenny was still in denial. She didn't hear the soft sound of footsteps that stopped suddenly at the corner of the hallway, and then pattered swiftly away. She didn't even hear the louder sounds of four pairs of feet treading cat-like toward her. The last sound Jenny Rhen heard was the burst of semi-automatic gunfire that sliced through the still air, ended her career, and left her husband a sorrowing widower. What was left of the reporter tumbled onto the messy tile, as a security guard's booted foot landed on her miniature camera, smashing it into a hundred pieces. A hand grabbed the back of the guard's shirt and heaved him back, slamming him into the wall.

"Idiot, we want to know who she was, and how much she knew!" A tall, sinewy man yelled at the guard. "Everything she carried goes to X. No one can know about us, especially until Operation Weed goes into effect on the 20th. And this spy might have told someone!"

"Understood, J," the guard gulped, nodding his hooded head a little too swiftly. This man was the eminent X's second in command, and a whim from J would mean death. "Nothing must hinder Operation Weed."

"Nothing must hinder our purpose; remember Operation Weed is just a small part of it," J growled. He motioned to the dead Jenny Rhen and snapped his fingers, done with the small talk. The

14

supple J watched dispassionately as the reporter's form was dragged past him, the same sort of bored stare one might give to a moth pinned on a card. It was a sentiment that played out in his life and his plans, and it was one of the main reasons X had chosen this man to be his third arm in his great enterprise. They would need such heartlessness to bring America under their control.

1

Simeon Lee's eyes traveled from his book to his wrist watch as the quiet hum of conversations not meant for him circulated through the rich, coffee-infused air. Someone laughed at a table across the room and Simeon turned his lonely gaze out the window to watch the moon slip into his sight, its silver rays beautifying even the small shopping center's parking lot. His eye landed on a black Nissan Z parked directly across from him, near the curb blocking the way into the slow street. The moon's enchanting light set it off well and he noted it was a very nice car. The convertible top was down and he could see the back of the driver, a brown-haired man sitting in an attitude of waiting. That would be a comfortable spot to wait. It was a pity that back looked so tense. Simeon sighed and stopped avoiding the point with himself.

It looked like the wild-haired young man that had suddenly accosted him on his way out of church Sunday and suggested this Tuesday evening coffee shop visit had stood him up. Oh well, he had accepted the invitation with a flutter of trepidation anyway. Despite the innumerable strange situations he had been in and out of, Simeon Lee still wasn't quite sure what was expected of him at an ordinary friendly visit. And that Mr. Tolliver had worn socks with dusty sandals to church, and was carrying a strange glossy black box under his arm. But even so, Simeon had thought it would be a nice change from his quiet duplex. Now it looked like Mr. Tolliver had decided an old man wasn't worth the effort. Or maybe he had simply forgotten about the distasteful chore he had made for himself on Sunday. He glanced at his watch again to see if he could

16

plausibly convince himself Mr. Tolliver was just late. Twenty minutes... Simeon had only been that late six times[2] in his forty-nine years, but he decided he would give this Vincent Tolliver a full half-hour before giving up.

Conversations filled the little room around him. Simeon sat silent, his eyes focused on the words in his little New Testament. The book was open to Romans, but he couldn't make himself comprehend the words. The empty chair across from him kept drawing his attention despite his efforts to ignore it. What would life have been like if someone had been able to fill that chair? He drummed his fingers on the table as he stared at the empty seat, and realized he recognized this mood. He needed someone to talk to. Or even better would be someone who would talk to him. Simeon pulled his flip phone out of his blazer pocket and navigated to the contacts quickly. Out of all the people who had come and gone in his life, there were three he knew would still always welcome him. One lived in the Caucus mountains and wasn't likely to answer his phone. Another was deep in the Mexican interior visiting his relatives and didn't have access to a phone. And then there was Saul. Simeon pressed the call button and put the trim black phone to his ear. It rang five times, the slow bell reverberating in his mind and making Simeon wonder if an echo could be mental. An automated message began to speak and Simeon snapped his phone closed without waiting for it to finish. He glanced at his watch, saw the thirty minutes grace period was gone, and stood up to leave. As he slid his New Testament into his pocket, Simeon's eye traveled to the large picture window in a well-formed habit of checking for possible threats before exiting a building.

---

[2] Simeon includes the time the greased dolphins and sea anemones hampered his movements in his list of times being late, but I don't agree. He wasn't actually expected at the undersea base and you can't arrive late to somewhere you are not expected.

A blond head whizzed past the window, the shaggy hair whipping around till it looked like some sort of writhing creature trying to eat its owner alive. Simeon watched Vincent Tolliver grab one of the white poles supporting the roof of the shop, winding himself around it to stop. His well-cared-for roller skates didn't fit with the rest of his shabby attire, but he was here. Simeon dropped his New Testament back on the table and moved toward the door as Vincent rushed in, the skates slung over his shoulder clanking against each other noisily. Simeon held out his hand, and the young man started to babble apologies for being late as he took it distractedly. As they strolled toward the counter to order, Simeon gathered he had run into weather that had increased his flight time while flying a freight somewhere. There was something about rabbits and pencils exploding mixed up in the rush of words. He held up a hand to stop the outpour and pointed at the menu.

"House coffee and Reuben," Simeon told the barista. He looked at Vincent Tolliver and raised an eyebrow inquisitively.

"Uh..." the young man started, blinking uncertainly at the menu. "Hey, you have hot chocolate here. One of those. With mint. And vanilla I think. And lots of whipped cream."

"Dinner?" Simeon insisted quietly, careful not to wince at that disgustingly sweet concoction. Vincent stared at the menu for a moment and shrugged. His stomach was doing somersaults and had been ever since he had looked at his watch and realized he was thirty minutes late again. This brother's spotless class and competent silence wasn't helping.

"I don't know. Just something like a sandwich I guess," Vincent told the barista, who was waiting with all the polite patience of the man with a tip jar. Their drinks were shoved at them

18

by a smiling girl, obviously proud of her quick time in getting them together. Simeon glanced at Vincent's wrinkled clothes, shoddy sandals, mode of transportation swinging back and forth on their laces, and paid. He waved away Vincent's objections and led the way back to his table. The two settled in the blocky wooden chairs, sipping their drinks and hoping the other would lead the way.

"You made a flight today?" Simeon broke the silence.

"Yeah, a cargo of tea needed to get to Boston," Vincent nodded. "I thought that was pretty appropriate considering the history of that town and tea."

"No Indians at the airport?" Simeon asked, a small smile breaking over his face. Vincent relaxed visibly at the lightened air of his companion. He did have a sense of humor, however slight. Maybe he would survive this meeting after all.

"Thankfully no," Vincent smiled back. "They would have had to carry it awhile before making it to the harbor, anyway. The turbulence wasn't too bad, and the fog made it kind of fun because when you can climb into clear air it's pretty keen. There's a lot of peace to flying. Have you flown a lot?"

"As a passenger," Simeon nodded.

"Being a passenger is even more peaceful, I guess. Do you like it?" Vincent asked. Simeon paused before he answered.

"No[3]." That conversation fizzled out. Vincent started another one to prevent the awkward silence that was trying to grow.

---

[3] He considered explaining that the eleven crashes, sixteen highjackings, and one flying torture room he had undergone had finally managed to give him a near phobia of planes, but decided that might be the wrong note to strike.

"So, you said you do something with the government, like most people around here?"

"An aide," Simeon nodded. "Paperwork mostly, in charge of the first batch through the office."

"A kind of first aide, huh?" Vincent grinned, and then looked quickly at his hot chocolate as the serious man in front of him still frowned[4]. "So, do you like the job?"

"Not entirely." Silence threatened to descend again, and in an attempt to forestall it Simeon expanded on his answer. "But I got too old for my other job. This one fell in my lap."

"Oh," answered Vincent a bit awkwardly. Simeon sipped his coffee again and tried to think of something else to say.

"I see your palm pilot in your pocket again. You like electronics?"

"Yeah, I'm also a computer engineer. My dad was a whiz at anything electronic. I guess I inherited some of his skill. Do you like computers or techy gadgets?" Simeon considered admitting he had looked on computers as enemies since they had begun to replace his favorite little note books, but chose not to.

"No, not really," he admitted instead. Silence reigned again.

"Have any family missing you tonight?" Simeon tried.

"No," Vincent said quickly, dropping his gaze to the brown liquid undulating lazily in his cup. That was an extremely touchy subject, and he didn't want to go into it right now. Tomorrow would mark a full year since his dad's accident in the lab had

---

[4] Simeon got the joke all right, he just didn't think it was funny.

caused a massive explosion, killing both his parents, just a few days after his nineteenth birthday. That was the reason he had been desperate enough to ask a random stranger at church for a coffeehouse visit. This whole year he had existed in a sort of numb sorrow, just getting by from day to day. And he was starting to wake up enough to realize it wasn't good and he had to do something to drive him out of himself. This little visit was Vincent Tolliver's first real attempt at the effort, and it had taken a lot of courage to get him through the coffeehouse door. But now that he was here, he didn't want to talk about it.

"Oh," Simeon said simply, and that conversation died the gruesome death of the others they had tried to start. This silence was beginning to be oppressive, and was getting more awkward by the second. There had to be some interest they both held! Simeon tried a different question while he attempted to think of something.

"Think you'll always be a pilot and computer engineer?" he asked. Vincent pondered that one for a moment.

"No, I don't think so. I want to do more with my life, you know?" The pilot shifted positions as he tried to find the words to voice his half-formed thought. "I know I can glorify God and share His gospel in the jobs I have now, but I keep thinking there must be something else I can do. The world is in such a mess! Every time I hear about another evil law passed, or another bomb planted, I feel so...helpless. Like I ought to be doing something to help." Vincent paused a bit awkwardly. That probably wasn't what Mr. Lee had wanted, a bared soul their first real conversation. But far from looking embarrassed or bemused, Simeon Lee nodded seriously.

"Same. I see people whose souls are dead and a world overrun with evil. Then look at the forms I'm filling out and think, 'futile.'"

21

"Right," Vincent agreed. "And as Christians it seems like our doing nothing is worse than if we didn't know the truth. Here we are on this earth, with a renewed heart and God's own words and promises. We have a reason to eliminate evil and promote righteousness and justice, and to help people. I guess I haven't really done much about it yet because I haven't found..." Vincent paused, his lips pursed slightly as he looked for the phrase he wanted.

"Haven't found the right place to jump into the fight?" Simeon suggested.

"Yeah, that's it exactly!" Vincent nodded, his freckled face lighting up with a sunny smile that Simeon Lee noted turned the young man into a very likeable character. "It is a fight, and it's an important one. It seems like Christians nowadays don't think about the fighting aspect at all. Sometimes you have to risk things for the gospel's sake, to reach people. You know, in the early church there was a group of Christians who risked their lives just to help the sick and dying. They ran toward plague victims instead of away from them, and called themselves the Parabaloni, the Gamblers, because they were gambling with their lives to help their fellow men. If there were more Christians like that around today, Christians who were willing to actually get up off the couch and risk some things for others, the world might not be in such an evil state. That's the way to let your light shine, and to be the salt of the earth! Be willing to risk everything for the sake of spreading God's light, and pushing back the evil!"

"You're right," Simeon said simply. The barista interrupted to ask who had which sandwich, and the conversation paused to get the food sorted out. As the coffee shop worker wandered away, Simeon noted with satisfaction that Vincent's sandwich was starting

22

to disappear. Aged fourteen or forty-nine Simeon Lee instinctively wanted to take care of people, and this young man was entirely too skinny. He decided he should allow Mr. Tolliver breathing room to chew, and started up the conversation thread again. "Our Savior risked everything for us. Risking some things for each other is necessary. Risks are a part of life, and taking on the right ones and avoiding the wrong ones ought to be one of a Christian's main concerns. That mindset also allows us to personally help restrain evil."

"You mean in our own lives?" Vincent asked cheerfully.

"Certainly. But also more. Police and FBI put out posters and warnings. If each Christian was willing to help catch criminals, consciously thinking about it as they live, few criminals would get away, and fewer people would be hurt."

"That makes sense," Vincent commented and went back to his sandwich. He had realized he was hungry when his stomach had stopped flipping. This Simeon Lee wasn't scary after all despite how serious he seemed. Simeon took a drink of his coffee and gazed out the window at the parking lot. The moon had moved past his line of sight but the same little Nissan Z was still there. So was its occupant. And he was squirming, as if he were worried. Simeon saw the man in the Z stiffen, and he looked quickly around the parking lot for the reason. A PT Cruiser had just pulled in. It circled around the other cars slowly, making Simeon quietly wonder if it was checking to see if the area was secure to stop. As the Cruiser drove past their window, Simeon caught a glimpse of the driver. Hawk nose, olive skin, thin, black hair, eye color – Simeon froze in his automatic assessment, his cup halfway to his mouth. Those eyes were deep and dark. And blank. He had looked into many of those kinds of eyes before and recognized the hollow emptiness, it came

23

back to him in some very nasty dreams. This man was an assassin. No one else had that look. The knowledge combined with the idea of wanted posters he had just mentioned to Mr. Tolliver, and Simeon suddenly realized he had seen that face before. He watched as the man placed a pair of sunglasses over his horrible eyes and slid his car smoothly into the empty space next to the Nissan Z.

"So are you going to do anything to change it?" Vincent asked, not noticing his companion's absorption. "I mean, are you planning on staying as an aide and just seeing what comes up?" The driver of the Cruiser held out his hand to the Nissan's driver window. A very large amount of cash was held in that olive hand. "I guess there's not really much choice, is there? I don't usually run into suicide bombers I have to shoot down when flying, and I guess you don't usually have militant anarchists you have to tackle." The Nissan Z driver found whatever he was looking for in his attaché case and handed it to the assassin. It was a very small something to have cost that much cash. "Any ideas on how to incorporate our good ideas into real life?" Vincent tried again, attempting to get some sort of answer from his companion. Simeon Lee turned his face from the window and looked at the young man across from him. Vincent suddenly had the idea he was being sized up.

"Go for a drive," Simeon answered, a little enigmatically. He slid smoothly out of his chair and looked back at the young man as he slipped his New Testament into his pocket. "Coming?"

"Uh...sure," Vincent muttered, wondering a little at the sudden turn of their quiet talk. Simeon headed for the door, moving very quickly for someone going for a peaceful excursion. Vincent had to break into a jog to catch up with him. He led the way to a very handsome brown car backed into a space in an unobtrusive corner of the parking lot. The sharp lines and tapered hood that

24

ended in a sort of knife blade style marked it as a car from some twenty years ago, but its sheen and new tires showed it was very well cared for. Its owner pointed a finger at the passenger seat as he settled behind the wheel. Vincent slid in obediently, wondering where they were going. Simeon pulled out so fast it slammed the young man's door shut for him. Vincent quickly buckled his seat belt and shot a very confused and worried look at the man beside him. Simeon zoomed out of the parking lot, straight across three lines of busy traffic. Horns blared, and the night air was split by brilliant headlight beams seemingly coming at them from every direction. Vincent yelped and grabbed onto the dashboard, as if that would protect him somehow. Simeon's hand left the stick to push a small red button over his tape player as he settled in the far right lane of the busy road. A whirring sounded and an instrument panel slid out from underneath the radio. Vincent glimpsed a button marked 'oil spill' and one labeled 'jet pack.' Simeon pressed one that read simply 'tracker.'

"PT Cruiser," the older man told his car. A cement truck pulled into their street, and Simeon whizzed around it, ignoring the red traffic light directly in front of them. Horns blared, and he immediately dodged in between two SUV's to hide his little brown car from obvious sight of the commotion. It wouldn't do to be noticed in their tailing. "White. License, HJK 657." Another whirring noise started up.

"Three lanes to the left, fifty-two yards ahead," an automated voice spoke up from the car's dashboard. Vincent's mouth dropped open.

"What kind of car is this? What are we doing?" he gasped, closing his eyes involuntarily as Simeon sped out from between the SUV's and sent his little car zipping across four lanes again,

25

seemingly without a glance at the lethal hunks of hundreds of pounds of metal moving swiftly all around them.

"A good one. Boss let me keep it when I retired from my last job. We're chasing a terrorist assassin."

"Oh. Right." Vincent swallowed, trying to let his brain catch up. It did. "What? What terrorist? Why are we chasing him? Mr. Lee, what was your last job?!"

"CIA field operative."

"Really?" Vincent gaped. Simeon nodded, his eye on the young man in the seat next to him. He was taking this very well. Much better than most, and Simeon liked him for it. He caught sight of the white Cruiser as it passed under a bright streetlight. Simeon shot across an empty lot to jounce over the curb and back into traffic. They were at a good tailing distance now, and he carefully modified his driving to blend in with the cars around him. All they had to do right now was remain unseen.

8:57 a.m. Monday, Feb. 11; Main St., Philadelphia, PA

Jack Leason honked furiously at the black Element that had just cut him off. Stupid people, they had too nice of a car to risk it in maneuvers like that. He pulled his own dinged, silver Taurus up to the curb with an expertise that showed years of practice at driving in the wild Philadelphian traffic. Jack navigated out of his car, skillfully juggling his coffee, blackberry, and wallet as he dug for his credit card to pay the parking meter. His active mind wasn't on what he was doing. It dwelt on a small, square room high up in the skyscraper beside him, and the single occupant there. Daniel Yates would be tapping his big, ugly desk with his fingers now, waiting to see if the investigative journalist was late for his meeting. Jack smiled grimly as he moved inside. He had done his research on this prospective boss and knew enough to be able to bargain his services well, but it was going to take some real arguing to get a good deal out of Daniel Yates. As he slid into the elevator and punched the button for his floor the reporter's mind wasn't on the silver walls surrounding him, or the slow humming movement carrying him up. It was going over the best methods of handling the man he was headed to meet. Jack stepped out of the elevator on the fourteenth floor and stalked toward the editor's office, his mind racing off onto another track. This had better be a good offer, he needed a real whammy of a story even more than he needed some ready cash. He stopped in front of the secretary's desk and exchanged his ill-humored frown for a businesslike stare[5].

"Dan Yates sent for me," Jack stated.

"In!" someone barked from the door behind the desk. The secretary sighed and waved a stressed hand in the direction of the door. Jack opened it and saw a small, square room with a large ugly desk, just as he knew he would. Daniel Yates, exceptional editor and king of grumpiness, was drumming his thin fingers on the desk. He was wearing green today, good. According to the latest fired secretary Jack had bought coffee for that meant Dan was in a decent mood. The wiry old man sat and stared, drumming his fingers with annoying rhythmic monotony as the reporter stepped in and kicked

---

[5] Jack Leason had just launched into free-lancing four months ago and hadn't quite decided if a good investigative journalist should wear a hardened scowl, or a knowing smile. After trying both expressions out on various animals at the zoo and getting no response, he stuck to businesslike stares until he made up his mind.

the door closed behind him.

"Well?" Jack prompted.

"Not very good manners," Dan Yates said, pulling his feet off the desk to look the young man up and down. "Too handsome. Too young. Drinks too good coffee. Dressed too well."

"What do you want, old goat, a wizened drifter or a really good piece of writing?"

"You did step in right on the dot of nine," Dan Yates mused, a smile curling his lip at the rude reply. "I've read some of your stuff. You don't mind pushing people and you're not afraid to state the truth as you find it. Your writing is too flowery[6]. But I guess you'll do. Here's the business: Jenny Rhen, a pal of mine and a really good reporter, was investigating a story connected with the Controlled Parenting here. She's dead now. Find out why."

"If you pay enough," Jack stated flatly. Inside his heart jumped, this sounded promising. He was sorry for whatever character had lost their existence in it but this sounded like good stuff; any story on the CP would bring scores of readers. The conservatives would read it to find out what gory things were going on now, so they could be freshly appalled. The liberals would read it to be certain they knew the current thing to cheer. Jack found himself running through the possible horrible scandals this research might elicit. And if it didn't elicit any, he could always cautiously hint at something he didn't have evidence for. Jack noticed Yates was watching him. He put on his hardened scowl. "So how much?"

---

[6] Dan Yate's actual opinion of Jack's writing had been stated earlier that morning to the flustered secretary: "If that fop wrote a piece on hobos needing alarm clocks, the Salvation Army would be buried under the flood of clocks gifted from the public in twenty-four hours."

"You've got a long way to go before the rest of you matches that scowl, kid," Yates grinned as he pulled a thin file out of his desk drawer. "But I'd rather have an eager pup who can write than a hardened tough who can't. Here's what I know about Jenny Rhen and the story she was working. It's not much to go on, she was keeping this one close, so you'll have to do your own hunting. If it's a good story I'll pay well. If it isn't, I'll still pay something."

"You'll pay well or you will certainly have no story. Let me tell you what my idea of good is..." Thirty heated minutes later the two men came to a temporary agreement, and Jack Leason left the office and headed for his car. He glanced at the file as he walked. His new interest was a *Mrs.* Rhen. Good, a marriage partner was always a fount of knowledge if you could just find what turned on their faucet.

2

"Okay..." Vincent muttered, his green eyes wide. "We are chasing a terrorist through Fairfax. What do we do if we catch him?"

"Don't." Simeon let go of the stick (missing a gear change and making the car jerk and jolt unhappily) to flip his black cell phone toward Vincent. "Call police."

"Right. Really? You mean you really are chasing a terrorist?" Vincent asked. Simeon gave a little smile at his doubt and nodded. Vincent dialed 911 and asked for the police.

"Police, how can we help you?" a bright young voice spoke over the phone.

"Hello. We are chasing a terrorist through Fairfax, Virginia," Vincent said. An amused note was in his voice and Simeon liked it there.

"Uh huh," the policeman said doubtfully. Vincent quickly flipped it on speaker.

"Hawk nose, olive skin, thin, black hair, brown eyes. Name of Asil Bakir," Simeon stated obligingly. "On your lists."

"Wait...you really are chasing a terrorist through our town?" the policeman stuttered. The sound of a chair being pushed back drifted over the machine, and a noise that might have been running footsteps, quickly supplanted by silence.

"How long were you in the CIA?" Vincent asked his companion as they waited for someone to return to the phone line. Simeon's driving had evened out nicely now that he was trying to remain unseen, and Vincent's nerves had calmed down with the car. Now he felt a burning curiosity and excitement beginning to spark through him, two emotions he hadn't felt in an entire year.

"Thirty-three very active years."

"Wow. That's a really long time. I mean, a long time to work there, not a long time to live..." Vincent's voice trailed off awkwardly before he added another thought. "You know, I sure stick my foot in my mouth a lot." Simeon laughed. It was a delightful laugh, more real and joyful than the laughter you hear every day on the streets because it was a laugh reserved for times its owner considered seriously humorous. Vincent suddenly found he liked this man very much.

"Are you still there?" a competent voice spoke over the phone. Vincent told it yes. "Can you describe the man you're following?" Simeon did, very accurately. He added in the other man in the Nissan Z and the exchange he had seen. The competent voice came again, but it was muffled this time, as the owner had turned to speak to someone else. "Over here, Gibbs! It sounds like him."

"Mr. Gibbs?" Simeon asked in surprise, as he hopped a curb and narrowly missed a skateboarder.

"Well shucks and howdy doo, it's Simeon Lee," a tired voice drawled over the phone. "Chief, that's Simeon Lee on the other end. If he says it's Bakir, it's Bakir. He was my best agent till he up and quit two years ago. Are you coming back again, I hope? Scratch that question, here's another. Lee, tell me about the other man again.

31

What did he hand over."

"Too far away to see. But very expensive," Simeon said. A debate started up between Gibbs and the Chief, too garbled for the two men in the car to understand.

"Who's Mr. Gibbs?" Vincent asked curiously.

"Old boss," Simeon answered distractedly, trying to stay invisible and still see his target.

"Who's that?" Mr. Gibbs' voice broke over the phone.

"Uh, nobody, just a Vincent Tolliver. Mr. Lee kindly took me along for the ride. Sir," Vincent answered.

"BIGG2[7]? Leave it to Simeon Lee to track you down when the American media has failed to a man," Mr. Gibbs chuckled, and Simeon glanced curiously at his companion, who was currently muttering maledictions over his unwanted title. He was turning out to be a surprising young man. "You're the one our testing division uses to get the kinks out of things, right?"

"Yes sir," Vincent admitted a little reluctantly into the phone. "Oh, speaking of which you would save me a phone call if you tell them their exploding pencils have too weak an explosive to be labeled as that, but make pretty good smoke bombs if you have to get out quickly. One made me get out of my house faster than I knew I could, but the rabbit who accidentally ate another one was still fine after it exploded inside him."

---

[7] Vincent Tolliver was an only child and inherited the millions his father's inventions made without a catch. His own inventing had caused Vincent's wealth to escalate even more, and if he hadn't been so good at hiding from them, the media would certainly have had fun speculating on what the young Mr. Tolliver did with his cash. But the American media had still given Vincent Tolliver a title of their own creation: BIGG2 (Billionaire Invisible [to them, anyway] Gadget Genius the second). The young man hated the name with a passion.

"Exploding pencils don't kill bunnies, but make people run. Got it." Mr. Gibbs sounded very amused. He grew serious again quickly. "Lee, we've had our eyes on Bakir since before he came back into the country. This morning he slipped all his tails. Your other man is Harry Jones, an inventor and small arms dealer who isn't particular about whom he sells his things to. If he sold Bakir something, Bakir's planning on using it tonight. Keep him in sight till we can get a handle on him. Hold on, the Police Chief's about to blow a gasket trying to ask something. What? Oh. Lee, where are you?"

"Turning into the Fairfax Metro Station," Simeon answered. Vincent looked up from where he had been avidly studying the strange instrument panel on the car. They were pulling to a jerky stop in front of one of the metro's parking garage arms. Simeon swiped his SmarTrip card and squealed into the garage.

"You're actually in the station?" Mr. Gibbs asked, a happy note in his voice.

"You want me to go in after him," Simeon stated, and Vincent noticed he was almost smiling. He got the idea his church friend was enjoying this. Personally, he was scared stiff. This was not what he had planned when he suggested a coffee shop visit.

"I do," Mr. Gibbs answered immediately. "Very much. And if Vincent Tolliver would agree to accompany you, I would be even happier."

"Me?" Vincent yelped[8].

---

[8] The note of frenzy was partially due to the way Simeon Lee drove in parking garages. Vincent had been in five fairly serious car wrecks in his time and was certain he was about to be in another with the way his companion drove.

33

"You're good enough that your name has drifted from the testing division all the way up to me, Vincent Tolliver," Mr. Gibbs said soothingly, and Simeon sent a second surprised glance toward his companion. He knew that was a long distance for one name to travel, and it meant Vincent Tolliver was very, very good at what he did. "Jones has skill, but not up to your quality. Lee can find Bakir, and whatever he bought from Jones. You can stop whatever it is. Please? Just for me? Well, actually because I really don't want Bakir killing his man." Simeon fishtailed into a parking place next to the empty white PT Cruiser and hopped out. He spun around and faced Vincent.

"Mr. Tolliver, I'm going to gamble," he stated. "It's not a killer virus, it's twice as deadly. If you really want to be a Parabaloni, now is the time. You coming?" Vincent hesitated for just a moment before answering, his hand resting on the palm pilot sticking out of his pocket.

"Yeah," Vincent said, and hopped out of the car onto the concrete. Simeon nodded to say he was pleased with the decision, snapped his phone shut, and began to run toward the tunnel into the station. Vincent felt like yelling as he followed, just out of feeling alive. That single approving nod had killed all his insecurity at the suddenness of this thing, scattered the numbness that had set in after his parents' deaths, and made him feel twelve feet tall. The hard jarring sensation running up his legs as he dashed over the concrete felt real. The smell of tires and gasoline and trash was delicious. He noted each detail of Mr. Lee's perfectly combed hair, sorting out the gray from the lustrous black. Even if he got killed by this assassin terrorist, it would be worth it just to feel this alive again after his year of numb existence.

7:45 p.m. Feb. 13th; 2413 Gregory St., PA

"I'll tell you, Mr. Leason, that woman never could remember to put my hammer away," Mr. Samuel Rhen rambled. He sunk farther down into his well-loved recliner, a sad smile playing over his face. Jack hoped he would get around to a point eventually. But he was careful to stay relaxed and sympathetic on the comfortable leather sofa. "I would always find it in a kitchen drawer somewhere. I told Jen again and again, 'If you don't put a tool back where it came from you might as well take it and throw it as far as you can, because you're never going to see it again.'"

"Women, they're always up to something," Jack agreed sympathetically, offering another roasted peanut. They looked a little like espresso beans in the dim, dusty light of this living room. Espresso. He needed a coffee. "Especially wives. There's always something unfathomable going on in their minds."

"Well, I'll tell you one thing, youngster. I'd give every penny I ever earned off my wood working business just to have Jenny back for one more day," Samuel said. He started to say something else, but it stuck in his throat. "Darned constricting throats, they make my eyes get watery," he complained, swiping a hand across his eyes.

"Some days eyes need to be watery, Sam."

"I guess that's true enough. What did you come here for, anyway?"

"To find out how you were doing."

"Look, Jack, my wife and I talked a lot. If she knew someone as handsome and rude as you, she'd have mentioned it. Don't think I don't appreciate your letting me bore you with memories for the last hour, but what are you actually after? Who are you and what do you want?"

"I'm an investigative journalist and I want Jenny's notes," Jack answered, deciding a dodge wasn't the right approach on this man.

"Really? First newshound to make it in here. You have a good approach, the insolence combined with peanuts put me on the wrong track. Sure you're not with the CP?"

"No. Not in any way. Why, have the cretins been slinking?"

"Well...slinking isn't just the right word," Sam mused. "There's been this one guy, a tiny meek thing, who keeps showing up. Reminds me of an earthworm."

"What's the earthworm want?" Jack asked quickly.

"Same as you, he's after Jen's notes," Sam answered easily. His eyes were on Jack's face, and the reporter jerked back the shout of triumph he was about to give.

"That's intriguing," he said calmly instead.

"You're not too good at pretending to be something you're not," Sam chuckled. "Who put you onto this story?"

"Daniel Yates. I'm working for him. Loosely working for the old goat-headed clock-watcher, anyway. I guess you knew about him."

"Oh yes, Jen and Dan went way back. I guess if he sent you you're okay. I Xeroxed a copy of the notes Jen took on the case she was on when someone got her–"

"Did she talk about her investigation for this story?" Jack interrupted.

"She was a little close mouthed about it, but she was cackling as she ran out of the house the morning she got murdered. Apparently it was something pretty exciting."

"That's all, she didn't tell you anything?" Jack said, not bothering to hide his disgusted disappointment.

"You're a newshound all right. Hold on, I'll get the notes," Sam chuckled as he creaked out of his chair and shuffled out of the dim living room. Jack leaned back on the couch and munched peanuts. It wasn't quite a wasted hour if he really got Jenny Rhen's personal notes. That was actually a very promising start. Sam's old recliner creaked as an obstinate spring moved into place, and Jack's gaze was drawn toward the sound. Poor old guy, he was pretty broken up. To suddenly find yourself a bachelor after being married for thirty-six years would be tough. Thirty six years... how on earth had they managed it?

"Found them!" Sam's voice called from out of the room. He shuffled back in, a file folder tucked under one arm. "I keep the originals, of course. I'm keeping them with her other things, and in case they turn out to be important. What, you're not going to say 'gimmie'?"

"I will if you hold it any longer, because I'm sure thinking it," Jack said, not bothering to check his eagerness as he stood up and held out his hand. Sam chuckled and handed it over. "Thanks. Say,

Sam, how did you manage thirty-six years of marriage?"

"That had better not be a part of your investigation," Sam smiled. He reached over to a bookshelf, pulled a little green book off the bottom shelf, and tossed it to Jack. The reporter was disappointed to find it was a Gideon's New Testament. "It's all in there. 'Love as I have loved.' 'Respect.' 'Charity.' Stop scowling at it, that little book is the best marriage handbook you'll ever find."

"Sure. Old dead men philosophizing about a superstitious religion from centuries in the past is just what every marriage needs."

"You might be surprised, Jack. If God made us it stands to reason His advice on marriage is the best you'll ever get. The inventor always knows his invention's inner workings best."

"It's the 'if' that makes me skeptical." Jack held up a hand to stop the old man's reply and headed for the door. "I don't want to get into scientific and superstitious jargon now, I want to go read your wife's notes. See you, Sam. I'll let you know if I come up with anything."

7:45 p.m. Feb. 13th; Fairfax Metro Station, VA

Simeon grabbed Vincent's arm and pulled him through the turnstile, swiping his card for both of them. He ran forward toward the station's railing, weaving expertly through the crowd. Vincent followed as best as he could, wondering why there were so many people on a Tuesday evening. Simeon stopped so suddenly Vincent almost ran into him. The inventor stood still, panting a little and taking stock of where he was. It was a clean, nice station with modern fixings and surprisingly few vagrants. This platform was on a second story level. The metro lines lay directly below him, running underneath his feet. Trains were coming and going quickly, and from this height the people getting on and off seemed like hundreds of mice busy skittering toward their holes. Simeon's gaze was raking the pathways below them. There are two metro lines running out of the Fairfax station. You enter one on the left, the other on the right, with metro tracks separating the two. If you go down the wrong escalator there's no hope of catching your train. Which line would Bakir want?

"I can't help thinking this is a little like *Where's Waldo*," Vincent commented. "Did he have a striped shirt and ugly beanie on? Because that would sure make this easier." Simeon spotted a familiar hawk nose stepping into the metro train to his left. He shot toward the escalator and Vincent sprinted to keep up. He had no idea someone of Simeon's age could move so fast. Scratch that, he had no idea any human alive could move that fast, that easily. Simeon kept his eye focused on the car where Bakir had disappeared. The train was getting ready to leave and he sped up.

"Doors closing," an automated female voice drifted out of the cars, with annoying cheerfulness. Simeon leapt through into the car and slid to an easy stop, Vincent right behind him.

"Doors closing," the voice said again.

"I noticed," Vincent panted, trying to pull his foot out of where the sliding door had closed on it. Simeon lent a hand as the train started to move. The door slid shut with a quiet thud as the foot was removed.

39

"A habit from your door to door sales, young man?" a lightly accented voice teased. Vincent felt a chill run down his spine as he looked up and saw it was Bakir. "When a door says, 'closing,' that usually means it is closing. Why did you not pick a car closer to the front if you were so pressed for time?"

"Sudden decisions make for hasty entrances," Vincent partially answered, smiling amiably. At least he hoped it was amiably as he followed Mr. Lee toward one of the old seats and settled on the ugly, yellow imitation leather. He felt like squirming after that strange sensation of a chill running down his spine. First time that had happened to him. Instead he just looked out the window as the train began to pick up speed. It rushed on, above ground at first. Vincent watched houses and stores and cars flash past his window, the only lights shining in the darkness of a late winter evening in the District of Columbia. There was a rush of noise as the metro dived into a tunnel underneath the streets of Washington. The lights of the tunnel began to flash past. They appeared and left in the window with such speed, it produced a strobe effect on the inventor's mind as he watched. Vincent turned his eyes away, blinking and feeling a little queasy. His church friend was sitting still, apparently reading a New Testament. Vincent pulled a screwdriver out of his pocket and began to flip it nervously.

As the young man perched tensely facing him, Simeon quietly looked over his companion's shoulder, surveying the sparsely occupied car. A man in a nice business suit sat in a middle aisle seat. He was staring moodily at his iPhone, an attaché case resting against his ankle. Almost certainly a smallish diplomat called back into town. A noisy family of tourists crowded the back. Two of them had a metro map open, deciding where to get out, while a stressed

40

looking woman tried to keep four young children sitting down on the strapless seats. Bakir was the only other occupant. He lounged comfortably a few seats in front of the diplomat, just in front of Simeon and Vincent. His eyes were still covered by the dark glasses so it was impossible to be certain where he was looking. But those glasses were pointed at the back of Mr. Tolliver's head.

"I am still trying to decide why you were so anxious to gain this particular place in the metro," Bakir declared, and Vincent spun around in surprise. Too quickly, Simeon noted with concern. He very much wished his little pistol[9] was with him instead of safely tucked under his pillow at home. "Were you perhaps testing your new sneakers? Or trying to catch an old friend?"

"Give it a rest," the diplomat complained, shifting to another position. Vincent glanced at Mr. Lee and saw he wasn't planning on offering any suggestions for a reply.

"I was looking for Waldo. I thought I saw him come in here," Vincent answered. Bakir smiled. His position didn't change, but his arm moved. Simeon moved with it, diving across the aisle almost as if he was attached by a string to Bakir's arm and had been jerked toward the terrorist. He collided into the tall man, and the two tumbled to the ground in between the seats. Vincent leapt up, but the antagonists were on their feet before he could move again. Bakir clutched a gun, a horrible bulge on one end marking a silencer. Simeon's viselike grip was the only thing keeping it from going off. The family in the back screamed while the diplomat dropped to the ground and covered his head. Bakir's knee shot up into Simeon's

---

[9] Simeon's little pistol could tell more stories than even I could. Most of them are highly classified though, and if a pistol could have its memory erased Simeon's certainly would have by now. I will stretch the rules, however, and say if someone tells you a .38 Ruger Special doesn't have the strength to stop a charging mastodon, don't listen to them.

middle with such a driving force it sent him crashing onto the floor. But he still kept his grip on Bakir's wrist and the dark man went down too. The assassin vindictively started spouting some foreign language Vincent didn't recognize as he tried to get his arm back. But Simeon understood it[10], and his face grew very hard. Bakir was taunting him with a terror growing inside America, maliciously telling just enough so Simeon knew of some unknown horror that no one would discover until too late. It was an old trick of a true terrorist; fear was always their best weapon. Simeon looked at him, furrowing his brows in a silent request for more as he smashed the terrorist's arm repeatedly into the floor to try and make him release the pistol.

"Thousands will die, thousands of those most innocent in your misguided eyes!" Bakir hissed in his native Turkish, trying to get his free arm around Simeon's head to gouge his thumb into his attacker's cornea. "X and his black boxes will destroy this country's peace forever, and change your precious America into a horror such as you have never dreamed!" Bakir suddenly lashed out with another driving kick to Simeon's kidney. The spy twisted viciously, jerking the brown arm he still clutched and blocking the kick with the assassin's gun hand. The man's words died in a gasp of pain and the pistol dropped from his numb fingers. Vincent darted toward the fight, brandishing his screwdriver and wondering what on earth he was supposed to do. He found the gun in his hands as he got closer, pressed there by Mr. Lee's tanned hand. Bakir shot toward the front of the car, propelled by a kick from Simeon. The family in the back screamed again.

---

[10] Simeon Lee is fascinated with languages, and has a particular skill in this area. To my knowledge he speaks forty-three different languages well enough to pass as a native, and that's not counting the some eighty different dialects and accents he has mastered within those languages.

"You're up, Mr. Tolliver," Simeon said calmly, using a perfectly starched handkerchief to wipe off a bit of blood dribbling from a cut eyebrow. He knew better then to let himself think about the disturbing idea just planted in his mind by his antagonist. There would be time enough to consider this 'X' and his boxes after Bakir had been dealt with.

"What?" Vincent gulped, eyeing the terrorist getting to his feet at the front of the car.

"Jones' weapon. It's been planted. Find it, stop it," Simeon ordered. He darted toward the front of the car, head down and shoulders squared. Bakir was waiting and a scissor kick shot out from the assassin. Simeon grabbed the flying leg and used it to bash the terrorist against the side of the car. Vincent pulled his eyes away from the fight and looked desperately at where Bakir had been sitting. It would be here somewhere, whatever it was. He slipped the pistol absently into one of his cargo pockets and pulled out his palm pilot, moving his screwdriver to his other hand.

"Finally!" his gadget spoke up in a pert automated female tone. "Do you have any idea how dark it is in your pocket? You should make me a light."

"I don't think I'm going to go around in glowing pants just for your benefit, Patricia[11]," Vincent muttered automatically to his gadget. He had been alone a lot this year, and when Vincent worked alone he talked to himself. This particular palm pilot had taken to answering him and was now in the rather abnormal position of being the young inventor's one and only good friend.

---

[11] Vincent Tolliver named everything. Well, everything but light bulbs. He had named light bulbs, but when he had burst into tears at five years old because 'Steve' wouldn't light and had to be thrown away, his mother had put her foot down on allowing light bulbs into friend status.

"What's going on?" the diplomat gasped from the floor. Vincent glanced to the front. Simeon slammed into the back of one of the seats, a knife blade slicing down at his head. Before the blade could reach its mark, the spy's head was butting into the assassin's chin, and Bakir flew across the aisle again as his knife sailed the other direction and lodged harmlessly in an empty seat.

"The good guy's winning. I hope," Vincent answered. "Pat, scan area for something powerful."

"What kind of power, you chump?" the palm pilot demanded. "You really are a daft-headed character–"

"Not now, Pat!" Vincent tried to interrupt.

"You can't just say something and assume I know what you mean. I might be brilliant, but I'm not a mind reader," Pat scoffed.

"If you're so brilliant why do you want me to make you a pocket light?" Vincent shot back. A gasping yell came from the assassin at the front of the car, and the inventor remembered what he was supposed to be doing, and that it was important. "I don't have to tell you details Pat, you're smart enough to know what I want when you find it," Vincent flattered. The flattery worked, the handheld started looking. Vincent poked things with his screwdriver as his electronic friend worked. There was nothing on the screws holding the chair together. There were no holes in the seat, nothing that could have been camouflaged as that ugly yellow stuff covering it. A rending crash came from the front and Vincent winced, but kept looking. He dropped to his knees and ran a hand quickly over the floor, searching for anything other than the dirty, bumpy metal. Nothing. Vincent leapt to his feet, feeling helplessly stumped. Bakir's very unconscious form slid down the middle aisle

44

and stopped by his feet.

"Keep looking, Mr. Tolliver," Simeon ordered in his quiet, rich voice as he pulled the limp assassin back toward himself and began securing him in a seat.

"Vince, there's nothing but cell phones and the metro itself making any power changes in this car," Patricia Palm reported disgustedly. So where was it? Vincent ran a hand through his hair as the automated voice came on again, announcing the next stop. The train slowed and he reached up for the bar running along the ceiling to steady himself in the rocking car. His hand closed around cold metal, and it felt refreshingly cool. Then the tips of his fingers brushed something that was a different sort of metal. Vincent leapt onto the seat and leaned over the bar. On top the thick metal bar, a tube of dull silver metal stretched for a full yard, a kink in the middle showing how Bakir had managed to transport the thing; it was designed to fold in half. Well it could, its folding days were over now. It was fused onto the metro car, and a slight discoloration of the metal showed this tube had been chemically treated to latch on automatically.

"Found it!" he cried. Simeon looked up from where he was finishing tying Bakir to a seat and saw his companion poking at something on the bar with a screwdriver. His hair was sticking straight up on his head, and his mouth was hanging open. Simeon smiled as he realized Vincent Tolliver's genius was working; apparently he was the smartest when he looked the stupidest.

"Wow, this is a fission bomb. Keen, Mr. Lee, this thing is awesome, I didn't know you could make something like this so small!"

45

"Make it stop, Mr. Tolliver," Simeon prodded, amusement playing over his face at the young man's reaction.

"What? Oh right," Vincent began to mutter to himself, his hand occasionally rubbing through his mane of hair as he poked at the bomb. "Oh, there's a lot of compressed U-235 in here, this is bad. I need the subcritical mass. Where's the neutron generator in this thing, and how is it activated? Oh hi, little foil, I found you! But I can't reach you, got to get through the tamper… This thing is really cool, I never thought of compressing one of these so small. Hey, it's a gun triggered bomb, which makes this easier. But altitude won't fire the U-235 bullet in here, so how's it set up… Hey, I know how this works now, Mr. Lee! This thing is amazing, it's got a U-235 bullet packed into a really nifty little gadget that can fire it at four thousand feet per second to start an impressive bit of fission, and the tamper set up here can make its efficiency almost a full 2.0 percent–"

"Can you stop it?" Simeon interrupted, finding his mouth was going dry as he realized what Mr. Tolliver was talking about. This was a miniature nuclear bomb. If it went off, it would kill more than just the people in this car, and contaminate at least a good portion of Washington.

"Right," Vincent reminded himself, one hand rubbing his hair again and making it stand up nearly a full foot above his head. "Yeah, the trigger mechanism's actually pretty simple, just an electronic thing. But it's about to fire, and then I can't stop it from exploding," Vincent said. The family in the back screamed again and the diplomat started frantically mumbling something that sounded like a mixed up version of the Lord's Prayer. The inventor's tongue stuck halfway out of his mouth as his brain raced. He grabbed his palm pilot and began pushing buttons furiously.

Simeon stepped closer, almost involuntarily. He knew he was watching his life in the hands of this young man. He prayed Vincent Tolliver was as good as Mr. Gibbs seemed to think.

"Sorry, Pat," Vincent muttered, pulling the back off the palm and sticking his screwdriver inside. For eight horrendous heartbeats, Simeon watched as the palm pilot complained and Vincent worked. A red light flashed from the bomb. Vincent slammed the palm on top of the light and let out his breath in a relieved sigh.

"Done?" Simeon asked.

"Yeah, it's done. Pat will keep it from firing now. Once the bomb squad–" Vincent broke off as the family in the back shrieked. Simeon motioned the inventor off the seat and toward the terrified tourists, including the cowering diplomat in his wave. Vincent headed to reassure them as Simeon pulled out his cell phone to try and reach Mr. Gibbs.

Two minutes later the metro drew to a stop at the Balston-MU station. Their car was immediately swamped. Police officers and FBI agents filled the small area indiscriminately, and Simeon quietly slipped out of the riot to the relative calm of the station platform. He watched the family of tourists escorted out, everyone assuring the poor terrified group it was safe now. The diplomat stepped calmly off the car a minute later, a pale face the only sign of the scare he had gotten. He stopped as he passed Simeon.

"Thank you," the diplomat stated, holding out his hand. Simeon took it silently, but nodded his own thanks back. Not many people stopped to say that. The retired agent leaned against a concrete wall, quietly wiping off his face with his handkerchief as the riot went on. Agents squeezed in and out. Police officers kept moving curious spectators along. Simeon began to get tired of waiting in the roaring, concrete station. It was making old Simon and Garfunkel songs get stuck in his head. Mr. Tolliver still wasn't emerging from that riot, and Simeon finally headed into the metro car again to find out why. As he got closer his acute hearing picked out Mr. Tolliver's voice among the babble of others.

"No. I am not leaving without her! It. I want it. It's mine. You don't need it anymore," Vincent was saying, in a very distraught voice. Simeon's lips pursed, knowing what the outcome of a conversation like that was going to be. He slipped into the car, weaving his way toward the blond mop of hair he saw poking above the other heads swarming around this car. A very stern FBI agent stood scowling at Vincent Tolliver. His arms were crossed moodily against his chest, and from his left hand dangled a plastic bag containing Vincent's 'Pat.'

"You'll get it back," the agent growled.

"I've heard that before," Vincent answered desperately. "You people still have my green gorilla finder, and my napalm wig. Look, it's the last thing my dad worked on for me, it has a little bit of him in its personality, you can't just..." Vincent broke off, knowing he wasn't getting anywhere. Simeon took his arm and pulled gently.

"Won't get it back here," he said.

"I'm not leaving without her," Vincent stubbornly insisted, his voice trembling.

"I will get it back for you," Simeon promised. "Just come on." Vincent reluctantly allowed himself to be pulled toward the door, but his eye stayed fixed on that little plastic bag the annoying agent clutched. After all that excitement and danger, to have his best friend snatched from him at the end was heartbreaking. Vincent glanced over at his companion as he followed Mr. Lee across the station platform toward a new train, and drew in a deep breath. It was okay. Mr. Lee would get Pat back.

3

Judy Leason scowled at her laptop screen as she leaned over the marble-topped bar where the machine was perched. Why did her boss want this will re-typed now? She had hoped to actually make dinner for Jack tonight. A sigh flew from her as she began to type and resigned herself to an evening spent shoving legal words around. It was a good thing she had married a man who liked frozen pot pies. Twenty two minutes later a key rattled in the lock, but Judy had a Pandora station playing through her iPhone's earbuds and didn't notice. Jack shot through the door and darted toward the bedroom. He stopped to give Judy a quick peck on the cheek, and kept running.

"Nice day, dear?" Judy muttered distractedly, her eye on her screen. No answer came, which was just as well. She wouldn't have noticed if Jack had given an animated five minute monologue. Eight minutes passed with her focused attention never straying from her work. A rending crash came from their bedroom, and Judy jerked her earbuds out.

"No problem, Sweetie, just the lamp!" Jack called.

"He spoke up mighty quick," Judy murmured suspiciously to herself. "Is it broken?" she called sweetly, slipping off her stool and quietly stealing down the dimly lit hall toward the bedroom.

"Uh, well...define broken," Jack called back as Judy carefully maneuvered herself to peek through the bedroom door. A grappling line lay stretched across the bedroom floor, the hook attached to the

50

floor lamp's shade. Jack was bending over it trying to make the hook retract without ripping the shade worse than it already was, muttering maledictions on his gadget. He was dressed entirely in black. He was even wearing black gloves. Judy slipped in and tapped him on the shoulder.

"Going for a light climb, dear?" she said pleasantly. "I think you should try something a little bigger; perhaps the lighthouse down on the beach."

"Now, Judy–" Jack tried to placate.

"Don't 'now Judy' me, Jack Leason! What do you think you're doing with that thing?"

"I know where this lamp came from, I can get another one–"

"The lamp? Who cares about the lamp, you crook-pated clotpole[12]! What are you doing in your cat burglar outfit?"

"Hold on, churlish canker-blossom, and let me explain!" Jack shot back. "I'm working on a story–"

"What story?" Judy interrupted. Jack knew that expression on his wife's face. She wasn't going to be satisfied with anything but the whole answer. He gave her the whole answer, all the way up to his walking out of Sam's door with the notes.

"Now I'm just going to go check a hunch," he ended soothingly. "I should be back before–"

"What hunch?" Judy interrupted again, and Jack sighed. Why

---

[12] Early into their marriage Jack and Judy had decided Shakespearian insults were much better and hurt less than the modern disparagements of the four letter type. They made a pact, and now when you hear them shouting Shakespeare, it's a sure sign they are very angry.

had he picked an intelligent woman?

"Okay, fine. Jenny Rhen found a distortion in the Controlled Parenting bookkeeping."

"Distortion? Like a misappropriation?" Judy was getting interested, and that's what Jack had been afraid of. Oh well, it was nice to talk it over with her, and he could figure out what to do with her later.

"Jenny Rhen thought it might have been more," Jack said, dropping his voice conspiratorially and stepping over the broken lamp to get closer. "She was thinking it might be a hidden agenda, something the Controlled Parenting don't want even their supporters knowing they support yet, and even vaguely mentions a group of murderers. These were funds not just taken away from the books, but shifted to another column. It was marked 'miscellaneous charities' in most of the books, but in the big cities she was finding one set of books that marked that column differently. They were special books of the top CP men, kept locked up, or somehow very specially apart from the other books."

"Come on give, what was the column labeled?" Judy breathed. Her dark eyes were bright with interest and she was re-braiding her long black hair; a sure sign she was fascinated.

"'X's fund – Feb. 20th,'" Jack answered her truthfully, and then tried desperately to think of a way to get her uninterested. He shrugged and returned to trying to get his grapple back. "I figure it's the date of a birthday, somebody big, someone they're trying to get in good with. It would take a lot of funds to throw a really good party."

"You do not," Judy said, shoving her husband off balance. "It won't work Jack, I'm interested. If I didn't have to type up a will tonight, I'd come along."

"You have a will going? Will, will, will."

"See, you didn't need to do all that sneaking around after all. Wait, you never answered my first question, hedge-pig. What are you doing in that outfit? What is it I would be going along with if..." Judy suddenly squealed as realization dawned, her dark eyes growing wide with alarm. "Jack! You're sneaking into the CP here in Philadelphia! If you're caught not even my boss could get you out of the lawsuit they would slap on you. No. No! No, Jack, you are not going to burgle the Philadelphia Controlled Parenting building! I forbid it."

"Forbidden by my wifey," Jack sighed melodramatically and kissed her cheek again. He was smiling as he drew away. "You know I'm going to anyway." Judy shoved him away irritably.

"I knew you would when I married you. You're always trying to get yourself arrested or killed for a story. Fine. But don't expect me to come to visit you more than once a week."

"Only once?" Jack pouted playfully.

"Well...for you maybe I'll visit the state penitentiary twice a week," Judy smiled. Jack grinned, but then lost it.

"You just gave in awfully fast. You're not planning anything are you?" he asked his wife's back as she headed toward the kitchen. She turned around, a mischievous smile playing over her beautiful face.

"Wouldn't you like to know?" Judy murmured mysteriously, and headed back to her typing. Jack chuckled as he hunted for his glass cutter in the bureau drawer. He did love that woman. He hoped she really wasn't planning anything. The picture of Sam forlornly alone flashed across Jack's mind and he chose the window as his exit. Better not push his luck; if he went out the door Judy might decide to follow him despite her avowals of disinterest. One lady was already dead from whatever this was he was digging into, his lady wasn't going to be the next one.

10:34 p.m. Feb. 13th; 100 42nd St NE, Washington, DC

Simeon pulled up in front of the Third District Police Station and hopped out of his car. Vincent followed in silence, the same silence that had mostly reigned since they had left that swarming metro car. It was somehow a companionable silence, Vincent reflected as he followed Simeon through the door into the hum of the busy station. Sort of easy and nice, with both of them knowing they didn't have to say anything if they didn't want to. Vincent stopped behind Mr. Lee's still form and smiled wryly at himself. He was trying to ignore the panic setting in after the adrenalin wore off. Vincent took a deep breath and focused on his companion's broad back as Simeon tipped his head on the side, listening for something. He was with Mr. Lee, so there was nothing to panic about[13].

"What are you listening for?" Vincent asked his friend, wondering what on earth he expected to hear over the busy hubbub of the station. Come to think of it, this place was awfully filled for a

---

[13] Simeon has this effect on most people. He inspires a calm trust that is very reassuring. Even in the presence of very angry, formerly-believed-to-be-extinct, hairy mammals Simeon's quiet presence breeds assurance of safety.

Tuesday night. "Are Police Station's always this busy at night?"

"No, but the FBI just invaded this station, dragging a terrorist in tow," a passing officer answered Vincent's question as she kept walking. "Why they couldn't take him to their own building I don't know…"

"Where?" Simeon asked quickly. The officer paused and studied the stocky figure.

"Straight," she answered. "Then take the first hall left, two halls right, and it's the second door on the left. You'll be able to find it okay, just follow the stream." Simeon began to pace through the bare hallways and passed closed wooden doors, following the officer's directions. Vincent kept in step, silently quieting his heartbeat and forcing himself to believe the obvious; he really was in the middle of a terrorist story. A tall man stepped out of a door on the left, his eyes searching the hall for someone. Simeon raised a hand and those tired eyes lit up in happy recognition. This guy looked like quite a man, Vincent reflected as he followed Simeon toward the stranger. He was probably well into his seventies but it was impossible to call him elderly. He was too vital, too alive. After one look at his chiseled, scarred features you knew he'd be much more likely to die tackling a suicide bomber or wrestling a cougar than quietly in an old folk's home.

"Lee," the tall man said simply, shaking hands fondly with Simeon.

"Mr. Gibbs," Simeon nodded, honoring his old boss with a smile. Mr. Gibbs motioned them into the room he had stepped from and Vincent followed Simeon in. It was large, but on the whole it was a room that looked designed to be unprepossessing. Bare, gray, and rectangular were the only three words that came to the inventor's mind as he studied this area. There were policemen and FBI agents everywhere. Some of them looked pretty impressive, but not one matched Mr. Lee or Mr. Gibbs in Vincent's opinion. Three tables rested on the opposite end of the room from him, stacked with an indescribable mix of things. Something made him think 'evidence' as he looked at the mix. But the main action was coming from the middle of the room. A thin, nervous man, somewhere in his thirties, was handcuffed to a chair there. Vincent recalled Simeon's descriptions earlier in this harrying night and realized he was looking at Harry Jones, inventor and small arms dealer. The D.C. police must have picked him up quickly, and now he sat in a metal chair, being questioned by about ten different agents. Vincent silently thanked God for keeping him honest and leaned against the wall next to Mr. Lee, listening with him. The two men stayed there, quietly watching. Fifteen minutes later they were still there and the questions shot out at the crooked inventor were beginning to be repeated.

"What did you sell Bakir? How did he contact you?" Agent Tyler barked at the cowering man in the chair.

"I didn't know what he was going to use it for," Harry Jones whimpered. "I wasn't even going to sell it to Bakir!" Vincent leaned closer to his companion as he heard they were starting over at the first question again.

"Why are we here, Mr. Lee?" he whispered.

"Your handheld," Simeon murmured back distractedly. Mr. Gibbs turned around at the whispered conversation. The CIA man stood taller as he caught sight of Simeon. He knew that look in his retired agent's eye, focused on Harry Jones. Simeon Lee had noticed something he found very interesting. Mr. Gibbs stepped a little closer and leaned down to compensate for their different heights.

"I'm not supposed to be here," he muttered. "CIA isn't allowed to work inside the country, remember? So you say something." Simeon glanced at his old boss, trying to tell if Mr. Gibbs had noticed it too or was just pushing him. But his insatiable curiosity was growing as he listened to Jones beginning his excuses again. There came that same phrase, with the same odd intonation[14].

"I wasn't going to sell it to Bakir, really," Jones whined. Simeon moved. The crooked inventor pulled back with a shocked hiss as a stocky stranger suddenly stood in front of him.

"Who were you going to sell it to?" Simeon asked. Everyone stared at the short, serious man. Most in the room had no idea who he was or why he was allowed in, but he had obviously latched onto something from the way the suspect reacted to the simple words. Harry Jones sat frozen. He stared at Simeon with his mouth hanging open, eyes wide with terror.

"It wasn't intended for Bakir," Agent Tyler murmured, realization dawning as he watched Jones. "You made that incredibly compact bomb for someone else, specifically for someone else. Who was it? What did they want it for?"

"No," Jones whispered. His voice was tiny and hoarse and his

---

[14] Simeon Lee is very good at reading people. The tiniest inflection of a tone, the way a glance drifts to the side, Simeon catches it all and deduced more than anyone else could. And you ought to thank heaven for this gift of the quiet Mr. Lee. Without it the world you live in so serenely would not be here. Why, just to think what would have happened if Simeon hadn't read Henry's love of lobsters in the fat man's eyes that day so many years — but no, that's classified. I would hate for you to have to have your memory erased. I had a bunny that my corgi chased into an industrial plant one day whose memory had to be erased after it saw... Never mind.

eyes never left Simeon. They were pleading, petrified eyes. "Don't ask me. Please." Agent Tyler shouldered Simeon out of the way to catch Jones gaze, determination in every movement. He began to demand answers to this new frightening line of questions. But Harry Jones sat still as if all the life had been sucked from him by the quiet inference of Simeon Lee. Simeon slid to the side of the room toward the long table filled with evidence. Vincent hesitated for a moment then trotted across to him. As he got closer, he saw Mr. Lee was looking at a strange collection that a label declared came from Harry Jones' car. A policeman stood beside the table, sternly watching Simeon as if he was afraid he might steal something.

"Wow. That's a lot of rifles," Vincent commented.

"Machine pistols," Simeon corrected. Vincent started in surprise and his hand shot toward a familiar little bag with Pat's shiny screen showing through the plastic. The policeman on guard was faster than the inventor, and he closed Vincent's wrist in his strong grip.

"No touching the evidence," the officer said sternly.

"But that's mine!" Vincent countered, as angrily as the mild young man ever got.

"No touching without the proper say so," the policeman insisted.

"Mr. Tolliver, what can you tell me about this?" Simeon broke in. The two men looked at him. He was holding a small, black box gingerly in his strong hands, a simple glossy square of about six inches by six inches.

"Hey, I said no touch–" The policeman started to say but Simeon held up his hand, cutting him off. His acute hearing had caught another hiss from Harry Jones. The man sat rigid in his chair, his eyes fixed on the box in Simeon's hands. Silence fell on the room again, everyone feeling this was another turning point in the strange situation. Simeon stepped forward, bringing the box toward the group in the center of the room. Everyone's eyes were on Harry Jones. The little man was petrified by that black square drawing nearer. Simeon stopped beside him.

"Yours, Mr. Jones?" he asked quietly. There was no response at all. "The replacement for that explosive, re-commissioned into this by the party you won't mention?" Simeon suddenly decided to make a wild guess and see where it took him. He leaned a little closer, his soft brown eyes locking onto Harry Jones' terrified blue ones, and asked one more question in a quiet, dangerous tone. "X?"

"You're one of them," Jones croaked, his eyes shifting from Simeon's serious face to the black box. "You're testing me, linking just enough to try and get me to spill it, in order to see if I can stick it out. I can. I will! You can tell X I won't say a thing, I know when to keep my mouth shut, and–" Jones clamped his mouth closed, his eyes fixed on Simeon's face. "I can keep quiet." Silence sank over the room and stayed for a full minute.

"Do you think it's worth my time to question him anymore?" Agent Tyler asked Mr. Lee, morosely watching the firmly silent Jones. The retired agent shook his head, and Tyler motioned an officer forward to begin unlatching Jones from his chair. Simeon handed the black box to Vincent.

"Jones, I get the feeling you would be a lot safer if you would help us with whatever it is you're mixed up in now," Agent Tyler commented. The unscrupulous inventor didn't seem to notice the advice as he was led out toward his cell; his eyes were still focused on that black box.

"Mr. Tolliver?" Simeon asked.

"I don't know," Vincent answered, turning the black thing around in his hands and tossing it up and down. "It's shiny."

"It's shiny. That helps a lot," Agent Tyler commented. "What made you pick up that particular bit of evidence?"

"Bakir mentioned an X with black boxes," Simeon replied.

"What did he say?" Tyler demanded, as Mr. Gibbs stepped closer, a sharp frown on his features.

"Hey, I just remembered, I've seen one of these before," Vincent interrupted, studying the box.

"What? Where?" Tyler and Mr. Gibbs barked.

"My pastor found it in the foyer this Sunday, hidden behind a potted plant. He asked me what it was, and I said I didn't know, but I would check it out for him. I took it home and forgot about it," Vincent said, turning the square around interestedly.

"Our church foyer?" Simeon frowned. That was a disturbing thing to hear. He was beginning to think this was very important, and quickly quoted Bakir's words verbatim to the FBI and CIA agents staring at him.

"Wow. Now I really want to know what this is," Vincent commented, tapping the glossy box on the top of a metal folding chair.

"I want to know that too," Agent Tyler took up irritably. "Who are you, anyway? And why are you touching my evidence? If you're part of the CIA you're not supposed to even be here."

"They're not affiliated with me," Mr. Gibbs broke in. "Vincent Tolliver has done some work on commission with my testing division, and Mr. Lee used to be affiliated with me. Look Tolliver up in your records, believe me, you want him to be the one handling that box. Lee, come with me and bring that inventor of yours. Vincent, don't drop the box. And stop banging it on things!"

"I will look him up," Agent Tyler called after the three men walking out the door, "and your Simeon Lee, too." Mr. Gibbs stopped and turned around, a little smile playing over his sleepy face.

"You won't find anything written about Simeon Lee in your files. If you did, I'd probably have to erase your memory. Call me when you decide what you're doing with Bakir." Mr. Gibbs waved a hand vaguely in the direction of the agent and made his way out the door. The CIA man led Simeon and Vincent down a long hall, opening rooms and peeking in as he walked.

"Here's an empty one," he commented at the fifth door. "Have a seat while I tell someone we're here and not to be disturbed." Mr. Gibbs stalked down the hall, his tall form looking sleepy even from the back. Simeon walked in, his eye running around in his accustomed new-room check. A bare white-walled square with a single small table and four metal chairs, one ventilation grate in the far corner the only option besides the door for an attack, or retreat. Not much to see. He settled in one of the chairs to wait. Vincent draped himself over a chair across from him, his expression showing a sort of depressed, overwhelmed feeling fuming inside.

"A lot to take in immediately," Simeon commented kindly.

"Yes it is. It would help if I had Patricia back," Vincent muttered, almost to himself. Simeon pulled a plastic bag out of his jacket pocket and slid it across the table. Vincent's mouth dropped open in delighted surprise.

"When did you-?" he stuttered as he pulled the palm out and began to check it over lovingly.

"You kept the policeman distracted."

"Ha! I meant to do that, right? Thanks, Mr. Lee. Thanks a lot." After a moment of watching the inventor relaxing with his machine back in hand, Simeon hazarded a comment.

"You must have loved your father very much," he said. Vincent looked up in surprise. He thoughtfully shifted the palm pilot in his hand and nodded.

"Yeah. That is why I get comfort from this old piece of bolts and wires, I guess."

"Old?" Pat's automated voice broke in indignantly. Vincent muted her quickly and took up the conversation again.

"He helped me put her together, and some of himself sort of stayed in her insides. Kind of weird, I know, but some electronics do absorb a bit of personality. Actually, I wanted to say thank you for more than just stealing Pat back," Vincent said, glancing at the serious man shyly. Simeon tipped his head invitingly and waited. "You're the first brother I've really tried to get to know since my parents died last year, and you've taken me in pretty thoroughly tonight. Thanks."

"Mutual. No friends?"

"Well...I did. But we sort of lost contact. I guess I let myself lose contact."

"The grieving shouldn't have the burden of keeping up. But if it has fallen on you, keep up, Mr. Tolliver," Simeon quietly admonished. "It's very important."

"Right. Of course, you're right. There is...there's one family we were pretty close to especially, Mr. Stevenson was one of Dad's financial advisors and helped him out with lab work, and we hung out with the family a lot. I'll call them when we get out of here." Vincent was surprised to see a smile spread over Mr. Lee's face.

"Do, Vincent. Friends are precious and important."

"Wait, you just called me Vincent," the young inventor said in happy surprise, feeling instinctively that it was a very special thing to be allowed on a first name basis with Mr. Lee. "What changed?"

"I've known many men who would chase a terrorist through a subway. I've only known one that accepted a correction as well as you just did," Simeon stated, but that wasn't the real reason for the change. Vincent Tolliver's conversation had told him something; by his immediate acceptance of his recommendation, and even opening such a hard conversation with a near stranger, this young man had just shown an immense amount of trust in his advice and friendship. Simeon sensed Vincent Tolliver wasn't made like most people, and had very little compunction about sharing whatever he happened to be thinking about at the moment. He prayed the shock of finding an untrustworthy person would never land on the inventor's skinny shoulders, and quietly accepted the confidence handed to him so obliviously by this young man. Vincent felt his cheeks burning from a happy fire fanned into life by the statement. But he had no idea how to reply to something like that. He was spared having to answer by Mr. Gibbs' reentry. The CIA man slammed the door behind him and dropped wearily into one of the metal chairs at the table. He regarded the two men silently for a moment, then a raspy chuckle escaped from him. Simeon raised an inquisitive eyebrow.

"Sorry, it just struck me how funny a pair you two make. Old and young, neat and sloppy, short and tall. Don't mind me." He stirred in his seat and regarded the two men with a calculating eye. "I have a proposition for you two. First let me tell you what this is all about. Do you remember the man in business casual?"

"The cowering diplomat?" Vincent asked. Mr. Gibbs gave him an amused nod and went on.

"His name is Henry Bruce and yes, he's a diplomat. He's a pretty ordinary diplomat working in an embassy in D.C. But he's doing some slightly unordinary things at the moment; he's working on signing a treaty with a little-known country in the Middle East. America wants the oil from the few oil wells they have working, but we'll only deal with them if they agree to move to a more democratic state of government. At the moment the government is at a crisis and could go either way, to being a despotic Muslim form, or one friendlier with the west. But there's a neighboring country that is thoroughly Muslim, and they will do anything to keep their neighbor from becoming so...un-Muslim, if you will. The Muslim neighbor has almost succeeded in getting their own people in power and the treaty Henry Bruce is working on is the only thing standing in their way. If the treaty is signed it will definitely mean an end to hard-core Muslim rulers for the little country and the beginning of pro-western thought, and the Muslim neighbor knows it."

64

"The Muslim neighbor hired Bakir to eliminate Henry Bruce before the treaty could be signed," Simeon clarified. Mr. Gibbs nodded. "Will the neighbor have another chance to stop it?"

"The treaty should have been signed about fifteen minutes ago," Mr. Gibbs said, glancing at his watch. "Since I haven't heard anything to the contrary, I assume it has been."

Simeon quietly tuned out the two other men as they dove into more details. He was recalling his conversation in the coffee shop and putting it together with what he had just heard from Mr. Gibbs. He had said that he wanted to do more for the world, to do more for God's kingdom. Now his actions (in part) had caused a whole country to be open to the gospel of Christ. In a land ruled over by Islam anyone trying to bring, spread, or accept the free gospel of Christ would be mercilessly squashed. But with another rule intact, one that linked the government with a somewhat Christian nation, there would be a chance for the seed of Christ's gospel to bloom in the soil of that little country. And if he hadn't turned into that parking garage, if he and Vincent had just gone back to their quiet coffee shop and their quiet lives, a whole country would have been plunged into the blackness of Islam. How many chances like this had he passed over because he was too focused on himself?

"Lee, are you listening?" Mr. Gibbs voice broke through his thoughts.

"No," Simeon answered truthfully.

"Well, do. Here's my proposition. I want you two to form an independent spy unit." Mr. Gibbs resisted the urge to laugh at the two men's identical shocked expressions, and expanded on his statement. "Here are my reasons behind the request. One: Lee is very, very good at finding things out and fixing things about to go wrong. You were my best agent, Lee, and I really want you back where I can call on your help. Mr. Tolliver is very, very smart and as he proved today is able and willing to become as good as Lee. He just needs a little training." Vincent's mouth dropped open involuntarily, but he made no comment. "You've already chosen each other; that helps the situation. You're even on a first name basis, which by the way, Vincent, is very special. Don't misuse the gift Lee just gave you. Two: anyone really affiliated with the CIA smells just a little of the department. There's something about our agents that make others able to tag them as agents. That won't be a problem for you two. Three: my main point, and one that I think will interest you. It has to do with that black box. Found anything out about it yet, Vincent?"

"Well, I think it's just a container," Vincent answered slowly. "Like most boxes. I doubt it's a bomb... I'll have to dissect it a little to find out more. But what's your point?"

"Whatever this black box business is, it's based in our country. Bakir told us that, and I think he was telling the truth, not just trying to scare you. Do you get the same idea, Lee?" Simeon nodded, his soft brown eyes very interested as he listened. "Jones was really scared. And that scares me, honestly. He wasn't worried about dealing with a terrorist assassin, but whoever this X is has him terrified out of his unquestionably smart wits. I want something that scary out of my America. I've fought too long and too hard, and watched too many good men and women die, and too many good boys and girls grow up here to allow something that scarily evil to be in my country." Simeon raised his hand a little, looking inquisitively at his old boss. Mr. Gibbs answered the look, and Vincent silently wondered if Simeon had lost his voice and been a

66

mute at one time in his past. He could certainly get things across well without words.

"Yes, I have more, a little more. I've heard rumors. Very small, trembling kind of rumors, the sort that undulate and contradict each other. But they all corroborate our Harry Jones' fright tonight. Senseless, sudden murders. People who used to be all for 'humanity's greater good' suddenly becoming hard, and even cruel. A quiet excitement, verging on fear, running through people and places that used to be at peace. Nothing that I can really stick in a report and send to the FBI, you understand. But..." Mr. Gibbs paused and leaned over the table, his eyes focused on Simeon. "But it's the sort of thing I know is real and dangerous. Very dangerous, and growing swiftly. And I'm scared. Lee, when I'm scared you're the one man that I want to calm me down. If I know you're on it, I know it will be all right. You never failed me –"

"Lapland," Simeon interrupted.

"It's not a failure when the entire stockpile of the enemy's cold war biological weapons disappears on them. I don't care if they weren't actually destroyed, or that because of that bug-eyed creep you weren't able to save the mastodons like– Where was I? Oh, yes. Lee, if you aren't affiliated with the CIA, you can work inside America. Without any of the paperwork and red tape that always goes along with missions like this. And if you start an official unit, even with just one other person (like Vincent here), I can sort of slip you a few credentials and cash when you need it. So, there it is. If you start an official spy unit you can look into this X box matter for me." Vincent laughed at the name and looked at Simeon to see what he thought about it all.

"Vincent, it's not easy to do what Mr. Gibbs is asking," Simeon stated, studying the young inventor with a kind of quiet sorrow.

"I get the unsafe part, Simeon," Vincent answered cheerfully. "But I also understand it's what we were both asking for in the coffee shop before we raced after Bakir. A chance to advance God's kingdom and drive evil farther back, to be the risk-taking Parabaloni who love enough to actually live God's love. That's something I'm very excited about, and something that makes me feel more alive than I thought I could be while still on this sinful old sod. Besides, it sounds pretty keen." He saw that Simeon was still hesitant to let him in on the business and quickly placed himself in the older man's shoes to try and answer his hesitation. "I don't really understand what it entails. I can guess, but I guess I won't actually know till it hits. But I know that if I go into something as ridiculous and unsafe and uncomfortable as this with you to show me the way... Well, somehow I don't think it would be the same level of unsafe and uncomfortable as a general training or jumping in on my own. And I don't have anyone to worry. Nobody but me, so no nail-biters waiting at home when I go out. Simeon, I've needed this for a while now, and am kind of hyped over it. And besides you'll get a free, private airline with me, and a free mechanic if your nifty car breaks down. I'm all for it! How about you?"

"What do you say, Lee?" Mr. Gibbs took up. "I don't know why you quit on me two years ago, and so don't really know if you want back in. And I don't really get what most of Vincent's statements had to do with anything, but I know you're curious about this X box. And if you have one fault it's letting your curiosity pull you in. Pull in with me again, Lee. Please?" Simeon picked up the black box and turned it over slowly in his hand, running a fingernail over a hairline crack his eye picked out. What was in this shiny, small thing? And why, why, why was there one just like it in his church foyer? No! What was he thinking? He was retired! He had promised himself he would retire when he got old, and when he actually found something to live for. Christ was something to live for and at forty-nine he certainly felt old, too old for this. But still... Simeon looked up and met Mr. Gibbs pleading, worried gaze. The last time he had seen him looking like that had resulted in one of the scariest, hardest six months of his life. There were still times when he woke up screaming with his sheets soaked in sweat from the nightmares over that business. But America and the free world was still here because of it too. Billions of souls were still living and learning to love. Simeon glanced to the side. Vincent looked very excited. The inventor was right, it wouldn't be so bad for him if he really let himself be led and protected by experience. And his earlier acceptance of a quiet reprimand had proved a spirit willing to learn and listen. Simeon took a deep breath and sat the box back on the table.

"All right," he said. "I'll gamble again. God help us, Vincent."

4

11:02 p.m. Feb. 13th; Outside the CP Office, Philadelphia, PA

Jack slid silently into the alley, finally certain he was alone. He pulled out his lockpicks and began to soundlessly work on the back door of the CP headquarters. A quick look shouldn't take very long. And if he was caught, it would just mean some embarrassing explanations. And probably jail. If he wasn't just shot dead as a thief. Jack swiped a hand over his sweaty brow, forgetting he was wearing a knitted mask and it wouldn't do any good. Why did he do these sorts of things again? The lock clicked as he succeeded in picking it open. A familiar pounding exultation swept over the reporter; he was on his way to solving another one. Consequences? Who cared. Jack stepped through the door and closed it softly behind him. He thought about locking it, but decided an opening for a swift retreat would be better. Knowing it was available would make him feel better anyway. Jack took out his pen light and flashed it around, noting he was in a back storage room. As good a place to start as any.

Twenty minutes passed in that little room. There were a lot of ledgers kept here, with a lot of columns in each ledger. Jack was familiar with this sort of thing and knew how to speed read a ledger, but it still took time. Book after book passed through his groping fingers, but nothing interesting cropped up. Minute twenty-one ticked into reality as he pulled another box off the shelf and was rewarded by a rain of gray dust on his head. He resisted the urge to sneeze and reached for another ledger that sat on the top of this box. Oh goody. Jack sighed and pulled the ledger out to flip through it. The cover bulged in an abnormal fashion. He opened it

70

quickly and noticed though the box was dusty this ledger wasn't. A small black notebook lay just inside the cover. It was thin and plain, but very interesting. Of course its main interest lay in the fact that it wasn't a ledger. He picked up the notebook and turned it over. It was of very good make. There was a symbol engraved in silver on the front; a sickly oak tree with a healthy one growing out of it, enclosed by a silver circle. Interesting.

Jack stopped, his finger poised in the act of opening the notebook. Was that a footstep in the room outside? A cold shiver ran through the reporter. He snapped his pen light off and slid the notebook into his pocket for later perusal. Jack moved quickly to the door connecting this room with the rest of the building and pressed himself against it, listening with every inch of his body. Something was moving on the other side of that door. The sound was very faint, but there was certainly something there. Half felt, half heard, Jack knew someone was moving. He was about to jump out the back door and race for his car when a thought occurred to him. There was hardly any sound. Whoever that was, they were being as cautious as he was. They were not allowed here anymore than him. What did this someone want? Jack's curiosity was almost as boundless as Simeon's, and it was less controlled. He opened the door he was leaning against and moved noiselessly into the next room.

Complete darkness and a faint cinnamon smell engulfed him. Jack stood still by the door, trying to locate the movement of the other person. A dim rustle came from his left, something like clothing brushing against wood. Jack moved slowly toward the sound. For one of the first times in his life he wished he believed in a god. Any god. He really wanted to pray whoever this was didn't have night vision goggles. Or a gun. Maybe he should have headed

71

for his car after all. A small bump came from his right and Jack froze, his heart feeling like it was going to pound out of his chest. That noise came from the other side of the room. The rustler couldn't have been the bumper, there hadn't been time to cross that space.

There were at least two people besides him in this room.

Jack stood frozen still, listening to faint movements that drifted to him from both sides of the room. They were far enough away that Jack wasn't sure the two noisemakers could hear each other. Not that that would make a difference, obviously they were here together. Weren't they? There couldn't be three different sets of people breaking into the CP headquarters tonight! That was too ridiculous for consideration. Of course it had been awfully easy to break in, but– Jack's mouth dropped open in horrified realization of his own stupidity. There had been no alarm. He had jimmied open a door and snuck inside, and no alarm had sounded. But there were always alarms on buildings like this. It had been turned off, in preparation for someone coming in tonight.

"Found it yet, K20?" a whisper drifted from the darkness on Jack's right. It was a nice, feminine voice and the quality surprised him almost as much as the sound itself did. "He said to look in a ledger, I haven't even seen a–"

"Shut up, R530, and keep looking!" a rough growl answered from the same area. That was more like what burglars ought to sound like. Jack gripped the doorknob of the little storage room door. He needed to get out. He needed to get out fast and silently. A hand closed over his hand on the doorknob. Quick as lightening Jack threw an uppercut at where he surmised this new threat's chin must be. A sharp crack sounded in the room at the impact of the

72

reporter's fist, and a loud thud followed as the owner of the chin fell to the ground. Jack dropped with it, judging someone with a voice like that K20 character would have a side arm to match. A flash from his right showed he was correct, but the impact of the bullet hitting the door was louder than the report of the gun. Jack bit back a terrified squeak and skimmed across the ground like a crab, toward the opposite side of the dark room. *"Silenced! Silenced! The gun is silenced!"* Jack's mind screamed inside him, as his fear quickly climbed into a full-blown panic. These were not nice people.

Light flooded the room. Jack's panicking mind went numb as his blinking eyes swept the room from his position crouching behind a bookshelf. Dark heavy wooden furniture, shelves lined neatly with files and boxes, and a delicate lighting spreading from old fashioned fixtures was automatically filed in his mind as he peered out, but the room itself hardly registered. He could see the other occupants now. The growling K20 stood by a small, tastefully designed desk. Over his face was a black hood with eye holes the only openings. Jack was convinced he had scars and an evil, leering countenance underneath that mask. Even if they didn't show on the outside, they would still be there if he used silencers, like the portrait Dorian Gray kept in his garret; you can hide the truth of yourself but it is still there. Only a hand could be seen of R530 from Jack's position, a well-groomed, pretty hand clutching the light switch. But Jack's mind didn't numb in shock over the sight of these two people, or even the Glock pistol with the large silencer screwed on one end that was sweeping the room under K20's deft work. He was staring at the hand that had closed over his, the person he had so swiftly knocked unconscious. That hand wore a wedding ring he knew as well as his own. He had placed that ring on that beautiful, limp hand.

73

Judy lay in plain sight, dressed in her own burgling clothes, her lovely black hair spread out around her like Elaine's limp tresses had as she drifted toward Camelot. What a horrible analogy! Jack swallowed and wished for the second time that night he knew someone to pray to. Judy must be alive, and must stay alive! Jack's eyes fastened on K20's silenced Glock. The reporter's eyes were dangerously determined.

7:02 a.m., Feb. 14th; 4601 12th Street, Fairfax, VA

The sound of the doorbell clattered through Vincent's thoughts as he lay awake on his bed. It was a firm, decisive sort of ring, like someone pushed the bell for longer than most. That shouldn't be ignored. Vincent couldn't decide whether he was glad or sorry to have to get up as he slipped out from under his throw and meandered toward the door. He nearly stepped on a test tube and swiped a hand across his eyes to clear them. Vincent told the door he was coming and hopped over a dismantled computer lying strewn around the hall. The young man rubbed his arms absently, thinking it was cold, and dark, and vaguely wondering why it felt darker inside him than out. His eye caught the kitchen clock and he idly wondered who could be knocking on his door this early. Well, even if it was the UPS man he would be tempted to hug him for giving him an outside influence this morning. Today marked a full year since he had come home from a peaceful flight to find police cars and firemen, and no home and no family. A year since... He pulled open the door and morning sunlight streamed in. It framed Simeon Lee, standing on the stoop. The retired CIA man held up a restaurant take out bag that smelled delicious and a cup holder with two coffee cups. Vincent pulled the door open wider and stepped aside to let him in. He tried to say something, but found it wouldn't come.

Simeon silently wondered if he was walking into a home, lab, experiment station, or scene of the latest hurricane. His new work associate was certainly not cut of the ordinary stuff. He stepped over a broken long board, a half-assembled jet pack, and a black rabbit munching on a shoelace, and steered for the kitchen he could see opening off the hallway. He passed a bookshelf and smiled as he recognized many of the titles. His eye caught one lying face up with a picture of modern veterinarians looking shocked in the middle of some medieval naval battle. *Crescent Tides*, Simeon read the title and reminded himself to ask about author Aaron Gruben sometime. Vincent slipped in front of him, mumbling apologies for the mess.

"I haven't picked up in...well, I haven't picked up at all, I guess," he ended his monologue, a half smile creeping over his freckled face. He closed the three laptops on the counter and stacked them in a corner to make room for Simeon's bag. "What's in there that smells so good?"

"Omelets, crepes, sausage, waffle, fruit. Wasn't sure what you liked," Simeon answered, handing Vincent one of the cups. The inventor took it a little nervously, knowing he would have to pretend to like the bitter coffee just for this morning. He took a drink and the half smile spread to a real one. It was hot chocolate. Really good hot chocolate. Simeon watched his companion surreptitiously as he began to pull things out of the bag. He was a sight this morning, with his uncombed hair flying everywhere and wearing the same wrinkled clothes he had on yesterday. But those nice green eyes were looking a little more alive every moment. If he

75

could keep him on this upward trend, those likeable eyes ought to lose even their heartbreaking redness soon.

"The porch table is almost clean," Vincent commented, watching Simeon try to find a place on the full counters to set the crepes. Simeon gave a relieved nod and shrugged back into his coat. The two men moved into the early morning sunlight streaming into the pretty backyard, Vincent grabbing the handiest thing to ward off the cold morning air on his way out. Simeon sat the bag on the oval glass porch table, handed his companion a fork, and motioned to the assorted foods. Vincent obediently picked the waffles and a few sausages and plopped on a mesh chair pulled up next to the table. The two munched in silence for a few minutes, the quiet murmur of distant traffic and the sweet sound of waking birds the only noise. Simeon took up the conversation as the sunlight grew stronger, setting off the fruit trees and landscaped bushes to perfection.

"Always like mornings."

"Right," Vincent said companionably. "I'm even starting to like this one. Thanks for showing up with food. Are we starting that X box thing this morning or something?" Simeon hesitated before he replied and Vincent guessed he was deciding on the 'right' answer. "Look Simeon, I'd rather not start out this new, uh...enterprise trying to guess what you're actually doing. Do you mind if we keep things out in the open? I'm not very easily offended, and I'm pretty good at keeping things under my hat."

"Good. Agreed. Not here on business. Read up on you a little last night, wanting to know where to start with training," Simeon answered, and went back to his whole wheat crepes and fruit. Vincent waited a moment to see if anything else would be offered. He realized Simeon Lee preferred to be taciturn.

"You found February the fourteenth in the file, and I already told you I don't have any friends to speak of. So you came over to get me out of bed and make sure I wasn't alone today," Vincent supplied the ending, smiling over his hot chocolate. Simeon nodded.

"Presumptuous?" he asked, allowing a hint of nervousness to show on his face.

"Beautifully! Thanks ever so much, this means a lot. A whole lot... It was just after my nineteenth birthday, you know...I wasn't going to get out of bed today. At all. Silly, I guess. I know Mom and Dad are in heaven and happier than anything I can imagine, and that I'll see them again too. I don't know why I get so depressed still. Just sulkily missing them, I guess. I ought to be happy."

"It's not sulking to miss someone you love. A Christian's death is never happy. Heaven is happy. Death is not. Death is a horrible reminder of everything wrong. It's unnatural, the most jarring reminder of our fall and the presence of evil there is. Don't try to be happy about it, Vincent. Hold to where they are, that you will certainly be there too. But here we have to live staring the effects of our sin in the face. Death is that effect at its strongest. It is a deep spiritual sorrow, as well as a real physical bereavement. Jesus is its conqueror. Keep letting Him conquer it for you."

"Okay. Thanks for being the Conqueror's aide today," Vincent sniffed. He decided to change the subject. "So, since you showed up early, do you have any plans for the day? Or was this just a morning stop before aide work?"

"Quit."

"Oh right, you're a Parabaloni now. You told me last night I was on trial until you decided if I could actually do this (whatever 'this' entails). What do I have to do to officially become your agent?" Simeon pursed his lips and shrugged apologetically at the young man. "I guess that means you don't really know till we start. That makes sense, I suppose. Well, I can live with not knowing till you figure out if I'll do. I hadn't thought about your quitting all other occupations to accommodate this new spy thing. Does that mean you get to stay all day?"

"Want me?"

"Awfully." Half a smile curved over his friend's face, and Vincent had the sudden notion Simeon liked being wanted. "So what are we going to do with ourselves?"

"What do you like?"

"Books, music, inventing, church, science, board games, praying, museums, playgrounds, and pie come to mind."

"Nice list," Simeon approved.

"Thanks, you must tell me yours soon. But right now I'm too curious about that box to bother much with the others. Do you want to figure out what's inside it today?"

"You up to it?"

"Yeah. I'd love to, actually. Now that you got me up into the sunlight, fed me really good food, and are planning on sticking around a while, I'm feeling alive enough to be very curious. But..." Vincent stopped and studied his companion hesitantly. Simeon tipped his head on the side to invite him to go on. "Last night you weren't too enthused when I mentioned flying. I'm not sure I want to ask now because I'm afraid you're the sort that will say yes just to be nice."

"I say what I mean."

"Well, okay. What about flying down to New Mexico? I have a whole workshop and a real lab down there in a mountain–"

"On?"

"No, in. It's a much better spot for tearing open X boxes without getting killed by whatever is inside. I don't have anything going for a couple of days. Do you have any family here, or anyone who would miss you if you're gone for the night? Wife? Girlfriend? Son? Daughter? Brother? Roommate? Friend? Dog? Cat? Plants?"

"No."

"Really? I'm sorry. Same here. Lonely, ain't it?"

"Rabbit."

"What? Oh, you saw Ivan. He's insurance against accidentally overdosing myself with poison gas, like a miner's canary. He bites and growls, and I detest him almost as much as he hates me. I toss a head of lettuce in the living room every so often and make sure the pet door stays open to the backyard, and that's about all our interaction. I wonder why I don't get a dog. I like dogs. Why don't I own one? Why don't you have a dog, Simeon?" Vincent asked suddenly.

"Like them too much," he shrugged. Vincent blinked confusedly, and Simeon explained. "Having your sole companion die every ten years is painful."

"Oh. Yeah, I guess it would be," Vincent mumbled, and

79

quickly changed the subject. "Well, if there's no one depending on us here, what do you think? Want to fly out west to open a box?" Vincent asked. What Simeon thought was more a feeling of terror at leaving the good old ground again. But he would rather fly than squash the eager excitement that had been growing in his new friend, and especially more than getting killed by whatever was in that box for lack of a good place to crack it open.

"Okay," Simeon answered. "Grab your things."

"Right on!" Vincent cried eagerly, leaping up and darting inside. Simeon slid to his feet and began to gather up their breakfast things and put them away neatly. If they stayed too long in New Mexico together he would have to teach Vincent to at least clear his place.

11:29 p.m., Feb. 13th; Philadelphia, CP Headquarters

The Glock stopped sweeping the room and settled over Judy's still form. A dark bruise was beginning to show on her temple. *"If only she was tall enough for her chin to have been where it should have!"* Jack berated himself, frantically looking for something to use against the pistol. His eye caught a box of pamphlets. "You be the chooser" they proclaimed loudly in a tastefully done type. Jack grabbed the box and aimed cautiously.

"K20, stop," R530 broke in, laying her pretty hand on his rough one. Something in her tone of voice made Jack pause, and he studied the woman for an instant. She was in plain sight now but a hood covered her face just as it did K20's and left little of note to be seen. A nice build though.

"No use asking for me to stop, whoever she is she shouldn't have been–" K20 started to answer, but R530 cut him off.

"Oh be quiet, I'm not going to plead for her life or anything stupid. Look at her head. Anything occur to you?"

"No."

"Someone hit her, you dolt! And it wasn't me, and it wasn't you, so there must be someone else here." A thick cardboard box hit K20 square in his face before he had the chance to think through the observation. Jack followed the box almost on the instant, darting through the snowing pamphlets. His aim was much better on chins he could actually see and a sharp crack rang around the room as the reporter's hard knuckles connected with desperate force. K20 staggered back against the door to the storage room, one hand groping for the gun that had fallen from his stunned fingers. Jack raced to pursue his attack while the man was off balance, but he slipped on a glossy pamphlet and found himself crashing on the floor. He didn't take the time to get up again but skimmed on all fours along the floor toward the pistol, every nerve focused on the one goal of closing his fingers around its black metal. A pretty, well-groomed hand picked it up while he was still a foot away. Jack reacted with the speed of adrenaline-fueled desperation. He drove his legs into the ground, propelling him toward the light switch like a Jack-in-the-box springing open.

Darkness spread so suddenly it was almost maddening. For half a second Jack felt he must have been hit, and was acting only in his mind as his life flowed away. But surely his mind wouldn't find

Judy so heavy. Jack resisted the urge to grunt as he snatched his wife from the ground and staggered toward the farthest corner he could remember in this room. Why did K20 have to be leaning against the door to his quick exit? But there must be another way out! Jack forced himself to focus, knowing he only had seconds before the light came back. He had briefly glimpsed another door and he shifted Judy to one shoulder to frantically grope at his nearest estimate. His hand closed on a doorknob.

Light filled the room, bringing with its instantaneous presence the panic of certain discovery. Jack jerked the door open and staggered in, closing the heavy wooden door behind him as gently as he could. This new place was dark, but it felt bigger than a closet. Promising, that probably meant there was another door or a window somewhere in here. He put Judy on the ground as gently as time would allow (meaning he bent down before he dropped her) and fumbled for a light switch. A soft yellow glow filled his new room, and the reporter glanced around. They were in a small, square office. There was no window and the only door led back into that room with the silenced pistol. Jack jammed the oak office chair under the doorknob and then slumped on the crimson carpeted floor next to his wife, feeling his stomach jumping and his throat constricting. What on earth were they going to do?

"It had better not have been you who hit me," Judy mumbled before he could come up with an option. Jack was so relieved to hear her grumble normally he pulled her up into a tight embrace. "We must be about to die, I just heard you sob in my ear. Jack did I get us in that much trouble?"

"We got us in that much trouble. Why did you have to follow me this time, Judy?" Jack said, exasperation coming to his rescue and hiding his desperation from his wife. The gruff sound of R530 and K20 arguing drifted through their heavy wooden door before Judy could reply. It would only be a moment before they found out where the two intruders were hiding. Jack motioned for silence and moved to switch the light off to make sure he didn't give them any hints. Judy stood up and stepped beside the door next to him, listening to the two people in the other room grumbling and searching.

"If only we could call the police!" Judy whispered in Jack's ear. The reporter's mind whirled away on the idea and he gripped his wife's hand ecstatically as he whipped out his phone with his other. Judy watched in confusion as he texted their position to the nearest police station. He held it up for her to read before sending, and Judy swiftly decided it would be a lot better to land in jail alive than get killed by whoever was out there. She took the phone from his hands and quickly made it sound more desperate. They would take hours to get here with Jack's calmly factual statements. Just as the notification popped up to report the text sent, the doorknob to their room rattled. And rattled again, harder. A shoulder bumped into the door and Judy slipped Jack's phone into his pocket and flipped on the light. If they were discovered anyway she would prefer light.

"How's your head?" Jack asked, eyeing the door malignantly.

"Oh, is it still on? I was thinking I was a kin of the Green Knight and it had become quite detached from me."

"That bad, eh? Sorry, sweetheart. Next time mention it's you before you grab my hand."

"I didn't know you were there, I just knew the doorknob was," Judy answered evenly. Jack pressed her hand quietly. He knew she was scared stiff, brave girl. So was he for that matter. The reporter moved to the ornate oaken desk and gripped it at the sides.

"Behind the desk," he ordered in a grunt as he flipped the heavy piece of furniture on its side, so the solid top faced the door.

"Why?" Judy asked as she obeyed. Something crashed through the door and made a small, round hole in the wall to her left. Judy sucked in her breath and tried to keep the tremble out of her voice at the sight of the quiet bullet hole. "Oh, that's why. I didn't hear a report, Jack."

"No, you wouldn't from here. He's using a silencer."

"A silencer?" Judy almost yelped. "Jack, only really bad guys own silencers!"

"I know, all right? I'm trying to think of something."

"Thick pate, get behind the desk while you think!" Judy yelled, pulling him down next to her as two more bullets crashed through into the wall. "What gun is it, when does it run out of bullets?"

"I know about guns, but I'm not an expert, and there's no way of knowing if he's really quick at reloading or if he has another side arm on him. Still, if I rushed him—"

"No!" Judy cried. A resounding crash filled the little room and the husband and wife knew their door was no longer any protection. They lifted their desk and charged with it, crouching low and tilting it up to offer as much protection as possible. There was no consultation or silent wink, it was a simultaneous realization it was their only chance. Wood splintered off above their heads as they ran, a shocked shot squeezed off in desperate surprise as the thuggish K20 found a large piece of furniture charging at him. Jack took charge of the desk as he felt them come in contact with their antagonist. He dashed it up and out, surprised by how clear his brain was and how light an oak desk became with the addition of adrenaline. He felt K20 fall under the impact. Jack dropped the furniture and jumped for the gun clutched in the sprawled K20's fingers. R530 aimed a kick at the reporter's head, but it never landed. Judy swept up the chair as soon as the desk was no longer in her hands and brought it down on R530 as the hooded woman watched her companion get run over by a mobile desk.

Jack staggered up, holding the pistol in what he hoped was a competent way. He knew lots of information about these things but had never actually used one. Somehow knowing the exact mechanisms and history of the machine in his sweaty mitts wasn't very comforting. K20 glared at him from the ground, his black hood sitting a little askew but still in place enough for two hazel eyes to burn into the reporter's. It wouldn't take very long for that malicious stare to turn into action, no matter how reckless. R530 was splayed unmoving on the ground under the broken chair. A siren's wail sounded distantly outside the building and began to get closer quickly. The sound was reassuring enough to allow for conversation.

"You were much smarter, dear," Jack commented to his wife, motioning to the laid out R530. "I didn't hit mine hard enough. As hard as you can is the correct way to act in this type of thing."

"Oh, Jack, stop! She could be dead for all I know," Judy said. There was a tremor in her voice, and Jack knew with the immediate danger down her nerves were starting to give.

"We're not out of it yet, honey," he murmured, sliding his ski mask quickly into a pocket as the wailing siren pulled into the parking lot. The door crashed open and officers waving weapons poured in. Jack quickly surrendered the one he was carrying and gave their names as Jack and Judy Lewis[15]. He began to deftly describe the way he and his wife were harried and hurt by these two hooded hoodlums. Judy backed him up in every point, adding just enough of the beautiful-female-in-danger touch to get the policemen on their side. It was working. If only they didn't ask what they were doing there!

"So what were you doing here to have surprised these two in their nighttime thieving?" Officer Georgeson asked. His manner suddenly grew a bit of hard suspicion and he glanced up from where he was scribbling in his notebook. "Come to think of it, why are you two all in black? And didn't Torez pull a ski mask out of your pocket, Mr. Lewis?" Jack waved a hand at a small, thin man who had been standing just against the door during most of these proceedings, called in by the police when they responded to an incident at his workplace. He looked upset at being pointed out. No, he looked plain frightened and his pale hands began to rub each other almost compulsively.

"Ask that CP employee," Jack hazarded, playing his card and hoping for all he had it was a winning one. "He can tell you why it's so busy in here tonight, when things are supposed to be locked up. I don't think he will have anything to say against Judy and me." Officer Georgeson turned toward the man, determined curiosity in his manner. Jack deftly began to move toward the door to the

---

[15] Mostly for fun, partly in case of trouble, the Leasons had created an entire extra identity under Jack's middle name of 'Lewis.' Every month they dined at the Lewises favorite restaurant, fed the ducks at parks around town, and professed to own a monkey. The Lewises even kept their own set of library cards (which came in handy when the Leasons' had fines).

storage room, taking Judy with him. The man was practically cowering under the officer's questions. Jack smiled as he ducked through the door into the dark storage room, and on out to the alley. The CP was too frightened by whatever they were hiding in their books and calling hooded criminals in to collect. It was going to be hard to explain tonight, especially with having deliberately disarmed the alarms. There was no way they were going to press charges on two non-existent people. Jack allowed himself a little hop-skip of joy as he reached his car with no other mishaps.

"Come on, Judy, let's go feed some ducks," he said happily.

"You're quacked. Feed ducks at this hour?"

"What? Even ducks like quackers at midnight."

"I think we had better do something, we're both getting too corny for any decent folk."

"Ducks like corn."

"All right, illogical one, drive on. I'll feed ducks at the midnight hour," Judy smiled. "I'm not in jail, nor am I dead. Judy has never felt so alive, Leason or Lewis." Jack agreed, feeling a little smug at having survived that mess and gotten out with so few scratches. And even with a very interesting notebook to look over later. *"Why did I think I needed help back there?"* Jack thought to himself as he drove toward the park with his wife beside him.

I expect you have heard the biblical phrase that pride comes before the fall. Jack Lewis Leason had no idea how fully he was to experience that harsh doctrine in all its flaring difficulties before the sun rose.

87

5

1:43 a.m., Feb. 14th; Wiggins Park, Philadelphia, PA

"Oh come on, Jack," Judy murmured sleepily. "What are you doing, fattening that one up for soup?"

"Duck soup is good, especially when made by you," Jack flattered happily. He tossed another handful of breadcrumbs at his favorite. "It's a beautiful night, the mallards are feeling just ducky about being awake. Why aren't you?"

"Because I'm tired, flatfoot!" Judy whined good-naturedly. "Come on, Jacky lad, let's go home."

"Okay, sweetums, anything for you," Jack sighed, and stood up to tie the bag of crumbs he had carried out of their car. For just an instant he had the uncomfortable sensation that someone was behind him. Then all other sensations were taken up in a burning pain as something very hard hit him on the back of his head. Jack fell forward on his hands and knees, pain sparking through him, his mind fuzzy and dark, and his body sluggish. He heard Judy scream beside him. The horrible sound cut through him, and was cut off abruptly. With the strength of a desperate love, Jack gathered his wits to himself just enough to be able to see Judy's limp form carried toward a moving truck with the strange motto 'We lug the rugs' painted on the side. The two people who carried her wore hoods, just like K20. Jack struggled to get his feet under him, fear and anger at Judy's manhandling giving him the power to fight the overwhelming tide of darkness and dizziness that was trying to send him to the ground. Another blow landed on his head. Jack crumpled to the grass, no chance of fighting it left in his agonized

89

mind. The last thing he comprehended before going entirely unconscious was the terrified quacking of his favorite mallard. Apparently the extra crumbs were weighing him down.

3:04 p.m. Feb. 14th; Rocky Mountains, NM

"I've almost got it..." Vincent muttered to himself. Simeon looked hopefully at the blond inventor, half straightening up from where he leaned on the kitchenette counter. The young man still sat plying his tools to that little black box, the tip of tongue sticking out of his mouth. Simeon relaxed against the counter again. He took another sip of his coffee and silently thanked God Mr. Tolliver Senior had liked the black beverage enough to install a good coffee maker in his workshop kitchenette. Simeon looked around again, once more trying to decide exactly where he was. It was a very big workshop, somewhere inside the Rocky Mountains. There was a garage, an airplane hangar, and a very large area that held everything even slightly useful for working on anything. There were piles of metal scraps, wires, rubber, bolts and screws, test tubes, beakers, at least three full chemistry sets, and tools of every conceivable size and usefulness from wrenches and screwdrivers to huge machines that looked as if they belonged in a body shop. Everywhere he looked there stood half-realized dreams in the form of unfinished inventions and piles of notes. Simeon's eye caught the airplane hangar where the neat little jet now rested. He shivered involuntarily and looked away. It was a very nice plane, he told himself again, trying to calm his fluttering heart. Vincent had flown them down here very quickly with that little jet and the trip had only been mildly terrifying; his new friend was a good and conscientious pilot. It was the end of the ride that had pushed him over the edge. Simeon quickly lifted his mug again, knowing the hot, bitter liquid was one of the few things that really steadied his nerves after losing it like he had on their arrival forty minutes ago.

Everything had been going well, Simeon had even managed to keep up his end of the bits of conversation that had gone on during the flight. Then Vincent had suddenly tipped his wings and headed toward a mountain. Realizing there was nowhere to land was the first intimation of terror in Simeon's mind. Next came the horrifying realization that his pilot was deliberately aiming for the mountain itself. Simeon didn't have time to scream a warning or jerk the yoke up before a black hole opened itself before the plane, they swept in and latched to something, and complete darkness enclosed him. Looking back on it now, as he leaned comfortably against the clean kitchenette, Simeon could see there was a camouflaged tunnel built in the mountain, designed to catch specially made planes and draw them into the underground hanger here in the workshop. At the time there had been nothing but the horrible darkness and nameless shifting, moving something outside his window, and the knowledge he was helplessly being drawn somewhere against his will. The state of terror he was already in, creaks and groans from the machines, and deep unabated blackness threw him back in his memory to Iraq twenty-eight years ago, to the unbearable– Simeon stopped himself quickly and stepped toward Vincent. At least the pilot had been more than kind about the holes Simeon's nails had dug in his passenger's seat. Vincent glanced up as he heard his church friend coming.

"You look a little better," he said, sitting his tools down and studying Simeon. "I'm really sorry I didn't warn you before the dive down–"

"Didn't tell you I needed it," Simeon quickly waved the apology aside. Again. The poor frightened kid had opened every conversation that way since they had landed. He must have looked pretty bad when Vincent had opened his door to help him out. "Almost there?"

"Yeah, almost. I think. It's sort of hard to know, this thing is really complicated. Usually I'd just grab a big mallet and whack it good, but I don't really want to do that with this one."

"No."

"You think it's dangerous then?" Vincent asked, standing up to stretch.

"Yes."

"My thoughts exactly. That Jones character was pretty terrified when you brought this X box near him, and there has to be something behind that fright. I mean, people only get scared for a reason," Vincent quietly dropped his hand on Simeon's shoulder as he said the last words, then headed for the kitchenette to get some water. It was an awkward, not very useful kind of comfort, but it was obvious the young man was trying. That he would try at all meant a very great deal to Simeon. He deserved an answer for that.

"Thanks. Don't ever go out on your own in this business, Vincent. If you don't have someone who knows where you are, and cares enough to try and get you out of trouble, don't get into it at all."

"Which business? The spy business?"

"Yes."

"I'll remember," Vincent said thoughtfully. He finished his water and headed back toward the box. "But I guess I don't have to do more than remember it now, I have you to keep an eye on me. It can get pretty tough sometimes?"

"Yes[16]."

"But you'll stick around as my partner, right?"

"Yes[17]."

"Thanks, Simeon. Me too, so you don't have to worry as we jump into this Parabaloni thing." Vincent paused and scratched his head with his screwdriver, a thoughtful frown on his face. It melted into a smile again. "If you're around, it won't be so bad. Besides, a little hardness will be worth it to do more stuff like we did yesterday. You realize our actions inadvertently opened up an entire country to the gospel? That's nothing to sneeze at, and that was only one night's work! What's it going to turn out to be next?"

"Get the box open."

"Oh, right, I guess that would tell us what might come next. It's the square thing to do," Vincent grinned as he went back to work.

---

[16] Reading conversations of this nature doesn't give a good picture of its reality. For instance, this 'yes.' Its inflections, the way Simeon's movements accompanied it, and the look in his soft eyes, said more than many sentences could have. Vincent was told a story of agony and sorrow and real heroic bravery in that single word that nearly broke his heart, and scared him quite a bit. It made him realize this was not going to be an easy job. The truth behind that little 'yes' would take up more books then I could ever write, and would probably scare you into realizing the world you thought was safe is actually out to get you. I will remain mum.

[17] In contrast, this 'yes' was a strong, wholehearted reply. It was a firm promise, and Simeon let his joy at being able to give it shine out to his new friend.

"A pun like that marks you as a square."

"You have to admit, this thing is trouble squared."

"Watch it, I'll box your ear."

"Warning taken, my poor corniness is boxed away," Vincent chuckled, and focused on the thing in front of him. Fifty minutes later the two men were still trying, each one gripping a side of the box as Vincent applied tool after tool to its shiny sides. They had both shed their jackets and were sweating profusely in the warm temperature of the enormous workroom. Ten minutes later the box shifted and a sliver of a crack opened directly down its middle. The two men looked excitedly at each other, but Simeon put his finger to his lips to check Vincent's triumphant outburst, his head tipped as he listened intently. He heard no ticking of a bomb or any clicks or hisses or churning cogs to activate a booby trap, and nodded Vincent on. They slowly worked the two sides farther and farther apart. Another forty-two minutes later the two halves were completely detached from each other. Simeon quietly gazed at one half while Vincent muttered things to himself and poked the other half with his favorite screwdriver.

"It's designed to spray something," Vincent suddenly piped up. "At a certain time, and (probably as a safety feature) it also has a lock controlled by remote. When the time is right, and its button is pushed, the thing will do…whatever it's supposed to do. But I think we broke the timing device getting it open."

"Can't tell when it was to activate?"

"No, and what's more disappointing I can't trace its remote to the other end, the thing that's supposed to finish activating it…" Vincent muttered, rubbing his head to help him think. "I think…just

94

think, mind you, it was sometime late this month."

"Fact-based guess?"

"I only give guesses I can slightly back up with some kind of a fact. Did you find anything in that one?" Vincent asked eagerly. Simeon held up a small, corked test tube. A globular liquid floated inside, its red color faintly iridescent. Vincent whistled and snatched the tube eagerly.

"I guess we had better not open it here," the inventor muttered disappointedly as he turned it around in the light.

"You good at lab work?" Simeon asked, glancing at the chemistry sets on the far wall.

"No, not really[18]."

"Call your friend."

"Right," Vincent sighed. He stood still, staring at the liquid undulating in the light.

"You need to be the one to do it," Simeon prodded.

"I know. I also know I should have done it a year ago, that's why I don't want to call him now. But that's just stubborn pride, and the longer I put it off the worse it gets. Here, you hold the dooly-mah-whatsit." Vincent tossed the tube to his friend and pulled out his cell phone. He paused and rubbed his chin, covered in blond stubble, a little hesitantly. "Look, Mr. Steve is a good guy, and a good friend of the family. He's going to want to check up on

---

[18] He had blown up his Virginia house twice just in the year he had lived there, and nearly killed himself with noxious chemicals more times than he remembered. The day he woke up a hundred miles from home talking to a lamppost, Vincent had admitted lab work might not be the best option for him.

me if I show up today. Can I tell him about all this Parabaloni stuff?"

"He a gossiper?"

"No, he's great at keeping his mouth closed, the whole family is."

"Then yes. Tell him we need results fast, we'll fly him the stuff this afternoon."

"Really?" Vincent said in hesitant surprise. "Simeon, I could just drop it off. You could stay here, there are plenty of comfortable rooms on the other floors. Flying scares you to death, I know that now."

"If Mr. Stevenson's a good man and a good friend of your father, he'll want to check out who you're with. Should be able to. I'll fly. Call," Simeon firmly ended the conversation. Vincent pressed the call button and walked slowly toward his plane to check it over for another flight. He heard the phone begin to ring in his ear, but his mind was on the quiet gentleman behind him. Simeon Lee was a very good man, and the bravest man he had ever met. And boy, what a teacher! He hoped he could survive Simeon's schooling when it started up. He was realizing just how much he wanted to keep this job.

Sometime in reality; Somewhere on Earth

Jack stirred slowly. His muscles screamed at the tiny movement and he gasped at the sudden pain. Or it should have been a gasp. There was something in his mouth, something fuzzy and large and that tasted like dirty oil. He tried to open his eyes, and after the second try he forced one bleary eye open. At least he thought he did. He still couldn't see anything. Jack closed his eye and tried to concentrate. Hopefully it was only a mild concussion he had to work through and not a full blown cracked skull, like it felt at the moment. Jack tried again. He was moving. It was cold. He was on something hard, and rough, and dirty. His arms and legs were behind him, and it hurt. Jack worked on trying to get his appendages back around to the comfortable frontal position, but they wouldn't work, and it hurt too much to try. The reporter lay still again, blowing hard and furious with his intelligence. He knew everything he was working so hard to figure out should be an instantaneous realization. Jack took a deep breath and forced himself to relax before he tried again. There. He was bound and gagged in the back of a moving truck, traveling somewhere at a pretty good clip. His head was hurt to the point of his brain feeling so jiggled it was hard to work with, and he felt sick. It was pitch black and he couldn't make a sound or move. Judy! Judy? Was she here? His wife's scream resurfaced in his mind, and panic engulfed him. He had never felt so useless, helpless, and vulnerable. What a fool, what a horrible fool he had been to think he had won! He should have…he should have done something. Judy was paying for his getting into this mess. Guilt flooded him, sharpened into an agonizing fiend by the fear running through him, and the uncertainty of Judy's fate. Fool! Fool, fool, fool, why had he jumped into this mess?

Jack lay immobile in the dark, fear for his wife making what little of his brain he could use feel numb. Then another fear hit him. It was as if the darkness, his impotent faculties, useless body, and solitude suddenly opened up a new darkness. It was like staring into a void, so deep and endless it engulfed his mind and made him shake in sudden terror of something he couldn't define. Vast and terrifyingly empty, and all around him...no it was from him, and around him, it was himself and only himself. Jack Leason had only himself, a useless incapable himself, and it horrified him. There must be something else, something besides his own useless, guilty self. There had to be something that could help! Something outside the void, something that could enter it and pull him out! He screwed his eyes shut and tried desperately to tell himself the blackness was only in his mind and the back of the truck. There was no void in reality, he had friends, and a loving wife... But it was still there, he still felt it. Empty, useless, unidentifiably horrifying in its very namelessness, a void of terrible proportions surrounding him. And worst of all, inside of him.

A snort came from the darkness in the truck behind Jack. His eyes flew open uselessly in desperate relief. There was someone near him in this material blackness at least. He stirred again in futile effort to see the one who made that sound. It was Judy, he knew it was. At the knowledge his wife was near and at least alive, his mind straightened out and he returned to his usual state of clear thought. He realized he could do that too. Jack snorted back, and Judy answered him. He considered another pig imitation, but decided against it. This was too serious of a mess for silly barnyard sounds. Jack had no clue why they hadn't simply been killed, but he knew the end of this ride was not going to be pleasant. He began to carefully flex his wrists in an effort to find out how he was tied. There had to be something he could do to get them out! There had to be something he could do to let Judy live, and to live a little longer yet. A bit of that empty feeling returned and Jack began to really struggle for life. Life could drive that emptiness away. As his brain began to function again, the empty void fell back into unreality and curiosity reared its invigorating head. Why had they been grabbed by these people anyway? What was this gang? And where on this globe were they being carted away to, like a couple of cheap rugs, in the back of a filthy van? Jack gritted his teeth and concentrated on the ropes, so tight around his wrists and ankles. He was going to find out before he died.

6

"Vince, it really is you!" Joshua Stevenson cried happily, practically running to say hello as the young man stepped into his lab. The red-haired analyst gripped Vincent's hand and held onto it for a moment in the joy of seeing him there. "Sorry I was a little short on the phone, I have had innumerable scam calls telling me they were you and trying to get information from me since..."

"Since Mom and Dad died last year," Vincent supplied to prove talking about it was okay. "They were reporters?"

"Yes, bother the nosy busybodies. You must have gone underground pretty thoroughly from the way they've been after me."

"Yeah. Look, Mr. Steve, I'm sorry I didn't–"

"Vince, I'm the one that needs to apologize," Josh interrupted earnestly. "You gave me your number at the funeral, and I...I didn't use it. The grieving party should not have to be burdened with keeping up."

"Forgiven, if I am too," Vincent said, a smile running over his face as he remembered hearing those words just last night. God was good to give him two wise men.

"Thank you, I am very relieved to hear it. My Mary will be too, we were both thoroughly convicted about our appalling lack of care for you when you called to get me back to work. What are we doing here instead of at our home, anyway? Oh, and do you need a place,

100

are you on your own? Thomas and Henry heard you called and both immediately said they'd double up if you wanted to share their room. And Mary already started her company chili and if you don't come over tonight for at least a minute–" Vincent laughingly held up his hand to stop the torrent.

"I always love how much you talk, Mr. Steve. Before I answer any of that, I'd better get you started on why we're here instead of at your wonderful home," Vincent grinned. He took the tube of red goop out of a small bag and held it out to the analyst. "Be careful with it, we think it's dangerous. Can you tell us what it is please?"

"Ooh, shiny. Certainly I can tell you, and I will be very careful with it," Josh said. He took the tube and began to putter about his lab, but most of his attention was on his guest. "Who is 'us,' Vince?"

"Me and a good man named Simeon Lee. He's out in the rental car because he knew you'd want to grill me first." Josh laughed and Vincent went on to explain about the past year and especially the past week. Josh Stevenson listened almost as well as he talked, and he was gifted with the art of multi-tasking. He worked as he listened. As Vincent went on from Sunday to the Tuesday coffee shop meeting, he began to find things out. He paused as his young friend arrived at the fight with a terrorist in a metro train, but quickly resumed. Whatever this red goop was, he was beginning to think it was very serious. Vincent finally ended and waited for the outburst of questions and comments he expected. It didn't come. Josh Stevenson stood staring silently at the sample of red goop he had isolated to test. Vincent quickly looked over the analyst's shoulder at the scribbles jotted down about this strange stuff.

"'Strain of andorsonii,'" he read off the notes. "What's that?"

101

"Well, I'm not entirely sure yet," Josh answered slowly. There was an almost frightened seriousness about him, and Vincent tensed. Whatever this stuff was it was nasty apparently. He quietly wondered if it was stress that made his head begin to throb right then. "But I have a pretty scary idea. Give me a minute, and I'll tell you about it."

Vincent nodded and began to wander around the lab, forcing his mind away from whatever Mr. Steve was working on. His eye landed on a series of drawings and old fossils in the back corner of the lab and he grinned at the cartoon style dinosaurs depicted in various violent poses.

"What's this?" he called, pointing at the strange mix.

"Oh, Thomas and I found some old velociraptor bones out in the desert. You know, little mean dinosaurs with large claws and teeth, and I imagine nasty tempers (kind of like poodles). I'm not satisfied with any of the dating methods and am working on one of my own that will knock the socks off the evolutionists. But never mind about that. Vincent, you say this stuff was in a box designed to spray out?"

"That's what it looked like, yes."

"Then I think I've learned enough to tell you this much. Your red goop is a deadly strain of adenovirus. That's usually the family that carries things like the common cold, and pink eye, and other things that aren't that serious. But this has a different genetic code to it… I think it's relatively harmless right now, contained in its own little cases. But if it is sprayed into the air it will almost certainly break out to become a live danger, having the possibility of infecting a very large area. And you know how you can catch a cold just from being in the same room with a sneezing person. But this stuff... I'm afraid this might be deadly."

"About how deadly are we talking?" Vincent asked, with a bit of difficulty, his hand straying up to rub his head. This sudden headache was getting really bad, the throbbing had already become more like a searing pain. Funny, he didn't usually get headaches.

"Well... I haven't finished, but as an idea still in the unproved theory stage... Or maybe it's a hypothesis." Josh blinked and rubbed his own head. He looked a little confused, and had to muster his thoughts before going on. "I would say very deadly. It looks like a strain a bit like pneumonia, but different enough that conventional drugs might not work on it. I should be able to tell you more in a few months...wait I mean hours. No, no... I meant...days. I should be able to tell you..." Josh Stevenson's words dropped away and he stood stupidly staring at the little tube, the red goop undulating mesmerizingly.

"Mr. Steve?" Vincent called in alarm. His voice suddenly sounded as if it was in a tunnel. He jerked his arm up in alarm but found it was sluggish and slow to move. He knew this feeling. Vincent grabbed Mr. Stevenson's shoulders and began to pull him toward the door, raking his gaze over the tables for anything that could be leaking Carbon Monoxide. A simple gas, but still deadly if breathed in too much. There was nothing. And the headache was developing very quickly. Vincent glanced back as he pulled the sluggish analyst toward the safe out of doors and paused in horror. One of the windows had a small hole cut in it, and a black hose filled that hole. This was no accidental leak, they were being poisoned on purpose! The room began to spin around him, and Vincent did his best to make his legs carry him into a run, dragging Josh Stevenson behind him. A wave of relief washed over him as he

103

reached the door and gripped the handle. Fresh, life giving air, just beyond it! But the knob wouldn't turn. He rattled it desperately, but it wouldn't turn. Vincent let go of Josh and jerked his wallet out to get the pin he kept there to pick the lock on doors he always forgot to carry the keys to. He could see the pin, but it was spinning so much he couldn't make his fingers grab it. The headache from the CO was debilitating in its intensity now, and still getting worse.

Something sailed through the wooden door and pinged off the concrete floor, an inch from where Josh Stevenson was lying. Vincent dropped to the ground and painfully pulled Mr. Steve away from the door. Someone from outside was shooting at them! They were not going to be allowed to leave. Vincent grimaced and gripped his stomach with a gasp. The nausea was starting. With the symptoms compiling in this fast, whoever was out there must be really pumping this gas in, at least at a level 3200 PPM. That gave them only minutes to live. Another bullet sang through the door and ricocheted off the ground, landing in a table two feet from where the men of science huddled. Vincent desperately fumbled for his phone, trying to make his stupefied brain remember Simeon's cell number. His finger frantically swiped at where his failing intelligence told him the lock was, but it didn't work...his phone was out of batteries. The cell slipped from his grasp uselessly. He gripped his head trying to get the horrible pain and dizziness to stop. A heavy metal microscope lay on the table above his head, and Vincent hefted it with all the strength he had at a window above the table. The microscope clattered to the ground, hardly even making a noise as it hit the window. Of course, Mr. Steve had his lab strengthened, so no one nearby would be hurt if an explosion accidentally occurred. There would be no breaking the glass. Vincent looked out from around the table, telling his Chick-Fil-A sandwich to stay where it was as he crawled painfully toward the

104

door. Another bullet hit the floor near him, and Vincent dropped to the ground. He didn't have the strength to get the door open anyway. *"If God wants us to live, someone else is going to have to step in,"* the inventor thought. He curled on the ground as close to the bits of air coming through the door as he could get and forced a yell for help out of his lungs. It was weak, and gravelly, and hard to get out while keeping his lunch still in, but it was an attempt. Vincent tried to raise a fist to pound on the wood, hoping Simeon would hear it, but his mind began to go dark before he felt the rough wood under his fingers. His last thought was a desperate prayer for God to nudge Simeon Lee out of that car and to their rescue. He would be dead in minutes unless help came first.

Daytime; Moving truck going somewhere

Jack lay still, gasping for air through the filthy rag and soaked with sweat. Sunlight had stuck it's hope filled fingers through the few cracks and chinks in the truck's metal body a few minutes after Jack and Judy's first porcine like conversation. At first the coming day filled Jack with urgency. Daylight probably meant their fate would be decided soon. The reporter began the fight with his bonds with more vigor than he thought he had. He realized he was tied to something metal and stationary, not just to himself, and it made him mad. That meant he couldn't even roll over to Judy, and he assumed she was treated in the same way. Minute after minute ticked by, and the truck roared on. The minutes climbed into hours and still nothing changed. Jack fought on as the heat rose in the metal truck.

There was a brief moment of excitement for the two people

105

trapped helplessly as they felt their ride slow down and begin to make turns. Jack could hear the noise of engines around them, and knew they were in a town. After some kind of time (whether it was hours or minutes was very hard to judge in that hot, humid truck) they stopped altogether. The sound of a door opening and closing drifted from by the cab.

"Do you think we can make it today?" someone said right outside their truck's metal body. Jack pictured a college boy dressed in stylish American Eagle clothes when he heard that voice.

"We'll have to make it, if we don't want X deciding we're useless," someone answered. That one was decidedly a large male with a lot of tattoos who carried a switch blade and rarely washed, Jack decided. "K20 said X wants us to pick up a corpse from San Antonio tonight and bring it along with these two."

"Why does X want these people again?" College Kid yawned, his voice growing fainter as he moved away from the truck.

"Something about that missing black notebook of his. It's not our business, kid. But if we miss our pick up, I bet we get ourselves blacklisted by the PDs," Switch Blade's gruff voice could just be heard by the straining reporter.

"We had better make this a quick stop then," College Kid said nervously. Switch Blade grunted something in reply, but it was too far away to hear. So X was a person. And that notebook tucked in his inner coat pocket belonged to this X character. And whoever it was wanted to talk to them. Talking could be okay. The memory of K20's hard pistol and R530's merciless tendencies reentered Jack's mind, and he shook his head in the silent knowledge the coming talk would not be pleasant. And then desperately whished he

106

hadn't as it increased his headache to the point of almost making him drop unconscious again. A snort came from Judy and Jack smiled[19]. She must have seen his head drop to the nasty metal truck again. He grunted back to say he was still okay and went back to work on his wrists. He couldn't decide if he had made any progress or not, but some moments it seemed like the ropes were just a little looser. If he could only get them off while they were stopped here!

The heat rose. The seconds ticked into minutes, the minutes ran together in maddening monotony. College Kid and Switch Blade came back to the truck. The roar of the engine started up and in a little time they had increased back to the smooth roar of a highway speed. Jack let his head drop on the hard metal again. The heat was still growing worse and his headache was making his whole body feel sick. Every muscle ached and groaned, he could feel the blood dripping from his torn wrists. Jack finally dared admit the truth to himself. He was helpless. There was nothing he could do to save himself. And that he was in desperate need of saving Jack knew all too well. He didn't know where this truck was taking them, or who they would meet but he was certain he would never stay alive to finish this story. Despair coursed through him, taking what little energy he had been able to dredge up, and exhaustion set in. Jack gave in to it, and let himself drift away.

7:07 p.m. Feb. 14th; Outside Liberty Labs, San Antonio, TX

A Brandenburg Concerto filled the little rented Fiat's interior.

---

[19] This is fairly difficult with a rag stuffed in your mouth. I had a bear once who loved to carry rags clutched in his teeth, and I don't think I ever saw him smile while doing it.

Simeon flipped his phone open, tucking his copy of Tennyson[20] back into his black overnight bag.

"Hello," he said simply.

"Sim!" a large voice boomed out of the cell phone. Simeon instinctively pulled it away from his ear and quickly turned the volume down.

"Saul," Simeon answered the greeting, his tone showing he was very pleased to hear from his old coworker.

"You called me yesterday," the big voice of Saul Korry explained. "Sorry I'm just now getting back to you, I was at one of Jon's concerts and you know how his annoying rock group likes to blare. Why can't my son play something nice, like a cello?"

"Drums can be nice," Simeon said mildly.

"Sure, when they aren't trying to be heard over screaming people and ridiculously loudly amped guitars."

"How is Jonathan?" Simeon asked.

"Good. He was the one who noticed you had called and he told me to say hello to Uncle Sim for him. He wants to know when you're coming to watch one of his games again. I wouldn't do it this season, the local college baseball team he's on kind of stinks."

"More reason to cheer them on."

"Well, that's one man's opinion. You do need to come and visit us, you know. Never mind what Michelle thinks, Jon and I

---

[20] Yes, even spies are allowed to have poetic souls. Simeon loved the old poetry and had confused many evil men by quoting favored lines to them in the middle of a fight.

want you and...oh, never mind. I know you hate to cause friction in a house, so I might as well shut up. Why did you call, Simeon? You didn't leave a message. You all right, little white bro? Is a normal job finally getting to you, or did you call to tell me you had gone back to Gibbs again?"

"Inapplicable."

"The reason you called me is inapplicable now? Then I missed you when you needed me again."

"Didn't say that."

"You never do. I'm sorry Sim. Why don't you get yourself a woman?"

"Good idea, trouble is finding one," Simeon said quietly. Saul recognized the depressed note underneath the tone and decided not to press it.

"Then what about a job you really like? Tell you what, you can come work with me. Come join the detective team and fight injustice again instead of pushing papers around an office all day. I could use another hand. Especially right now." Saul sounded tired and disheartened suddenly, and a thrill quietly coursed through Simeon. That mood in his big friend meant serious trouble.

"Why?" he asked.

"I guess the best way to get you up here to Wyoming is to prick that dangerous[21] curiosity of yours. Listen up then; I had a

---

[21] Curiosity can be dangerous, dear reader, and Saul knew it well. The two men had been thrown together when Saul was 21 and Simeon 16, and even than it was the younger man's curiosity that had nearly killed them and did save them in the end. Having gone through CIA training together, and from there to twenty-seven different missions around

grieving grandfather come in three weeks ago. He had a grandson named Tom Smith he was especially close to, a neat guy about Jon's age. He was a little slow mentally, and a deaf mute from some genetic thing. The old guy told me a lot about him (he was so broken up I just let him sit there and talk for a while). Tom showed up dead one day. Just dead. The doctor's said it was heart trouble, but his grandfather is determined it wasn't so simple."

"Murder?"

"So he said. He always took Tom to his doctor appointments and knew his insides almost as well as Tom must have. Grandfather Henry even brought Tom's medical records to me and I looked them over. There was nothing wrong with that kid's heart, Sim. And there are a lot of poisons that can make a healthy heart stop."

"Then?"

"Then I said I'd take the case, and started working on it myself instead of assigning it to one of my underlings like I usually do. I liked Grandfather Henry, and felt awful about his losing Tom. After I started looking into it I began to agree with Grandfather Henry, that Tom had been bumped off. But I can't find a suspect, not really. Tom got around and knew a lot of people. Folks were always in and out of his parents' apartment, where he lived. Then I started to come across something. Tom's brother has a girlfriend, and she has a brother, and I didn't like the girlfriend's brother. That's how low I had sunk, Sim, I was following a feeling."

"Worked in Singapore," Simeon comforted.

---

the world officially, and plenty more unofficially, Saul had thoroughly learned the dangers of the curious. Everywhere they went Simeon's curiosity found adventures, most of which put the two men as near death as you can come while still remaining on this earth.

110

"Only because you were the one with the feeling, and with the way you read people it made it almost a fact. Anyway, I was following Tom's brother's girlfriend's brother, an annoying kid by the name of Stu. He's such an ornery thing I didn't even feel sorry that he had a name like that. Little by little I realized he's into something, and I'm pretty certain Tom was a victim of whatever it is."

"That's not clear."

"No, it's not clear to me either Sim, that's why I'm not explaining it well! Look, it's just sort of vague and I can't seem to break into it deeper yet. It has something to do with an insignia (a dying oak tree sprouting a healthy one), and the initials PD, people wearing hoods, a Plant, and black boxes... I'm not sure what I'm on to Sim, but there seems to be a lot of people involved in it. And I don't like it in my country. We fought too hard to keep America safe. Just thinking about all we went through in Dubai makes me hopping mad to think there's something this evil running through our country. I'm not going to let a bunch of bozos make my America unsafe for nice kids like Tom Smith, and I wish you were here to fight it with me instead of pushing papers around in D.C."

"Black boxes?" Simeon asked, having latched onto one thing in his friend's confusing tirade. Then he noticed something. As he waited for Vincent, Simeon's eye had been running idly around the street, automatically watching the happenings around him. Now he saw a hole appear in the door of Liberty Labs. Simeon had seen holes appear like that before, and he knew Vincent was in trouble.

"Saul, I'm in San Antonio, Liberty Labs," he said quickly[22]. "A

---

[22] Simeon knew from hard-won experience that having someone know where you were when trouble started could save you years of trouble and pain.

sniper's after a boy of mine. Saltsburg arrangement[23]." Simeon snapped his phone closed and focused on the door.

---
[23] Neither man will tell me what the 'Saltsburg arrangement' is. Whenever I ask they just grin at each other and say things like, "I'm awfully glad that blimp was there."

112

7

Another hole appeared, just as he knew it would, and this time Simeon could tell the angle. The shooter was a story higher than the lab, directly across the street. The agent stepped out of the little rented Fiat, covertly drawing his pistol as he moved, and glanced behind him at the office building towering over the few cars driving down the skinny downtown street. The second story only had one window open and there was a dark silhouette showing. Simeon snapped his pistol up and fired, darting toward the brick corner of the Liberty Labs building as the bullet sped out of the barrel. He kept his eyes focused on the window and saw the silhouette jerk with the impact of his shot. But he couldn't tell from that shady silhouette if he had dealt a killing blow or just winged them. The tip of a sniper rifle protruded from the window, sweeping the street as the shooter tried to pinpoint the new threat. Apparently they were still pretty whole. Simeon was about to lean around the corner and open fire when he realized he was getting a headache. That was very strange, he never got headaches, not since the remarkable surgeon in the Yucatan had put him back together when an IED had blown him up eleven years ago. As soon as the recognition of the growing pain in his head came, Simeon's remarkable hearing picked a sound out of the myriad of noises coming from the city around him.

Someone was operating a pump nearby. A bullet pinged off the bricks near Simeon's head as the sniper across the street found his hiding place, but the agent hardly noticed it. He was spinning around and racing for the sound of the pump, his heart in his throat as the facts slid together in his mind and he realized how much danger Vincent Tolliver was in. His shoes made hardly a sound as he flew along the concrete alleyway toward the back of the building. He spun around the corner and saw what he expected and dreaded.

A black hose stretched from the window of the Liberty Labs to a tall pump machine. It looked like a moving dolly, but there were several red switches and buttons, and one deadly cylinder attached to the other end of the black hose. A man stood beside the pump, most of his face hidden behind a gas mask. But two blue eyes regarded Simeon with shocked fear as the agent burst around the corner. Simeon didn't bother to give any melodramatic warnings, special judo moves, or even order the guy to shut the machine off. Time was too sparse. He took in the situation the instant he spun around the corner, and his pistol barked. The man collapsed in the alleyway, screaming and clutching a fractured shoulder. Simeon kicked him unconscious out of mercy (and to stop the distracting noise) as he flipped the machine off with one hand and fired rapidly into the reinforced window with his other. Three bullets spun from his barrel to land in a small circle in the center of the pane. A sharp crack sounded in the alley and the window shivered into thousands of shards. Simeon dove through the glass as it fell, ignoring the sharp stings as they slid into his hair and down his shirt, holding his breath as if he were diving for pearls[24] instead of a strange inventor. He spotted him immediately. Vincent lay curled near the door, completely unresponsive to the commotion that had just happened. Simeon's heart twisted and his stomach churned as he darted over and scooped the young man up. Joshua Stevenson's shock of red hair caught his eye and he shifted Vincent to one shoulder in order to heave the analyst under his other arm. He willed himself not to

---

[24] A relatively brief career from Simeon's past. He spent a three month stint as an expert pearl diver while working undercover to unmask a gang of deadly shrimp dealers.

114

think of how heavy the two men were as he trotted to the broken window. Simeon kicked a wheeled table under the smashed window, dropped the analyst on it, and clambered up. He sat on the sill and pivoted himself so he was in the open air, dragging Stevenson along with him and keeping Vincent steady on his shoulder. With a burst of strength he jacked himself to his feet and trotted up the alley, away from the deadly gas now seeping out of the lab into the air. He grunted his way around the corner and dropped to one knee. Simeon allowed himself to breathe again, gently dumped his charges on the concrete, and darted up to the alley's entryway with his pistol out in his hand.

The sniper was in plain view, trying to find the threat that had so suddenly appeared and then disappeared. And probably wondering what that screaming had been about. Simeon could see one arm was held stiffly against a slight form, and guessed it was a woman, and he had winged her earlier. As he came into view he saw her raise the sniper rifle and aim at him. She was good, to have spotted him immediately. But Simeon's pistol was already raised, and it spoke before the big gun. The sniper spun away from the window and dropped out of sight. Whether dead or not, she was out of the reckoning. Only then did Simeon allow himself to run back to Vincent and check him for life. He held his gun's slick metal against the young man's nose and saw a faint mist cover the silver. Simeon went limp with relief, and found himself gasping out a thankful prayer. He had gotten there in time, Vincent was alive. As the wave of relief hit him and he turned to check on Stevenson, Simeon realized this young man who paid enough attention to be kind had already become very dear to him.

Tires screeching on the road rang out in the busy city air as someone slammed on the brakes just at the top of the alley. Simeon

115

was grim as he reached into his pocket to see how many bullets he had brought for his Ruger and prayed he could keep Vincent alive long enough for the young man to come back to the waking world. This was an unknown situation they had wandered into, and he had no idea what to expect from his enemies. Car doors opened and closed from just beyond his sight in the street. Simeon glanced up at the buildings that made this alleyway as he heard an alarming number of feet beginning to pad softly his direction. The two tall buildings were basic brick make, but the one on his left boasted a pretty balcony on the second story. Simeon leapt up immediately, scaling the bricks and ducking out of sight of the alley below. The light from the street darkened a fraction, and Simeon peered cautiously through his balcony's flimsy iron railing to see why. Eleven people were crowded there, beginning to inch toward him. They were of all different types and makes, from a slender figure that looked like it belonged to a highschool girl, to a wizened drifter type with a beer belly. But all of them had black hoods covering their heads and draping their shoulders, almond shaped eye holes the only break in the smooth black. And all of them were well armed with machine pistols. Machine pistols and hoods? Who on earth were these folks!

Simeon quickly curbed his curiosity, knowing he had to concentrate. He took a deep, silent breath, aligning every thought and movement with the here and now as he watched the eleven people moving swiftly and competently up the alley. All their eyes were focused on the two men lying still on the concrete. Simeon let them pass under his balcony, and then silently hopped over the side. He hung by his fingers, weighing the feeling of his body, strength of his arms, and the distance from the nearest bad guy's back. It had been a while since he had done this.

"Are these the ones we were supposed to toss in with that snoop and his girl?" the potbellied one growled, and Simeon paused. The man prodded Vincent's back with his machine pistol. The inventor stirred, and the pot-bellied one stepped back with a curse.

"They were supposed to be dead!" a tall man said, and Simeon placed the accent immediately; a young Texan just back from gaining an Oxford education, almost certainly by means of a foreign exchange program.

"M29 didn't tell us why we were suddenly supposed to come pick them up instead of just letting P52 do it. Maybe the plan was changed. The snooper's still alive. Or he was last report I got from the rug truck," a contrastingly short individual drawled.

"I don't like it. I'm going to make sure the plan stays the same," Pot-belly grumped, and raised his gun to his shoulder to finish the botched job. Two Teva shoes hit him directly between his shoulders, and the weight concentrated in those loafers all but broke his back. Pot-belly slammed into the concrete and lay still. Simeon was not so restrained. He lashed out immediately at the slight girl, catching her in the chin with his toe, where he knew it would keep her out of the fight but would do her little permanent damage. As his foot worked on that, his hands ripped the tall gent's gun out of the man's grasp and snapped it into his middle to bring him to his knees. Timing himself carefully, Simeon leapt sideways on the wall and ran along it, grabbing heads to keep his balance and smashing them into the bricks after he was done with them. Timing was everything, if he stayed in one place for more than two seconds it might give a bright boy the opportunity to shoot him. As soon as his feet landed on the concrete again, Simeon's arm shot out and grabbed a lady that smelled strongly of horse and was trying

117

desperately to get her gun muzzle lined up on the agile agent. He slammed her backward into a big fellow, and followed the move with a leap onto the big one's shoulders that insured he would stay down, and that gave him the momentum needed to catapult himself onto the three remaining bad guys. As they crumpled below him, Simeon caught one of their machine pistols out of a falling, limp hand and began to check it over to see if it was in decent condition and loaded. He heard a low whistle and looked up to see Vincent staring at him in shocked wonder.

"Well that was a sight worth waking up for!" the inventor murmured, his green eyes very wide as they glanced around him at the alleyway. He swallowed and wrinkled his nose at the sharp iron smell invading his nostrils. "And that's a lot of blood."

"It's not mine," Simeon shrugged. He stepped on top of the Texan-Oxford guy, slamming his stirring form back into the concrete, and pulled Vincent unceremoniously to his feet. "And it was about to be yours and Mr. Stevenson's. Vincent, lesson one: always remember the bad guy is a man, and is out to get you. Only kill if you have to, but be quick and merciless in knocking them out of the fight. Lesson two: got to have more strength than you think you do, in order to help others." Vincent slumped against the brick wall, his legs so shaky he felt he must have the support. Simeon shoved the red-haired analyst into Vincent's arms. His head was spinning horribly, his stomach was still extremely nauseous, and he felt weaker than he ever remembered feeling in his twenty years. Vincent's knees buckled and he felt the rough bricks scraping his back as he started to slide helplessly to the concrete. Simeon's hand caught his collar and pulled him upright again. Vince told his legs to straighten out and he strove to stand up without help, thinking it was a fool's errand, but determined to try anyway. He was shocked

118

to find he could do it when he made himself.

"Good man," Simeon praised, as he busied himself taking all the bullets out of the machine pistols. Vincent felt like he could have run up the alley if Simeon ordered it. "Get you both to the Fiat, we have work to do."

"Right," Vincent panted, nodding his spinning head and immediately regretting it as the alleyway spun out of focus. He got his vision under control again and realized Simeon was nowhere in sight. The girl by his feet started to stir, and Vincent quickly began to drag Mr. Stevenson toward the top of the alley and their rented car. He grimaced and stumbled as he felt his feet stepping on the softness of people sprawled across the concrete, but kept going and didn't look down. Mr. Steve started to stir as Vincent poked his head out of the alley to take stock of the situation in the street. He saw cars milling past, a smashed window in the office building across from him, a few peaceful pedestrians walking the sidewalk, and their rented sports car waiting for them by the curb. He wondered what he was looking for anyway, and quickly crossed to the blue Fiat. Josh Stevenson murmured something about chili as Vincent pulled the back door open and pushed him inside. The inventor stood swaying a little on the sidewalk by the car, wondering what he was supposed to do now. Where was Simeon? Was he supposed to help him?

A hairy arm suddenly wrapped around his throat and jerked him backward off his feet. Vincent choked, feeling thick muscles rippling under his chin, and desperately clawed at the sinewy arm that held him and was dragging him backward into that alley again. Then he suddenly remembered he had legs, and they were long, and he kicked furiously at where he judged his attacker's knee to be. It was an instinctive action that had no training behind it, but a

119

good deal of desperation. The man yelped and the arm loosened a fractional inch as Vincent found himself falling with his enemy. He shoved himself backward and when they crashed onto the concrete the inventor landed heavily on top. The arm loosened more, and Vincent pulled away from it, gagging and coughing. Stars were sparking in his vision from lack of air, but at least the world had stopped spinning a little, and he could see enough to punch hard at the black hood of his attacker. Vincent pulled his fist back with a sharp hiss, shaking his hand and marveling that a punch could hurt that much. He felt someone else suddenly grab him around the waist and jerk him toward the road. This time before his panicked mind could react he found himself shoved into a passenger seat and the door slammed in place. Vincent, still gagging and trying to get his breath back through his bruised throat, scrabbled desperately for the door handle.

"Simeon!" he managed to croak.

"Here," Simeon's steady voice came from beside him, and the inventor spun around and realized he was sitting in their rented car, with Simeon beside him and Mr. Steve reviving slowly in the backseat. His racing heartbeat began to slow down, and even his breathing managed to even a little. He glanced up and felt his peace leaving again as he saw his prospective boss was glowering at him.

"Told you to get in the car, Vincent," Simeon almost growled as he flipped the little car's engine on and whipped into the road.

"No, you said, 'Get you and Mr. Stevenson *to* the car.' I was looking for you, to see if I could help, when gorilla arms jumped me," Vincent defended immediately. They clipped the side of a shiny Honda Accord, bounced two feet to their right to almost ram into a Charger in that lane, and Vincent closed his eyes and sank

120

farther into his seat. Joshua Stevenson, who had just begun to comprehend he was squished in the back of a tiny sports car, was flung against the left door and sank blissfully unconscious of the wild ride. Simeon opened his mouth to reply then shut it again as he realized that is what he had said, and that the inventor had kept his head enough to handle the threat. But he also knew it was a mistake on both their parts and had almost killed Vincent. He was going to have to learn some things about commanding young men under him if this was going to work. A non-committal grunt was his only answer to Vincent now. Simeon concentrated on driving, whizzing in and out of traffic, entirely ignoring all speed limit signs and traffic signals, and wishing he had his own car with him.

"What are we doing?" Vincent gasped as he felt their car spin around a corner on two tires, and heard about ten frantic horn blasts from the traffic around them.

"Looking for something," Simeon answered. "Could use your help."

"Now?" Vincent almost squeaked, then quickly sat up and did his best to look capable. "Right, okay. What do you need? Oh boy." The last was an involuntary ejaculation as he saw they were about to speed through a busy intersection. Simeon whipped around a SUV, spun the other direction to miss a red Lincoln's bumper by centimeters, zoomed under a passing semi-truck into the relatively clear street past the intersection, and then took the time to answer the young man gasping in panic beside him.

"Square truck. *'We lug the rugs'* on the side," Simeon said.

"What?" Vincent murmured, opening his eyes again with a great mental effort.

"I didn't make the quote, just watch," Simeon said. "Saw it turn this way."

"Why are we looking for a truck lugging rugs?" Vincent asked, swallowing carefully and beginning to watch the traffic around them.

"Mentioned by the black hooded creeps. Might have someone needing help," Simeon saw another question forming from his companion and a slight frown curved over his face. "Vincent, if we are going to do this, going to have to make a choice about what's most important to us. Our prerogative."

"Okay," Vincent nodded. "And it has to do with the rug lugging truck?"

"The only reason to go around shooting and hitting people is to protect those who can't protect themselves," Simeon said, the sharp clarity in his tone showing he would accept no triviality about this subject.

"Right," the inventor nodded seriously. "So let's go get this someone out of trouble. Left, there it is, left now!" Simeon jerked the car left and found himself facing a tall glass office building. He spun the wheel desperately and the little Fiat bounced over the curb onto the sidewalk and managed to only take out the lower story windows as it banged into them. Simeon glanced aggrievedly at Vincent and quickly shoved his foot down on the accelerator, ignoring the screaming people from the offices, and those diving away from the car as he drove up the sidewalk.

"'Left now' in normal terms means turn left at the next street!" Vincent shouted, one hand draped over his eyes to shut out all the pedestrians screaming and diving out of the way.

"Not in normal terms now," Simeon said, jumping the car off the curb onto the road they wanted.

"Lesson three: if I say now, I'd better mean it?" Vincent asked, and received a short emphatic nod from his potential boss. A square metal truck with the hideous logo they were hunting for was pulling ponderously around the corner about three yards ahead of them, and Simeon fell in behind it very quickly. He noticed the young man beside him was nearing hysterics.

"How many wrecks you been in?" Simeon asked abruptly. Vincent shot him a glance as he shifted positions nervously.

"Five."

"Anyone died?"

"No. But there were some nasty injuries in a couple. Sorry, I'll calm down–"

"Twenty-seven plane crashes," Simeon interrupted the apology, shooting the young man a little encouraging smile as he carefully tailgated the van. "Sometimes you just have to find a way to live with the fears."

The back of the truck flew open before Vincent could respond, and things started happening too quickly for him to think about how scared he was anymore.

Evening; Back of a Moving Van

Jack lay still, and his mind was as still as his body. He didn't want to think anymore. He couldn't think of anything hopeful, or good, or fun, or cheerful. They had turned off the highway some time ago, but that movement only brought more dismal fears with it. As long as they were helpless prisoners, a stop only meant more trouble. Besides, this truck just kept moving. And everything just kept hurting. The rag still tasted like fuzzy, dirty oil. Minute followed minute, and they ran together agelessly. As he lay so still with his ear pressed to the metal bottom of the truck, Jack dully noticed the sound of some car zooming up on their tail. Not that it mattered. Jack didn't even have the energy to wonder why someone might do that. Then a gasp came from behind Jack. A real gasp, not a snort!

"Yuck," Judy murmured hoarsely. That single word brought life flooding into Jack. He twisted his head around for the thousandth time to try and see behind him. This time a face more beautiful than he had ever seen greeted him. Judy was filthy and sweaty and her hair looked like a homeless bum's hanging in sweaty, dirty strands over her shoulders, but Jack had never seen anything lovelier. She reached a shaky hand over and pulled his gag out, then went to work on his ropes.

"Hey, gorgeous, what are you up to tonight?" Jack croaked.

"Running away with you, handsome," Judy whispered back. "Oh Jack, your poor wrists!"

"I'll let you weep over them all you want later, just get them free now!" Several pain-filled moments later they were free. Jack silently moved his arms to try and get them back into operating order as Judy worked on his ankles. He knew if he tried to talk right now it would probably come out as a scream, but Judy wasn't so handicapped.

"Let's feed the ducks, you said. Just a few more minutes, you said. The ducks are happy, you said. Home is dull, you said. Why do you want to go home and go to sleep, you asked."

"The ducks were happy," Jack gasped as he felt his ankles suddenly free. He gave a shaky laugh and caught his wife to him. "Darling, next time you say you want to go to bed this poltroon will listen."

"I want to go to bed. Come on–" Judy was interrupted by a partition separating the cab from the truck's body flying open with a metallic clang. A gun muzzle hove into view held by a seedy looking character, greasy dreadlocks hanging by his sneering chin. Jack did the only thing he could think of. He grabbed the latch to the back and flung it open, holding Judy's arm protectively. The gun went off and a bullet ripped between the husband and wife. Judy screamed and dropped to the ground, as she had read somewhere you should when gunfire started. Suddenly losing hold of Judy made Jack's shaky leg's falter. He felt himself stumbling and knew he was about to get killed by that gun. But Judy! As he stood indecisively swaying, the truck gave a sharp forward jerk and the momentum threw Jack out of the van.

He hit the top of a hot little car that must have been tailgating the van pretty fiercely. The car swerved away at his sudden impact, and Jack heard someone yell inside as he wildly grabbed for a hold to keep himself from slipping down the hot hood. The car jerked to the side and Jack heard Judy yelling something angrily and another gunshot from inside the van. But he had no time to think about what was happening back there, this hood was slick and he was slipping farther with every swift rotation of the wheels. He was about to be underneath the black tires.

8

The back of the rug truck flew open with a sudden metallic zing, and a filthy couple could be seen facing a greasy hoodlum with a gun. A bullet spun out of the barrel between the guy and girl and pinged off the blue Fiat's hood. The girl screamed and dropped to the ground, and the guy teetered weakly, obviously not at his best physically. Simeon saw the gun muzzle swivel to switch targets from their car to the man, and pushed his foot onto the accelerator, deliberately ramming their Fiat into the truck's bumper. The stranger crashed backward onto their hood, missing the bullet aimed for him by centimeters. The hoodlum's gun followed the man and Simeon quickly swung the sports car to the next lane and shoved his foot down again, trying to get this stranger out of the range of that pistol. Vincent yelped as a bullet sang through his window and slammed into Simeon's seat, his arm coming up instinctively to protect his face from the hundreds of tiny glass slivers spraying from his window. Their car swept up level to the van's wide metal side before any other chances offered themselves to the hoodlum.

"Get him," Simeon ordered, one finger lifting off the wheel to point at the stranger sliding off their hot hood. The inventor leapt up and leaned out his window without a second's thought. As the inventor leaned out, the hot, humid wind whipped around him and made his long blond hair suddenly turn into thousands of little whips that stung his face and neck relentlessly. But through the infuriating blond storm he could see the stranger slipping farther down the hood. His peripheral vision caught the hot black asphalt

127

of the road racing underneath them, and for an instant Vincent froze. He leaned rigid halfway out the window, paralyzed in terror as he realized what he was doing. His mother's motherly horror stories designed to keep an inquisitive child from dying swung across his mind; arms torn off because they were stretched out the window of a moving car, mangled bodies under smoking car's tires because they had leaned too incessantly against the door... In that instant of terror and uncertainty, the stranger's eyes suddenly caught his. They were alive and bright, and entirely desperate. Vincent's long arm shot out and caught him by a bloodied wrist. The stranger gripped back with the vice-like pinch of instinct, and the inventor winced as he leaned farther out of his window to grab the guy's shoulder and drag him closer. He suddenly realized how close he was to the van's metal side and pressed one shoulder against it for balance as he dragged the stranger closer to himself across the blue hood. One mighty heave, that Vincent had no idea he had in him, and both of them sprawled gasping and numb from fright in the passenger seat of the Fiat.

"Talk to him," Simeon's voice sounded vaguely through the roaring going on in the inventor's head, and he heard himself muttering something unintelligible in reply as he moved to try and sit up. He blinked and got himself back under control. The stranger was lying panting on top of him, his face holding the blank look of exhaustion and shock.

"Hi," Vincent said, smiling at him and shaking his hand gently. "I'm Vincent Tolliver, nice to save your life. How about you?"

"Jack Leason," the stranger murmured in a dull automatic way, too groggy to be cautious with strangers. Then he suddenly came back to himself, snapped into a sitting position, and yelled.

"My wife is back in that truck! Turn around, get me back there, I've got to get to Judy!" His hand went for the door handle, and Vincent yelped in the sudden fear of seeing that racing asphalt underneath him again, and caught his wrist unceremoniously. Jack yelled in pain, and then felt an incredibly strong grip take the back of his shirt and jerk him backward. He found himself sprawled in the miniscule back seat of this little sports car, accidentally slamming a squirming red-haired character back into the door as he landed on top of him. The squirming underneath him stopped rather suddenly, and Jack felt a slightly hysterical giggle rise in his raw throat. He forced it down and scrambled onto the seat, making himself comprehend what was happening around him. They had dropped behind the van. The back was still open and Jack could see the dirty metal floor with the rough ropes still lying there. But there was no Judy.

"Vincent, take the wheel," Simeon said, unbuckling his seat belt and checking over the machine pistol he had snagged from the alleyway. Vincent gulped and reached over to grip the steering wheel, carefully moving his leg around to get at the pedals as Simeon perched in the driver's window. A bullet sang from the partition into the truck cab, and Vincent automatically ducked. But it wasn't aimed at the car, it was aimed at the stocky man climbing out of the car. Simeon wasn't overly concerned. He had seen that man's ability with a pistol, and while it was a threat, he was hardly a crack shot. His shoes found a suitably steady hold on the window sill and he leapt for the back of the truck.

Simeon landed in an easy roll and kept going to rest with his back firmly against the metal under the partition. He closed his eyes to focus on his hearing and pinpointed two people moving in the cab, one at the wheel and one shifting nervously against the partition, directly above him. Simeon came up with a sudden spring, spinning in midair so he faced his opponent, and diving into the cab of the truck as his hands gripped the hoodlum's neck where he leaned nervously trying to get a bead on the spy. Simeon's knee smashed under his enemy's thick chin as he vaulted in, and he spun to land on his fingers and toes facing the driver. A pair of terrified young green eyes stared back at him and the truck jerked suddenly to the left. Simeon delivered a simple right hook, jerked the unconscious man from behind the wheel, and slid in himself to straighten the big vehicle out in its lane. As he slowed down to the speed limit he was furiously wondering who this gang was that had its ranks filled with people like the well trained sniper back at the lab, and now this greasy hoodlum and scared kid (who had obviously never faced a fight in his life).

But there were other things to think about now. A pretty woman was hunched against the passenger door. She obviously needed seeing to, and her frantic husband in the sports car needed to know she was alive. The wail of police sirens sounded in the distance, and Simeon pulled law-abidingly to the side of the street. He flipped the engine off and reached around to dig into the two bad guys' pockets as he saw Vincent pulling up behind him. There was an ordinary array of stuff there, nothing particularly interesting. A small hardback copy of Well's *War of the Worlds* was crammed in the driver's pocket, with an inscription signed simply, 'To Q90 from X.' That was interesting. The ID's were carefully removed, Simeon noted as he flipped through the two wallets. There was a list in the hoodlum's bill fold though. A hand-written list of names, in a fine script that he doubted was written by this greasy character. He tucked the list into his pocket for later use, tossed the wallets onto the seat, gathered the woman gently into his arms, and slid out of the truck onto the sidewalk. Jack was there

130

waiting, and swept her out of his hands, murmuring frantically, his dark eyes searching his wife's unresponsive face then snapping up to beg Simeon for a good report.

"She'll be fine, Mr. Leason," Simeon reassured him, and carefully took her back as he saw the reporter's knees begin to tremble with the effort. He was in no state to carry anyone. This guy was hardly able to stand, and his nerves seemed shot too. Jack teetered after Simeon, holding Judy's hand and beginning to look a little more like his normal sharp self in the knowledge they had both survived.

"I saw you take something from a wallet, what did you find," Jack said. It wasn't a question, it was a demand, and Simeon regarded him for a moment as he waited for the husband to open the back door for him. Police cars whizzed past, sirens blaring, finally headed to where someone had called in the smashed window, sniper, and pile of people with machine pistols in an alleyway.

"Reporter or PI?" the agent asked, carefully sitting Judy on the backseat. Jack murmured something that Simeon magnanimously decided to ignore as he slid in next to his wife, carefully avoiding stepping on the analyst still splayed on the floorboards.

"Investigative reporter," Jack admitted grumpily[25], watching Simeon settle in the driver's seat and start the Fiat moving down the road again. He started to gently rub Judy's temples as she stirred and sighed beside him. "Now what was it that you took out of that wallet?" Simeon flipped his cell phone to Vincent instead of

---

[25] He liked to think he didn't look like a reporter, and was always annoyed when someone pegged him right off. So far the only other one to know immediately was the remarkable bearded lady from the Hungarian circus.

replying. The inventor caught it automatically. He was slumped dazedly in the passenger seat, wondering if it was actually all over or something else was suddenly going to show up and try to kill him.

"Mr. Gibbs," Simeon ordered Vincent. "Need a safe house for the Stevensons and Leasons."

"I'm not going to skulk in any safe house while those hooded murderers are running around my country!" Jack declared vehemently. Judy gave a little groan and he shifted her gently to lay on the seat, then turned his attention back to their stocky driver, a furious scowl on his face. Vincent found himself smiling, amused at how different the reporter's manner was toward his wife than to his two rescuers.

"You two going to a hospital, then safe house," Simeon said evenly.

"'Peace, ye fat guts!'[26] You can't make me do either of those things, and I'm sticking to whatever it is you just snagged, and I want to know who you are and what you're doing following these hooded horrors around. I'm not going anywhere!" Jack took a deep breath and calmed himself down. He leaned a little closer to the front, changing his tone to a conspiratorial murmur. "Listen, let's make a deal. I have a notebook I found yesterday that these guys were really interested in. And you have whatever it is you just took. So let's put them together, compare stories, and see what we get. I have the feeling both of us together would stand a better chance at figuring out what this is all about." The reporter found Simeon's gaze focused on him by means of the rear view mirror, and he met the unwavering brown eyes steadily, knowing he was being sized

---

[26] From Henry the IV, Part 1

up.

"Mr. Leason, if you can square it with your wife, you've got a deal," Simeon said after a moment. His finger flicked at Vincent, and the young man pushed the call button and put the phone to his ear. He realized his head was pounding and there was a fierce ringing in his ears as he waited for Mr. Gibbs to pick up. The inventor glanced down and saw his clothes were covered in dirt and grime, and even blood, and his hands were no better. Then he glanced to the side and noted with awe that Simeon's pants were spotless and still perfectly pressed, and not a single hair was out of place. A deep sigh welled from him as he realized how much he had to learn of this business, and how incredibly difficult and painful it was going to be. But, oh boy, what a teacher!

2:16 a.m., Feb. 15th; Parabaloni HQ, NM

Vincent leaned forward to flip Percy's[27] engine off and let himself keep leaning, his head coming to rest on the yoke of his little jet.

"It takes a while to get a big family like the Stevensons settled in a safe-house," Vincent muttered through his leather yoke.

"Yes," Simeon answered evenly. Vincent smiled and shifted his head to look at his companion.

"You made it back on the ground with flying colors this time,

---

[27] Vincent Tolliver named everything, and his small jet had earned the name Percy.

Simeon."

"With the cockpit light on, I can wing it."

"I guess it's not a terminal illness then," Vincent grinned tiredly.

"That pun was plane awful," Simeon complained. "Your jet doesn't even require a terminal."

"Well, to be a good pilot requires a sunny altitude," Vincent chortled. He yawned again. "Now that I'm back in my New Mexico place, I don't want to go back to Virginia," Vincent murmured, more the ramblings of a man in sleep than a comment to his companion. Simeon resolutely held back a sigh. He hated to have to invite himself into things like this, but Vincent was definitely too much the absent minded professor to catch a delicate hint. Besides, he had already promised to keep things above board and just state what he was thinking, and if it made him uncomfortable the feeling was not to be heeded.

"Roommate?" Simeon asked.

"What?" Vincent yawned.

"There's lots of room here?" Simeon asked, deciding to ease into it.

"Yeah. Dad kind of got carried away with the building project. Why?" Vincent yawned.

"You said there's an herb garden up there?"

"That's right. Mom had a good one, up on the next level from here. A sort of greenhouse that spills out onto the mountain side."

"You own this place?"

"Yeah..." Vincent said, his mind waking up a little as he began to wonder about the purpose of these questions.

"Many people come here?"

"Nope. I'm the only one that even knows it's here, asides from a few choice friends like the Stevensons. The nearest town is a cute little thing about twenty minutes stiff driving, and the nearest real town is two hours driving time away, so it's not like there are many neighbors dropping in."

"Do you like it here?"

"Yeah. This is actually where we lived, Mom, Dad, and me. I liked it so much I've avoided coming back on my own. The Virginia house is more like just an apartment I don't have to pay for, not a home where I have to deal with memories every day. It's nice to be back, with you here. Why are you asking all this, Simeon?"

"For good effectiveness in Christ's service or in spy work a good partner is an enormous aid, and nearly crippling loss if absent. Likely our different personalities will get on each other's nerves. But it isn't part of God's plan for His people to live alone, need the accountability and encouragement. Here it sounds big enough we could stay out of each other's hair, but be close enough to help. Willing?"

"Wait, you're offering a roommate situation," Vincent finally caught on. "Keen! You as a roomy sounds kind of astoundingly great actually. I'm all for it, and I'd love to settle here again." Vincent suddenly lost his happy excitement. He swallowed and tapped his finger on the yoke. "I guess everything will be just the

135

same as we left it last year. I cleared out some of our other spots, the apartment over in Las Cruces, and the house in Virginia, and the penthouse in New York...but not here. I'm a weak chicken and don't want to have to go through their bedroom." A surprised look flew over the inventor's face and Simeon raised an eyebrow inquisitively. "I just realized everything will be just like we left it a year ago. We had burritos and watermelon last, with quite a few leftovers."

"I'll spring for a new fridge in exchange for a new headquarters," Simeon smiled.

"I guess throwing the old one out would be the best plan," Vincent grinned back, twisting around to poke their passengers. Jack muttered something and went back to sleep. "I still think we should have taken them to a hospital, just to be sure they were all right."

"Dangerous," Simeon frowned, studying Judy's young face.

"You think these bad guys could be in the hospitals too?" Vincent grimaced.

"Might be anywhere, don't know." Simeon indicated the Leasons, still frowning. "Should have stayed at the safe house Mr. Gibbs set up, with the Stevensons."

"Jack didn't like that idea much. I thought he was really going to attack you for that list you stole. He sure is rude for a guy we rescued," Vincent grinned. He suddenly changed moods again, looking away embarrassedly. "It was nice to be able to rescue them from the bad guys, whoever these people are. I'm sorry I panicked back there, and I know I failed the first test you ever gave me. I... I hope I get a second chance?" Vincent asked, looking up at Simeon.

"Did well. Just came out from under poison gas, first time in a car chase or under rifle fire." Simeon considered for a second and then nodded. "Very well."

"Seriously?" Vincent started a whoop and it turned into a yawn. "I think I'm going to have to sleep on that."

"Good plan," Simeon said, poking Jack again. The reporter slapped his hand irritably and twisted around in his seat. Vincent chuckled, hopped out of his pilot's seat and pulled Jack to his feet.

"Come on, reporter, since you insisted on not letting that list out of your sight, you have to walk to your bed."

"How about just sleeping here?" Jack complained. He woke up enough to look out the jet's windows and noticed what an interesting array of stuff lay around him. "Nix that idea. Judy, come on sweetheart. It's bedtime."

"What do you think I'm doing?" Judy mumbled.

"Hot shower?" Vincent offered, and Judy sat up hopefully.

"Next you'll be telling me you have a clean change of clothes in this garage shop," Jack scoffed.

"Well, you look about the same size as my parents," Vincent mused, eyeing the two people speculatively. He hesitated a moment and the reporter wondered why he seemed so fascinated with the floor suddenly. His green eyes snapped up in decision, and a sort of sad smile played over the inventor's face which made Jack very curious. "Which means, sure, I've got plenty," Vincent finished his earlier thought. Judy opened her mouth to ask another question, but Simeon got tired of waiting for them.

137

"Out," he ordered. Jack and Judy climbed out of the jet and the party trekked through the piles of fascinating junk littering the workshop, toward a glass elevator. Vincent pressed a gray button and the elevator moved smoothly upward, through solid gray rock. The Leasons gaped as it shot out of the rocks to show a beautiful moonlit snowy mountain scene. There was even an elk drinking out of a little pond in a valley below their feet, and it couldn't have been more enchanting. The elevator slid to a stop at the edge of a round rocky room and the party stepped slowly out. A glass partition shut out the cold New Mexican night, while a small dribbling waterfall running down the outside of the glass wall created a shimmery aura of enchantment. Jack thought what a lot of papers he could sell with a description of where BIGG2 was living now as he stepped out of the elevator and limped deeper into the mountain after Vincent. Judy thought she might see a dwarf pop out of one of these numerous doors opening off the main room, hewn out of the raw rock of the mountain. Simeon quietly studied the glass wall and decided the waterfall was a very clever, beautiful way to mask their presence here. The inventor's drawl broke into his thoughts as Vincent worked on getting the Leasons situated for the night. He sounded completely exhausted. Simeon trotted toward the little group to take over.

"Go to bed," he ordered the inventor.

"Right," Vincent yawned stupidly. He waved a hand around the gray room and started to weave toward a pale yellow door close to the glass. "Pick any door. They all have beds, most of them have bathrooms attached. Let me see about clothes..." He paused at a red door and stood frowning at it. Simeon quickly crossed to him.

"I'll find clothes tonight and clear it out later," Simeon promised quietly in the inventor's ear. "Go to bed." Vincent's green
138

eyes grew suddenly wet, and as he lifted them to give Simeon a profoundly grateful look, a little of the wetness spilled down one cheek. But he only nodded, and headed to crash behind the yellow door. Simeon quickly prodded the Leasons into picking a room, made certain they had towels, soap, and a first aid kit, then turned to trot toward the red room again to see what he could find for them. He opened the door, flipped on the light, and paused. It felt strange, and not very nice to be stealing into Vincent's dead parents' room in the early morning. He felt like murmuring an apology and saying he wasn't there to take their place. Simeon Lee's colorful and rather violent life had taught him to expect such feelings when entering the room of someone who had passed on, especially for the first time since they were gone...but the hollow, silent sorrow was still there. He was very glad he was able to spare Vincent the task. With the familiar eerie quiet in this room, the times he had lost those dearer to him than his own life resurfaced in Simeon's heart and memory. Old heartbreaks opened again to bring perfect empathy, and he felt almost sick for the nice young man a few rooms off. Simeon stepped in. He went about his business, beginning to try the numerous closet doors, looking for the one that held the clothes. On the seventh try Simeon finally found the right closet. There were full suits or worn out t-shirts with ratty old shorts in Mr. Tolliver's side of the closet. Apparently he had been an all or nothing sort of man. Simeon picked a pair of crimson pajamas and a suit with a vest for Mr. Leason. Mrs. Tolliver had apparently been a bit more diverse. Simeon raised an eyebrow in quiet amusement as he grabbed a pair of hot pink pajamas with yellow ducks all over them as the quietest print available, and chose a tie dyed dress with nice brown leggings. It might not be Mrs. Leason's style, but it looked comfortable at least. Simeon paused on his way out and allowed himself a look around. The room was filled with a very

139

eclectic collection of knickknacks, each one looking like it had a long story behind it. A bookshelf stood next to each side of the bed and gave a very nice picture of two very different people living together in harmony.

Simeon closed the door softly behind him and headed toward the dark blue room the Leasons had chosen. Clearing out that room was going to be a sorrowful, interesting chore and he was glad he was able to spare Vincent the heartbreak of packing it all up. But first he had to find out who was running underneath his country killing good people. The memory of Vincent curled on the lab floor unconscious flashed across Simeon's mind, and his jaw squared in angry determination. Saul and Mr. Gibbs were right. They had fought too long to keep this country safe. He wasn't going to let any group terrorize his America, with God's help he would still keep it the best country in the world. Simeon quietly prayed the Leasons had some leads as he knocked on their door. Tomorrow they would start to try and piece together the different facts they had picked up here and there. Simeon handed over the clothes to a bleary eyed Jack, picked his pocket to retrieve the notebook the reporter had mentioned, and headed toward the yellow door. He wanted to call Saul again tomorrow, that big lug was onto something, Simeon could feel it. He knocked softly on the yellow door, wanting to be sure Vincent was safe, and stood still analyzing himself while he waited for an answer. The protective, paternal love he had noted outside the lab today was certainly there, bother it all. And yet, not bother. Now that he recognized the growing feeling Simeon Lee chose not to chase it out. Vincent Tolliver could use someone looking after him, and heaven only knew how much Simeon Lee needed someone to care for. He just would never, ever mention it aloud unless specifically asked for from the inventor. If he never admitted his heart was wide open to this boy, it couldn't be tossed

140

out and shattered again. A haunted frown at his own frailness was on Simeon's face as he knocked for a second time. There was no answer and Simeon quietly pushed the door open. He saw stars. It was a round room with glowing stars laid out in aerial perfection across the domed top, the deep blue of the ceiling dripping down to meet the pale yellow walls in a beautifully haphazard way. As his eyes followed the wall toward the rest of the room a smile curved over Simeon's face. He hadn't seen a room in this state of chaotic shambles since Afghanistan guerrillas wrecked his hotel room three years ago. Vincent was splayed over a large bed on the far side of the messy space. He had been too tired to even pull back the poofy, blue comforter, much less climb out of his dirty clothes. Poor kid, Simeon thought silently as he closed the door again. Having been nearly incessant in his own life, he didn't remember the first time he had been almost murdered and then shoved into more violent actions. But he could still guess the first time's effect. He must be very brave to still want in on this business. Simeon silently prayed Vincent would sleep well tonight, with no dreams at all, as he picked up his small night bag and chose an ordinary brown, oaken door across from the yellow one. Sleep did sound very nice. For the few hours he could allow himself, anyway.

Eight hours later, Vincent started to stir. His stomach growled and it woke him up all the way. Vincent yawned lazily, glanced at his clock, and bounded out of bed in shock. It was noon! It only took a moment to wade through the stuff thrown around his room to the closet and toss on some fresh clothes. Vincent stepped into the gray room and followed his nose toward the kitchen. It took him up a tunnel carved out of the rock, with beautiful slits of windows that let in plenty of light. The tunnel ended at a blue room, with another glass wall where the waterfall tumbled outside. A large entertainment cabinet rested at one end and comfortable blue

141

furniture was artfully arranged around it, surrounded by shelves full of books and odd little knick knacks. Vincent ran his hand along the shelves with a thoughtful smile on his freckled face, as he headed for another tunnel and started up its bare rock. This one emerged in a cheerfully bright, large kitchen. The first thing he noticed was the missing refrigerator. But the smells emanating from the oven and stove drew his interest and he didn't bother with the disappearance of a large white appliance. Vincent opened the oven to find two beautiful quiches keeping warm there, and removed the lid off a pan on the stove to find a sauce that smelled divine.

"Where on earth did the stuff for this come from?" Vincent muttered. His eye fell on a note sitting beside the coffee maker, and the words answered his question well enough.

'Good morning. Found the car, found the village. Nice. Breakfast (or lunch) staying warm in the oven and cold on the porch. New refrigerator's on its way to Las Cruces, backordered. Find me when you're done.' Vincent grinned and went to go find whatever was on the porch. Simeon was going to be a sweet guy to room with. And what a teacher! Life was turning good once more with him around. He came back shivering and clutching a beautiful fruit salad.

"Close the door!" two voices yelled at him as he slipped in, and Vincent looked over to see the Leasons stepping out of the elevator. They looked good in his parents' things.

"Good morning to you too," Vincent smiled.

"Sorry Vincent. Good morning," Judy apologized.

"Anything left for the late risers?" Jack didn't apologize.

"I think everything's left for us," Vincent answered. "I just got up too, it must have been the smells that did it. Check out this fruit salad Simeon somehow came up with."

"It's winter in a ridiculously remote place and Mr. Lee finds beautiful fruit like this," Judy laughed, moving to hunt for the bowls and plates.

"And he wrestles a filthy refrigerator away on his own," Vincent grinned. Jack suddenly stuck a hand in his suit pants pocket.

"And steals my notebook while I slept!" the reporter yelled, and turned on Vincent furiously. "Where is he?"

"I don't know. Eat lunch, then we can find him," Vincent shrugged. Jack looked like he was about to throttle something, standing on the black and white tile with his fists clenched and his jaw working.

"Since you obviously want to do something violent right now, grind the coffee for me," Judy smiled, handing him a bag of beans.

1:00 p.m. Feb. 15th; Parabaloni Headquarters, Library, NM

Simeon's watch beeped the hour and he looked up from the note he was doodling[28]. He put the page neatly on top of a pile of similar drawings and sat back, looking at the four neat stacks of 'notes.' His research had been very interesting this morning. That

---

[28] Notes sometimes helped Simeon's agile mind work better, but he preferred doodles to regular notes. No matter how clever you were with your codes, a note could be cracked. A nonsensical doodle cannot be cracked.

list of names stolen from the young man's wallet had turned out to be decidedly interesting. Some of the names had checks next to them, and some were unchecked. The name that interested him most was near the top, checked decisively; Tom Smith. Joshua Stevenson was on the bottom of the list, still unchecked. Almost certainly a hit list for these people. The notebook Jack had snagged held mostly financial figures. Very large financial figures, given voluntarily to something. The names of the donors were placed with the donations they had given, and Simeon recognized most of the names. Some were well known scientific institutes, others large liberal groups. But the most interesting thing about the notebook to Simeon was the watermark on each expensive page. It was a drawing of two trees, a dying oak tree with a healthy strong tree growing out of it. Underneath the picture was a statement, what could almost be called a battle cry.

"PD: We will advance the human race; we will create the next evolutionary step."

Simeon slowly picked up his own notebook again, studying the watermark on the open page. Putting together what he had come up with this morning and his brief conversation with Saul yesterday, he was beginning to have a glimmer of an idea who they were up against. People who spoke of the 'advancement of the race' always meant the human race's evolutionary advancement. They were the atheists who denied any God over them, usually so they could feel as if they were their own god to satisfy their pride and do whatever they wanted. (A picture of a large glowing throne set in clouds appeared on a note, with a thought bubble drifting from it saying, 'Ha ha.') Simeon knew them well. He had been an atheistic evolutionist most of his life. But when he heard of 'the advancement of the race' what came to mind was the wild eyed sciences

144

professors who spoke much and did nothing. (A caricature of a man in a lab coat wildly waving his arms on a soapbox began to appear on the note.) But what if someone who really believed the evolutionary theory decided there had been enough talk? (A particularly foolish looking chimp was quickly sketched on the other side of the note.) If a person really believed in evolution, and had the charisma and funds to collect others who also believed it around them, what would their group look like? What would it stand for? Simeon studied the watermark again, his face grim and hard. Out of a sickly family tree rises a new and better race... If evolution was true, the most lasting thing you could work and strive for in this life was for the race to leap on to better heights of evolutionary advancement. (A puny man staring up at a towering giant in a cape flew from Simeon's pencil.) There were other things you could strive for as an avid evolutionist, but they were all sidetracks compared to the glorious idea of mankind growing up. It was in nearly all the sci-fi books and movies, and hinted at in plenty of scientific writings. (A flying saucer with monkeys in it began to appear on one of the little notes.) Come to think of it, Well's *War of the Worlds* would be prime reading for someone like that, it would explain why such a well-read copy was in the truck driver's pocket, inscribed by the mysterious X himself.

It sounded harmless enough in Well's book, and in theory, but in reality? There were plenty of people that would dare to hold humanity back from such a leap. (A cheerful baby with a hearing aid and glasses took shape on Simeon's paper.) The Tom Smiths of this world, genetic weaklings, would have to be kept from polluting the race. And as there was no practical use for people like that a quiet death, like putting an animal to sleep, would be the preferable method. (A grim chalk drawing swiftly went around the happy baby.) The Joshua Stevensons, who dared to oppose evolution itself

145

and kept the race tied back to the ancient anchors of religion and old time morality, would also have to go. Mr. Stevenson had put himself in the limelight by preparing to publish that article on new dating methods. (A cartoon style velociraptor was quickly sketched.) How many others would come under the heading of those holding back the race? Simeon picked up the list again, reading the names that were checked off. Janet Southerly. Thomas Smith. Nathan Cross. Aban Madani. It was like reading a list of names on a memorial, the sober death knell rang in Simeon's mind with each one. Aban Madani sounded like a Muslim. Of course they would oppose an evolutionary dream like this too. And so did whole churches. (A simple box appeared on Simeon's note as he remembered that little box found in the foyer of his church in Virginia.) A cold chill ran down Simeon's spine. How many other churches held those lethal little boxes? It was time to move.

Simeon hopped up and tucked the list of names and the notebook into his pocket. He stacked his notes neatly again and walked swiftly toward the large library door, running a hand appreciatively along the grand piano's keyboard and his eye around the shelves, reaching five feet above his head and filled with a lovely eclectic array of books. He could learn to love it here very quickly. Happy thoughts of replanting the neglected herb garden, reading by the giant fireplace with Vincent on winter nights, and having someone to fill the chair across from him at meals filled Simeon's mind. For a moment they pushed the sorrowful knowledge of evil at work away, and he let them play in his mind as he headed for the kitchen. He found an unexpected conversation going on at the little table as he stepped into the bright, homey kitchen.

"Right?" Jack was saying to Vincent in a supercilious tone as warm sunlight spilled through the winter frosted porch windows onto the round wooden table. "What is a right, even? We all define them differently, and you have no 'right' to tell me what my 'rights' are."

"Oh come on, you don't really believe that," Vincent scoffed good-naturedly. "There is a set of rights that everyone agrees with, that God set down in the very beginning." Judy snored gently from where she lay against her husband, very asleep, and Simeon wondered how long the conversation had been going on.

"Oh, you believe in the God theory. I don't have a need for that," said Jack with his reporter air of any-man-that-does-is-little-less-than-an-uncouth-idiot. The argument went on, courteous but very adamant. Simeon didn't bother to join in the debates[29], but he was very interested to find where Jack stood on life and listened in. And so while Jack and Vincent argued vehemently over the existence of God, Simeon started to wash up the lunch dishes. He put the last pan away and turned to the two men. He had let them have as much time as he could, he needed his pilot.

"I have your notebook, Mr. Leason," Simeon said, thinking this would probably be the quickest way to get the two philosophers to break back into more solid things.

"– so there's no way you can say that you 'know' God," Jack concluded.

"But there's no way you can prove there isn't a God," Vincent

---

[29] Simeon Lee had never much enjoyed arguing over things that couldn't be proved one way or the other, and while he recognized that this was often very necessary, he preferred to stick to the things he could actually prove whenever possible. He was what has been termed 'a practical man.' This very practicality usually made him win any arguments he did get into of the intangible sort, for they almost always hinge on the practical application of the idea.

countered.

"The notebook I stole, Mr. Leason?" said Simeon.

"But you can't prove there is one. And to say that everyone in the world has to conform to a certain way of thinking about 'good' and 'evil' because of a God you can't prove, is incredibly arrogant," Jack said.

"Your arrogance is just as clear in saying we have to conform to your way of thinking. And what you're arguing for is complete reliance on man for all that we know and do. That's the most depressing and dangerous thing I can think of!" Vincent objected. "And what if you're wrong?"

"Mr. Leason, you promised your story," Simeon tried again.

"It's only the truth, even if it does depress you so much," said Jack. Simeon gave up trying to reach these two in the normal manner. He slid the slim black notebook out of his pocket and dangled it in front of Jack's eyes. The reporter's feet slipped off the table to the floor with a bang as he grabbed at the book. Simeon whisked it back in his pocket and stepped away.

"Hey!" Jack shouted, hopping up to face the ex-CIA man, inadvertently making Judy wake up with a start. "You can't just take it like that!"

"Already did," Simeon said evenly.

"But I was the one who found it in the first place!"

"Can't say you have a right to the notebook, you just said there are no rights," Simeon refuted. "I took it. Now it's mine." Silence reigned in the kitchen for a moment. Vincent was trying hard not to laugh at Jack's shocked expression as he watched Simeon quietly pour himself a cup of coffee.

"I'll fight you for it if you really want it," Simeon commented, as he turned back to the table. "That's your only logical position now." That was too much for Vincent; he chuckled audibly.

"No thanks," Jack muttered, at a loss as to what to say to this physical outcome of his purely intellectual debate.

"Apparently I missed something," Judy yawned. "What's going on?"

"About to hear your story," Simeon said, sliding onto one of the wooden chairs across from Vincent.

"Only if you promise to give yours too, and I want to know what you're doing. And who you are, Mr. Lee!" Jack declared.

"Oh stop it and sit down," Judy told him. "You tell things better than I do Jack, so get on with it while I make a pot of tea. You keep a very good selection here. Well, go on poltroon, tell them what the past few days have been like!" Jack obeyed. He told stories like he wrote them, and Simeon and Vincent were both a little surprised by how good he was. As he spoke the events came to life in their minds. They could feel the despair and triumphs, and almost smelled the wood from the desk the husband and wife had crouched behind and the dirty metal of the truck floor. It was a tale told with realism and imagination mixed so well the story fit any human like a glove. Jack only left out that brief moment of hallucinating despair when everything in and around him had been that horrifying emptiness. When he grew still he still felt just a hint of that horrible void around him. Jack hardly dared admit it even to himself, but one of the reasons he had started that philosophical debate with Vincent was a feeling that had been growing inside of him; something ought to be able to fill that void. Jack was hesitantly beginning a hunt, a hunt for what he had no idea. But finding a Christian that could actually debate sensibly was a surprise, and very interesting. He wound to an end with being pulled into the Parabaloni car and looked at Judy.

"Oh, my little bit after that is very uninteresting," Judy said, nursing her cup of lavender earl gray. "The big seedy guy with the gun climbed through to the back of the truck and tried to grab me. I hit him hard. But he hit me harder, and I woke up with Jack in the backseat of that poor little car of yours."

"I hope you broke at least his nose, Mr. Lee. Preferably his neck," Jack growled. He looked at Simeon and grew determined again. "So now you." The agent tapped the table for a moment, studying the man in front of him.

"Mrs. Leason, how reliable is your husband's word of honor?" Simeon asked.

"Whatever other things he defaults on, Jack always sticks to a pledge of honor," Judy smiled. "One of his greater grandfathers was a southern gentleman, you see."

"Mr. Leason, your wife keep her word?" Simeon turned to the reporter.

"If you try to cast any aspersions on Judy, Mr. Lee, I'll..." Jack paused and took a breath, swallowing his words and starting a new sentence. "Yes. If you can actually make her promise something, Judy always keeps a promise."

"Mr. and Mrs. Leason, I want your promise that you will not

150

make a story out of Vincent Tolliver, no mention at all of the Tolliver family unless he gives permission," Simeon said.

"Yes!" Vincent cried pulling a balled up fist down through the air in a display of victorious delight.

"Oh, you don't have to worry about me," Judy smiled. "I don't do stories, and I don't gab to people."

"Very good, Mrs. Leason. Mr. Leason, also want you to promise you will not have anything published about what you hear from us without first letting me read it and having my approval. No dodging out of it by employing clever newsman tricks. Agreed?" Jack didn't like it and he quickly began to wheedle, trying to get Simeon to let him have a little room to squirm out. It was like arguing with a rock. After Judy and Vincent both got bored enough to head off on a tour of the headquarters, Jack sighed and agreed. He duly promised, on his honor, to treat the Tollivers as totally un-newsworthy and to let Simeon read over anything he wrote about the doings of the newly formed Parabaloni and wait for his changes and approvals to get it published.

"Find Vincent, tell him he can explain our part in the business," Simeon said, giving the reporter a nod. Jack stood up without another word and headed to go find the ragged billionaire inventor. Not newsworthy indeed! The whole of America wanted to know more about the reclusive Tolliver junior; homeschooled his whole life, making brilliant patents by age twelve, sole owner of billions and billions of dollars... And he had so many good ideas about announcing Ted Tolliver's accidental death and what his son was up to currently, all down the drain now. Confound Simeon Lee's farsightedness! That serious toughie was a fascinating character. Jack found himself wondering what kind of a man they had landed with as he walked toward the blue room. Whoever Simeon Lee was Jack somehow knew the story of his life would make the best tale any writer ever got a hold of. Too bad he was never likely to divulge it. And if he did he'd probably make people promise to clam up anyway.

Simeon watched Jack go and smiled. He was beginning to like that man who spouted Shakespeare insults before cuss words and could argue like a Socratic thinker for a good story. And his wife was certainly a gem. Bother him and his quick temper though, he would have to wait while Vincent explained the past week now. Well he could employ the time well. Simeon slipped to his knees by the kitchen counter and began to pray for the Leasons' salvation and this boxy situation he and Vincent had landed themselves in. He stayed kneeling in prayer for nearly an hour, giving all his thoughts and fears and suspicions to his good God. When he rose Simeon's knees hurt. He was suddenly reminded he was no spring chicken anymore, and sighed as he limped off to go find Vincent. But despite the sober reminder of his age, he felt refreshed and refocused. His God was real and good, and they were going to win this one. Simeon found the three people gathered on the Leasons' bed. Simeon quickly stopped Jack's outpour of questions as he came in, and gave the husband and wife the task of trying to find connections in the list of names, to keep them quiet and occupied. He collared Vincent and headed him toward the workshop.

"Where are we going, Simeon?" Vincent asked as he walked.

"Virginia. Need the X box Pastor sent home with you. Date."

"Oh right, I didn't think about that. We broke the date the last one was programmed to go off on, but we can figure out when it was from this new box. Brilliant! You think it would be the same

152

date as the one we found?"

"Yes."

"Are we going for anything else?" Vincent asked as he hopped into Percy and started to run over his pre-flight checklist.

"Have a plane that can carry a car[30]?"

"Sure, Perry. He's a good big jet I have parked over in the Dallas airport. Want to stop and switch for him?"

"I would like my car."

"You got it, chief," Vincent said cheerily. He motioned Simeon in and started the engine. Simeon steadied his nerves and hopped into the passenger seat. Vincent talked his way out of the hanger all the way to being sling-shot out of the mountain into the brilliant blue of the New Mexican sky, explaining each step of the process, and glanced at Simeon as he leveled out over the Rocky Mountains. His prospective boss seemed to be handling flying all right now that he wasn't surprising him with dive bombing into dark mountains. The subject of his thoughts looked over and caught the pilot's eye.

"Vincent, listen up," Simeon started. He began to explain what he had found and decided in his morning's research. Vincent's sunny face was clouded and thoughtful as Simeon finished.

"Wow," the pilot breathed. "I guess it all fits. And it makes sense too. Once you take that step to say there is no God that holds a transcendent moral code, and we all really just happened from lower animals murder is no longer an issue. Not really. If we are all

---

[30] Simeon was already beginning to assume his young companion had everything or could make everything. It was the first time in his experience asking for something as ridiculous as a plane equipped to transport cars seemed perfectly natural.

just animals, killing off the weaker ones is fine."

"So long as you can get others to see it from your point of view," Simeon nodded.

"Right. In fact if you can get others to see it from your point of view, it's a small step to getting them to see it as a good thing."

"Encouragement in numbers. Gather more who believe as you do, and you go farther down your intellectual path. In a country like America, a real republic, if you can get enough people who believe what you stand for, in sixty to a hundred years you can do almost anything. Googled a few of the names on the list. Killing more than just the weak. They're including those who oppose their ideas."

"Wait, so you're saying these PD X box people are killing off those they know would oppose their murderous plans to remake the human race? I guess if they are really looking at the future of humanity they would be concerned with society's evolution too. If they get rid of the people with the right view (the ones who think life is life and messing with it is murder), society would start to 'adapt' itself and these X box people's goal would be gained. Not that it would do any good, even if they got that far. We're degenerating under the curse as a race and world, not evolving to higher things. Silly people, aren't they taught to observe? Hey wait, Simeon...in America it's the Christians who oppose this horrible practical evolutionism the most! Well, Christians and the law enforcement that works off Christian ethics. Is that why that box was in the foyer at our church in Virginia? Simeon, how many other churches have those boxes hidden in them, set to go off? So many people come and go in a church, if Mr. Steve is right and that really is andorsonii-whatever that will contaminate, infect, and kill...we're talking a death plague of Christians. On top of all these other people

154

this PD gang is killing off for other reasons!"

"Yes."

"Wow. We've got to find that date fast. Wait, Simeon, we've got to find out who's behind this! We can't stop it without knowing that, no matter how many dates we have. How do we find that out?" Vincent asked[31]. Simeon sat silent for a moment, and the pilot had to shoot him a look to get him to speak up.

"I've lived a fair while, Vincent."

"Okay... that's a good thing," the pilot answered a little confusedly. Simeon ignored him.

"At the risk of sounding silly, I'll let you know something experience has taught me. I've learned not to ignore my ideas just because I can't place where they come from. No idea why, but I think Saul Korry has the answer to who is behind the X boxes."

"Should I know that name?"

"Not unless you've gone to a private detective agency in Cheyenne. Saul's bigger stunts were before your time."

"Keen. Like a modern day, cowboy version of Richard Diamond the singing detective," Vincent commented, and was surprised when Simeon chuckled at the allusion[32]. "How do you

---

[31] Simeon's quiet presence inspired those around him with the idea he had everything covered. It even worked on animals. I remember the wolf pack in Iceland, if Simeon hadn't stood so calm and still in that pack of caribou I don't know what would have happened to our president at that time, and America's influence on the rest of the world would certainly have been lost for good.

[32] Saul Korry was more of a singing detective than Vincent knew when he mentioned the old time radio PI. Simeon's mind was on an instance in his early career when he and Saul worked undercover in a London Opera company. A fascinating web of intrigue was

know him? Did you have a need of a Cheyenne detective?"

"He was a coworker before retiring into PI work."

"Ah, a spy," Vincent grinned. He was starting to enjoy the idea of being in a world of espionage and secrets. "So, Saul Korry knows who the guy behind the X boxes is, we think. Does he know he knows?"

"Don't know. Won't answer his phone. The big lug."

"Ouch. Whenever I do answer mine it's just a poll calling, or something just as dull. I wonder why I even have a cell phone."

"So I can keep track of you."

"Hey, that's right," Vincent beamed. "Okay, so we wait for Mr. Korry the lug to call us back and work on finding that date in the meantime. Say Simeon, why didn't you tell Jack and Judy about what you had figured out? Do you think they won't take it well?"

"Didn't mention it because it would take too long. But left the notebook and Jack is smart. Don't think I'll have to explain. But don't know how they'll take it."

"Yeah," Vincent muttered a little damped. "I'll up my prayers they accept the truth soon. So do you think we'll be on time? I can't imagine those boxes are meant to sit there for weeks without going off."

"We will have to be on time," Simeon said, and dropped the conversation as Vincent headed over a thunderstorm.

---

uncovered in those two years of Simeon's life, which unfortunately I don't have time to go into here. But bats and fourteen different countries were involved.

9

Vincent stood awkwardly on Simeon's front porch rug, looking into the spotless house. He wasn't sure he should bring his dusty feet onto the white carpet. How on earth did his prospective boss keep a white carpet that spotless? Simeon paused on his way into the living room, noticing the inventor's firm footfalls had stopped behind him. Vincent noted he was waiting and walked in. He saw more neatness. Everything was spotlessly in its proper place. And the silence of the place was complete, and a little unnerving. He glanced at Simeon, quietly putting a few things into a reusable grocery bag in the little kitchen attached to the living area.

"Do you actually live here?" Vincent asked, and then quickly fumbled for a nicer statement. "I mean, do you like it here, I was thinking..." The corner of Simeon's mouth moved up in his little amused look.

"Live here now[33], don't entirely like it. Prefer a home to a house. Relax, Vincent. It could use some dirt."

"Right," Vincent grinned. He plopped on the entirely too unwrinkled leather sofa, pulled a screwdriver out of one of his cargo pockets and began to fiddle with it idly. Simeon finished collecting his organic foods, favorite herbs, and special blend of

---

[33] Simeon Lee's experience of living accommodations ran the gambit of the nightmare-givers to the extremely opulent. His favorite up to date was a tiny farm in the country of Georgia where he had once scratched a living, in the company of – but that's his story. I really shouldn't tell it without his consent.

coffee and sat the bag by the front door. He motioned Vincent to follow him and headed into a long hall. Vincent had assumed they were headed to his bedroom, but they passed a bedroom instead. Of course that could be the guest room. It was sort of hard to tell in this house. Simeon stopped at the end of the hall at a closed, white door with a security keypad on it. The lock scanned his eye and clicked open. Simeon swung in and motioned Vincent to follow. The inventor stepped into the middle of the room and turned in a slow, awed circle, a low whistle escaping his lips. There were rifles and machine pistols, machetes and bazookas, and things he couldn't even name covering every wall. A few of the larger weapons even hung tastefully from the white ceiling. This room was a very well stocked arsenal.

"What is that thing?" Vincent muttered pointing above him at a long, heavy looking mass of metal. He was half afraid a loud noise would set something off.

"RPG," Simeon answered. Vincent looked blank and Simeon restrained a sigh. He had a lot to teach. "Rocket Propelled Grenade-launcher. Anti-tank system." Simeon opened a closet, tossed his friend a duffle bag, and began to load things into it. Vincent looked on in silence, wondering what they all were. Simeon could tell what his prospective employee was thinking and began naming what he was putting in the bag.

"MP7, powerful delivery, easy to carry. MP7's extra clips, extension. Cornershot, used in indoor fighting and house to house. AK47, standard, first automatic rifle you'll learn on." He paused and glanced up at the inventor. "Never seen even one?"

"Sorry, no. My dad had a .45 rifle I shot once or twice, that's the closest I've come to any gun. Do you really use all these? Am I really going to have to learn about these? Wait, I'm going to have to really use these!" For just a moment a look of amused pity showed on Simeon's face. Then he stood up and handed Vincent the AK47. He pointed through the open door and stepped behind the young man. Vincent looked and saw a small target hanging gracefully on the white painted wall at the end of the hallway.

"Seriously?" Vincent muttered in shock, shifting the weight of the large weapon uncomfortably in his hands. "What will the neighbors think?"

"Soundproof," Simeon answered, and Vincent stared at him. "A construction company owed me a favor," he explained, and motioned down the hall as he looked up at his companion. That look clearly said, 'If you think you're going to do this you had better listen to me now,' and the inventor understood it. Vincent took a deep breath and lifted the weapon. He sighted as carefully as he knew how and pulled the trigger tentatively. Nothing happened.

"Safety," Simeon informed. He showed Vincent how to flip the safety on and off and stepped back again. The inventor tried again. This time a line of bullets ripped down the hallway and the silent house was filled with the metallic cough of automatic rifle fire. The recoil drove Vincent back a step and he swiftly pulled his finger off the trigger as he knew his aim had been thrown off. The inventor stared at the ragged black bullet holes running in a line along the neat hall's wall on up to cut into the white ceiling. A piece of plaster quietly crumbled off the ceiling onto the white carpet as he watched. Vincent swallowed nervously and glanced to the side at his friend. It looked like he got to learn how Simeon reacted when angry this evening.

"Not awful," Simeon said, eyeing the target critically.

160

"I just busted your ceiling and that's your response? Hey, maybe I can do this!"

"Again," Simeon ordered. He stepped beside the smiling Vincent and silently showed him the best way to fire the weapon. Vincent tried again. And again. He was starting to have fun with the exercise, and actually hitting only the target under Simeon's deft directions. He carefully slid his fourth empty clip out of the AK47 and tossed it toward his teacher. Simeon caught it but held out a new gun to his student instead of another clip.

"All right, a switch!" Vincent exclaimed, eyeing the strange looking little rifle in Simeon's hands. "This is that Cornershot thing, right? Street fighting and indoor use?"

"Yes," Simeon answered. He switched the rifles on the young man, took his arm, and repositioned him beside the door, facing the wall.

"Uh... Am I supposed to shoot the wall?" Vincent asked, doubtfully eyeing the spotless whiteness three feet from his face. "Because I really don't want to. It's too nice looking, and clean. And there are pictures near it, I'll probably hit them by accident and they look much prettier and more important than any old wall." Simeon reached over and moved something with each hand on the gun. The first half of the rifle rotated around the door's frame, and a digital screen shot out of the side with a clear picture of the hallway flickering into life. Vincent yelped and dropped the rifle in shock and the scene on the digital screen changed to show the ceiling. Vincent felt his cheeks flare red, but he spun around to apologize. One look at his boss alleviated his fears of getting fired at least. Simeon's hand was over his mouth in an effort to be polite, but his soft eyes gave it away as he looked at his student.

161

"Didn't know guns could do that?" Simeon asked from behind his hand. A chortle escaped and he gave up and started laughing.

"No, I didn't know guns could do that, and a warning might have been nice," Vincent grinned. He picked up the gun and ran a hand over it. It took him three seconds to figure out the mechanism that made the gun rotate, and learn exactly how the little screen was hooked up. He aimed carefully around the doorframe and a line of bullets ripped down the hall and crashed into the target. Simeon nodded in approbation.

"Did I do well that time? I did actually hit the target," Vincent commented.

"Picked it back up on your own and figured it out. Good," Simeon quietly praised. "Try again." Simeon went back to packing his bag as he watched Vincent practice. He wasn't so bad. Quick learner, really listened, ready to apologize when he made a mistake, tried again when he failed, and even didn't mind getting laughed at. Vincent Tolliver had good character. Maybe this would work out. Vincent finished the clip off and carefully lowered the gun. Simeon kept packing his bag, so he wandered over to the far wall to look at the pictures. There were eight of them, each with Simeon Lee at a different time of life and a different companion. At least he was pretty sure it was Simeon Lee…the face was different at different stages, in the young pictures he was kind of mouth-droppingly handsome, actually. But yeah, it was Simeon. The build and stance was the same. Something must have happened to make him have his face remade a time or two, Vincent decided, and the inventor idly wondered if he wanted to know what disaster had caused it as he turned his mind to Simeon's pictured companions. A big black man who looked like a smart football player, a little Hispanic with a great grin, an elegant Englishman, a corgi, a chubby baby of some

Eastern decent, a cute woman with Simeon's arm around her waist, a basset hound... Vincent paused at the eighth, smiling at its differentness. A Simeon somewhere in his thirties knelt on one knee in some sort of European peasant folk clothes. Huge, beautiful mountains rose up behind him, and a young boy and girl stood cheerfully by his side. That Simeon looked so proud and happy as his arms rested on the children, it made Vincent smile. He wondered about the story behind it, instinctively guessing it was a very good one.

"Where is this, Simeon?" Vincent asked, pointing at the picture. Simeon glanced at where his friend was pointing. His face dropped into a stiff mask, and even his soft brown eyes grew harder.

"Georgia," Simeon answered curtly, and immediately held up a vest to the inventor. It looked almost like a metal plate shirt of the old medieval era, with many different layers of thick metallic material running down its impressive length.

"Am I supposed to wear this?" Vincent grunted as he took the heavy vest and accepted the silent order not to press into Simeon's past life. "What is it?"

"Dragon Skin body armor. That's yours. Wear it, get used to the feel. Should be familiar when you have to use it."

"Dragon Skin, keen," Vincent grinned. "I shall name it Smaug and it shall be my friend. Does it go over or under my shirt?"

"Under. Unless you want people to run and scream when they see you coming," Simeon smiled, helping his bizarre friend into the heavy vest. "Hungry?"

"Yeah. And tired, even if I did sleep all morning. How about picking up something on the way to my place, to get that black box pastor sent home with me?"

"All right. Then back to New Mexico to sleep. Wake you early, we can get it open first thing tomorrow."

"Smaug and I vote for something like a hamburger, or steak," Vincent grinned, doing a quick jumping jack to see how the heavy vest felt. "What kind of fast food do you like Smaug? 'Meaty!'" Vincent hissed in a very nefarious voice, meant to be the vest answering back. Simeon shook his head in silent amusement and went to grab a few things from his bedroom before racing off again.

Both men needed a good rest, and Simeon was experienced enough to know it was best to sleep while you could. Once they got back to New Mexico with the second black box, he allowed them till six the following morning. But he insisted on speed after that. It turned out a good thing he did insist, this box stuck. It was three in the afternoon before they were able to break it open. The shadows grew deeper, the sunlight faded, and it was after five before they finally pulled the two halves apart. It was rough, nerve-wracking work. Every time they moved the box both men felt a cold sweat start up as they thought of that little red tube of goop inside breaking open. As they pulled it apart finally and saw the stopper was still safely in, Simeon sat up with a weary sigh and decided he needed another refill on his coffee. Vincent began to dig eagerly for the timer and Simeon headed to the kitchenette, managing not to groan over all the aches and cramps from his long day leaning over pulling and prodding that little black box. As he filled his clay mug again, Simeon's phone broke into a Brandenburg concerto. He flipped it open and put it to his ear.

164

"Sim, thank heaven you always answer!" Saul's voice broke over the machine before Simeon could get a word out. The usually large voice was low and quick, and Simeon could hear his friend's breath coming in strained gasps. "Listen up, bro. I've stuck my big foot in another hornet's nest and I'm about to be cornered again. I think I have a card to play to keep myself alive, but if I don't...look out for Michelle and Jon for me?"

"Promised I would take on all family for you thirty-three years ago. Talk, Saul."

"You old rusty anchor, you always sound so steady," Saul chuckled. It broke off into a retching cough and Simeon winced and began to pray for his old friend's safety. "That X Plant finally realized I was getting close. I'm not sure how, but they tagged me. All day they've been showing up, from my morning donut to my afternoon coffee stop. They could have gunned me down a hundred times today, which makes me think my card will keep me alive all right. I got a little banged up when they caught up with me a few minutes ago. I'm more out of practice at this than I thought."

"Where now?"

"I'm heading back to my office, it's the safest place for me to hole up. I think I lost them for a while and I'm going to toss anything that could be tracked as soon as I stop talking to you."

"Not a place of yours, go to a friend's. Where they wouldn't look first and you aren't alone."

"I'm not bringing anyone else into this, Sim!"

"Alone in your office? Not a good idea," Simeon said, but he knew his friend wasn't going to pay any attention to him. Saul

Korry was not a good listener.

"I can see my office roof from here," Saul said, not listening. "Sim, I haven't gotten to the worst part yet. You can't call anyone in. And you can't let anyone know you're coming." Saul sounded terrified suddenly and Simeon felt a familiar sick tightening of his stomach.

"Jon and Mrs. Korry."

"Yes, just two minutes ago I got a text with a video attached. Sim, these murderers have my wife and only son! I don't know if I could live if I didn't get them back, I'm not strong enough to go on without them! I can't–"

"Saul, breathe. Demands?"

"Don't call in anyone and stop fighting back. All they want is me, the text said. I have till midnight tonight."

"Forward me the text and video, toss the phone. I'll be there in three hours. Only three hours to hold out, Saul."

"Okay, I'll make it. Sim, thanks for dropping everything for me again." Silence came over the phone and Simeon knew his old coworker had hung up. He pulled it away from his ear and stared at the screen as he ran across the concrete of Vincent's workroom. A beedle sounded to show he had a text as he leapt a pile of junk and skidded to a stop by the inventor.

"Smaug and I finally dug up the date, and it's freakily close!" Vincent commented, his eye still on the box. Simeon grabbed the inventor by his collar, jerking him to his feet and pushing him toward the plane in his haste.

166

"Saul's in trouble. Cheyenne, now."

12:37 a.m. Feb. 16th; Library, P. H., NM

"'Conscience is but a word that cowards use,/Devised at first to keep the strong in awe./Our strong arms be our conscience, swords our law[34].'" Jack stopped reading out loud and let the book drop to his lap. Judy stirred where she was warming her toes by the large library fireplace and looked at her man. The fire's warm glow danced over Jack's handsome features where he sat framed by the enormous backdrop of shelves and shelves of magnificent books. Judy found she was smiling just out of enjoyment of the scene as she spoke up.

"What's wrong, Jack? Nasty old Richard is about to finally get what he deserves, and a better king take his place. Are you getting too tired? I can finish it."

"No, I'm not tired, it's just... Judy... Why does Richard deserve what he's about to get?"

"What? Oh, you're getting philosophical on me again. Because he murdered seven people who didn't deserve it and stole a crown that wasn't his. Turnabout is fair play, as some say."

"'Conscience is but a word that cowards use,/Devised at first to keep the strong in awe.'" Jack quoted again. "That's what these hooded wackos would say, you know. If I'm reading that purpose

---

[34] From Shakespeare's Richard the III, Act 5, Scene 3.

167

statement in that notebook right, they wouldn't have much of a problem with old Richard the III, provided he murdered for the right reasons. And now that I come to think of it, I have no reason to say that he is wrong. I mean, what do I have to base a statement like 'murder is wrong and so you deserve death' on? I don't have a thing."

"What about the people and the families of the people that die? There's a lot of suffering that comes with a murderer's actions that affect other people. And we have tradition on our side."

"Tradition," Jack snorted. "Now we sound like Tevye and his little town."

"If it upsets you that much, just stop thinking about it," Judy shrugged. "Finish the play and let's go to bed instead. When we wake up we get to attack that list Mr. Lee left for us to check out. There's an idea, Jack. Mr. Lee is obviously a very good man, and I think he would have your answer to why we can state a murder is wrong."

"But what if I don't like his answer," Jack muttered, more to himself than to Judy. His wife sat and blinked at the fire, and didn't hear his quiet comment. The reporter didn't realize it, but she was pondering his question. Philosophy had never interested Judy. She was practical, like Simeon, and rarely bothered with abstract ideas as she could always explain them by something more tangible. But her hubby had stumped her this time. Why could you say it was wrong for someone to murder someone else? Jack sighed and picked up the filigreed copy of the Shakespeare play again. Judy was certainly right about something. It was time to finish and go to bed.

9:01 pm. Feb. 16th; Outside 467 Cummings Ave., Cheyenne, WY

Simeon gently pulled his car to a stop across the street from the restored old two story house, painted beautiful shades of brown and green. Saul had picked a nice place for his PI office. Everything was dead still. Simeon refused to assume the silence meant what he knew it should, and instead flipped his cell phone open.

"Going in, Vincent," he spoke into his friend's phone.

"Right," Vincent's shaky voice came out of the cell. He sounded terrified. "Simeon, I'm kind of terrified right now. I really think you should be the one to get this Jon and Michelle Korry out!"

"There?"

"Yeah, Pat and I found where you say that video was taken all right. There's a light on in the right room, but nothing seems to be happening."

"No one on the street?"

"Not that I've seen, no. Pat's scanning for me." Patricia Palm's saucy automated voice could be heard in the background reporting something. "She says there's no one near, and that she can only find three people inside the building."

"That means just one guard, and you can do it. Go in. Keep your gun ready, extra clips handy, but only fire if you have to."

"But you're the one that knows–" Vincent broke in

169

desperately, and Simeon cut him off.

"Hostage situations are uncertain, I've explained this. The bad guys might suddenly decide they don't need them anymore and choose not to wait till midnight to murder. Vincent, we need them out. Now. And I need you to do it. You can handle this. I wouldn't have sent you if there was any doubt of it. I have to go in." Simeon hung up and slid silently out of the car. There was new fallen snow all around him, and it made a beautiful picture as a sliver of a moon peeked over the rooftops. Simeon wished he could appreciate the beauty as he slipped silently toward the house. He stuck his hand into his jacket pocket just to be sure his .38 Ruger was still there. It was, and the touch of the familiar, cold metal made Simeon feel more confident as he slid up to the side of Saul Korry's branch office. Simeon had always liked this office. He prayed Saul was there now, waiting for him just beyond the door. Something inside him sapped his hope and spoke of darker things. Oh, if God would just see fit to include his old friend amongst His chosen own! Simeon pushed his fears away, resolutely refusing to listen to them, and took hold of the door knob. It was locked. He made a decision and knocked for someone to answer it. No answer came from inside or outside. Simeon was very stern as he moved toward the back of the building, but he kept his thoughts focused on the job. The back door was just as firmly locked. A quick glance around showed no one was in the area, and he pulled a jackknife out of his pocket. The door was jimmied silently open within a second. He slid inside and locked the door behind him. Simeon stood in what would have been the laundry room if this had been an ordinary house. Now brown file folders and miscellaneous papers poked out of cardboard boxes stuck on shelves all around the agent.

"Saul?" called out Simeon as loudly as he dared. His voice

sounded small and lonely in the old wooden building. Simeon placed his hand on his handgun and left it there as he walked forward slowly into the reception room. It was a mess. Files were everywhere, a flatscreen computer monitor was lying smashed on the floor as if it had been flung against the wall on purpose. The basement door was flung wide and hanging by a single hinge. Simeon pulled his pistol all the way out of his pocket, crossed quickly to the basement, and switched on the light. He moved halfway down the stairs till he could see the lower offices laid out below him. There was no one there, and it looked too neat to be interesting. Obviously whatever had happened on the first floor hadn't gone down in the basement.

Simeon shot up the basement stairs and on up to the second story. This is where Saul would be if he was anywhere in the building. But he wasn't anywhere in the building. After a quick and thorough search, Simeon came up with a complete blank. He was the only person in the branch office of Korry's Investigative Services.

10

Saul's office was wrecked. Simeon dully began to pick up the papers littering the ground everywhere and set them on the enormous oak desk resting by the frosted window. His heart felt numb and empty and his mind little better. Saul had been a rock in an evil, stormy world since the day they had met, when Simeon was sixteen. As he stood in the wrecked room, Simeon's mind shot back to that day when the enormous, black hand dropped onto the back of his chair and Saul's booming voice asked if he wanted help with his math. No one had ever offered him that. The feeling of gratefulness and the quiet hope kindled in him from that simple act of kindness came back in full force now as Simeon picked up the scattered papers and replaced the pictures on the desk. Saul had always been like that. He was the brother Simeon had needed growing up and had stayed his brother through all these years. If these people hurt that big bass... A protective fire began to burn in the hole Saul's absence created. They wouldn't have the chance to hurt him. Saul said he had a way to stay alive, at least for a little while, and Simeon would find him before that time was up. He began to put away the papers with real purpose, looking them over as he worked.

There was such a myriad of facts contained in Saul Korry's paperwork, Simeon assumed they must be from several cases. He quickly sorted them on the big wooden desk. There was a stack on someone named Heinrick Nuemenoff and his wife. Looked like they could use some marital council. There was another stack dealing with a robbery of some show llamas near Fort Collins. Then there were two very interesting stacks to Simeon. He settled in the oversized desk chair facing the second story window and picked up the thickest pile. It was a stack of papers dealing with various murders and unexplained disappearances. There wasn't much of a connection except for their very unexpectedness. But Simeon Lee already had a connection to work with and he ran each paper in this stack through a mental checklist. They all fitted neatly in these X box people's agenda; a pastor fighting for a school to allow Intelligent Design within its doors; a pair of twins, genetically malformed; a young college student trying to start a Creationist club on campus...the list went on and on. Simeon pushed it away with a shudder and reached for the last pile. This one was thinner, but the most interesting of the lot. It was newspaper, magazine, and Who's Who clippings, all on one man. Saul Korry had taken a great interest in an Edward Plant. Simeon knew the name and only glanced at the clippings. Edward Plant was a few years older than Saul, an independently wealthy playboy of an unusual sort. He played mostly with various charities and organizations. Glancing over the stack of papers Simeon remembered a long forgotten fact. Edward Plant always endorsed things 'for the furtherance of mankind.' It was his favorite phrase and he used it often, in nearly every press conference, which he called periodically to endorse something new.

A half-heard noise registered, and Simeon paused to listen. He had a sudden feeling he wasn't alone in the building anymore. Simeon slid silently out of the chair and glided toward the door to the hall, pressing his ear against it and letting every sense concentrate on that one ear. Someone was down stairs. They were moving nearly silently, but they were moving. Simeon slid away from the door to the window. It was starting to snow, and the pain of glass was freezing to the touch. He pulled a small vial of oil out of his jacket pocket and rubbed a little over the lock and hinges. The someone was inching up the staircase. Simeon began to open the window slowly, to avoid any noise in the old frame. A blast of freezing air blew in through the new crack in the window and he didn't bother to be stealthy anymore, knowing the breeze would be felt by the someone on the stairs. Simeon jerked the window open, slid out so his fingers gripped the sill and his arms were extended, and let go. The cold of the sidewalk made it feel especially hard, and the force of the fall jarred upward through Simeon's legs to his skull. He heard someone turn and ducked instinctively. A soft pop came from the darkness by the front door and a bullet whined over Simeon's head. He turned and dashed for the corner where he had parked his car, unlocking it as he ran. Getting killed or caught would not help Saul. Besides, before he died he wanted to tell Vincent he was proud of him for taking on a hostage situation so early in his new career.

Simeon counted as he ran, estimating the time it would take an average gunman who owned a silencer to get a bead on the new position of his target. It would be now. Simeon dropped to one knee on a patch of ice forming on the road, using it to slide the rest of the way to his car. A familiar round ding appeared in his driver's window, where his head would be if he hadn't ducked. Simeon pulled the door open and dived inside, thanking God again for allowing him to keep his company car with its bullet proof windows and armored sides. A flick of the key brought the little sports car to purring life, and Simeon sent it skidding over the patch of ice to grip the road and shoot toward the heart of Cheyenne. A blue BMW pulled out behind him. Simeon saw a pistol waving through his rear view mirror and moved his finger from the four-wheel drive toward the button that launched the oil spill. A wash of black oil spurted from the little sports car, spreading over the road in a quick, even sea. The streetlights were dim and the Beemer didn't see the release

174

of the black liquid. The first he knew of it was the sudden lurch of his car and the terrifying realization he had no control over his vehicle. Before he could comprehend what was wrong, his door smashed into the lamppost, a rending screech of metal reached him, and the terrifying sound of something enormous tipping over, and the metal top of his car folded down on his head as the falling streetlight bent the roof in half.

Simeon turned law-abidingly onto a side street, working his way toward the airport and running a quick bug check to make sure these people hadn't been smart enough to track him. He doubted it, but it was healthier to assume your enemy was better than he was, than to get the nasty shock of discovering you underestimated them. This was an interesting gang, but their mix of trained fighters and amateur goons was destroying their image. It was as if they pulled in whoever they happened to find on the streets. But then, that might be precisely what they were doing. There were enough ardent evolutionists in America to allow for such a method. It was an uncomfortable thought, and Simeon was frowning as he pulled open his phone to report an accident and dangerous driving situation on Cummings Avenue.

An old moving truck shot out of an intersecting street. It smashed deliberately into Simeon's car door, flinging him to the right with the horrifying violence only a car wreck can, and filling the air with the hideous screech of metal on metal and tires scraping over a frozen ground. Simeon dropped his phone, shoved his car into fifth, and jammed his foot down on the accelerator. His little car obeyed on the instant, shooting away just before it could be smashed between the truck and an apartment building. Two more pairs of headlights appeared in his rearview mirror as more of these people rushed at him. Simeon's face was grim as he dashed through

175

an intersection and skidded around a corner on two wheels, to go zooming through a tiny alleyway. Something told him these were not going to be easy people to shake.

9:15 pm. Feb. 16th; Outside, Cheyenne, WY

Vincent stood in the shadows of an alleyway and gazed at the dilapidated building in front of him. He rubbed one leg against the other nervously and shifted the weight of the Cornershot hanging over his shoulder. It was really cold out here.

"Looking isn't going to make it go away, lunkhead," Pat drawled through the Bluetooth slipped in his ear. Vincent sighed and nodded. The single light he had been watching had already gone out. He felt desperately unprepared for this. But Simeon needed him and Vincent Tolliver wasn't going to let him down by not even trying. The pilot darted across the street and headed toward the dim doorway, trying to remember everything Simeon had crammed into his brain about hostage situations during the three hour flight over here. Vincent twisted the doorknob of the dilapidated old building and darted through faster than he knew he could, to keep from being framed in the doorway by the dim light of the moon. His heart was pounding in his mouth and his scrambling, running footsteps seemed amplified as loud as rifle shots in his mind. There was no other sound in the darkness engulfing him. At least it was fairly warm.

"Dark, isn't it?" Pat spoke up through the hidden Bluetooth, making her man jump. "Now you know how I feel in your pocket."

Vincent resisted the urge to answer and knelt on the floor in what he thought might be a corner to fish in his cargo pockets. He pulled out a pair of goggles he had been fiddling with and tapped the night vision feature. The room showed up in eerie yellow and Vincent had to make himself keep still and not leap to his feet with the sudden change. A quick glance around showed only dust, ancient broken furniture, and stained old walls. Vincent stood up and crossed to a door hanging crookedly on a rotting frame. He touched it and a squeal sounded from the single hinge.

Immediately, a noise split the silence. Vincent felt something crash into his chest, driving him staggering back into the room. His heart hurt, but he didn't give himself time to think about it. Remembering Simeon's lessons, the inventor dived through the door headfirst in a roll. He spun upright on one knee, and swung his little rifle around toward the middle of the room. His goggles showed a man with a hood over his face standing a yard away, and two people right behind him bound in metal chairs. The hooded man was raising a large, automatic rifle and pointing it toward Vincent. A sick feeling twisted the inventor's stomach; his aim wasn't good enough to risk a shot with the three of them clumped together like that. Vincent threw his Cornershot. The little rifle hit the hooded man square in the face, and he staggered back, more in surprise than pain. He tripped over one of the chairs and the pilot used the moment to his advantage. Vincent darted forward and punched the struggling hooded figure hard in the chin. The stranger spun around and rammed into the wall with a hard thunk that rained a shower of dust off the ceiling. Vincent snatched up his gun and smashed the stock into the hooded head, adding in another punch for good measure. His opponent crashed on the ground and lay still, while Vincent danced in place, shaking his hand and wishing he hadn't hit quite so hard.

177

"Why are you dancing?" Pat asked interestedly. "Having a ball are we?" Vincent ignored her again, and turned to the two people he could see yellowy bound in metal chairs.

"Hold on, I'll get you lose," Vincent told them, just to say something as he dug for his knife in his bulging cargo pocket. He looked at them as he began to use his knife to get them free. Mrs. Korry was pretty, with a ton of nice crinkly hair, somewhere around Simeon's age probably. She looked livid. Vincent decided to let her get her own gag out as he began to let Jonathan Korry loose. He was somewhere around Vincent's age, a well-built kind of guy, and he looked pretty scared. His eyes were searching when they turned toward Vincent, and the inventor wondered why he didn't want to meet his rescuer's eyes. The last rope came off and Vincent grinned at himself for a fool. He had forgotten he and his antagonist were wearing night vision goggles. The Korry's couldn't see anything in the blackness. Vincent moved to the wall and flipped the light switch, hoping the ancient wiring didn't start a fire just yet.

"Well it's about time!" Michelle Korry spoke up acidly as Vincent flipped his goggles off and turned around.

"Hoity-toity, don't you know we just rescued you?" Pat answered, and Vincent was glad he was the only one who could hear her.

"Look out!" Jonathan cried, a slim finger pointing toward the man on the ground. Vincent followed the finger and saw the hooded guy had revived enough to grab something out of his pocket. Vincent identified it as a gas bomb, jerked a plastic cover out of his cargo pocket and threw himself across the floor to slam it over the bomb. A dull bang sounded in the room, but the sickly green gas stayed enclosed in Vincent's little round plastic, another gadget he had been commissioned to make for the CIA. Before the inventor could congratulate himself on his quick thinking or pick himself up a heavy body landed on his knees, pinning them to the ground, and strong hands wrenched his arms behind him, hard enough that he felt his joints pop and his sinews cringe. Another ounce of pressure and he would have two dislocated shoulders, and that wouldn't help anybody but the bad guys. Pain shot through him, and fear flooded the young man as he realized he couldn't struggle free. A metal clunk rang out in the busy room and the strong arms went limp. Vincent flipped around, panting and trying to look semi-competent, and saw Jonathan setting his metal chair back on the ground and the hooded man lying very unconscious. The inventor laughed shakily and hopped up.

"Vincent Tolliver," he said, holding out his hand to the young Korry. He resolutely held back a gasp as his shoulders moved, and wondered if strange pains like this were going to become normal for him.

"Jon Korry," Saul's son introduced back, taking the inventor's hand. "Thanks. Can we get out of here please?"

"I want to go home!" Michelle cried piteously.

"Come on, let's go figure out where we go from here," Vincent said, quickly leading the way out as he fished for his phone in his immense pocket to call Mr. Gibbs about another safe house.

"My dad," Jonathan said, catching up with Vincent as Michelle followed behind, whining and sobbing quietly, "these creeps were after him. I don't know who you are, but please tell me you people have him safe somewhere!"

"I'll check," Vincent said, opening the car door on his silver

179

rented Accord for Mrs. Korry. She pulled the door handle firmly away from Vincent and flounced into the seat, her face livid. The pilot resisted the urge to stare and slid his phone unlocked. He had a text from Simeon. *'No Saul. Tagged, on the run through town. Call when safe.'* Vincent quietly prayed for Simeon's safety, and let his fear rest in the knowledge Christ could help. He started the car and sent the Honda sliding into the comparative safety of Cheyenne. Things had worked out on his side, but his heart was still pounding as he dialed Mr. Gibbs.

"Jon, I'm with Simeon Lee," Vincent finally answered the young Korry as he listened to his phone ring. "He didn't find your dad, but that could mean lots of things, not all of them bad." He hoped he was right about that as Mr. Gibbs' tired voice answered, giving instructions on where to take the Korrys. As the inventor hung up, Michelle began to berate 'Little Lee' heatedly. Jon took up for 'Uncle Sim' as Vincent tried to get Pat to tell him where to go. The argument grew, both Korry's obviously very passionate about their opposite opinions on the quiet Simeon Lee. Vincent was about to yell at them both to be quiet so he could call the object of their fight when Michelle's yells suddenly disappeared into soft panicked sobs. Jon slumped down in the backseat looking very tired and frustrated. Vincent rather bewilderedly instructed his phone to call his prospective boss. The phone rang twice and gave out a click to show it was answered, but Vincent didn't hear anything.

"Hello?" the inventor said doubtfully. The sound of tires skidding noisily came over the phone, accompanied by the sharp crack of gunfire.

"Safe?" Simeon's even voice drifted to Vincent's ear.

"Yeah, all three of us," Vincent answered. "We're headed

180

toward another Gibbs sponsored safe house. What about you, can I help?" Something banged very loudly from Simeon's end.

"Finish, get to plane, call police," Simeon said.

"I want to help my dad," Jon spoke up from the backseat, loud enough so he knew he could be heard over Vincent's phone. Simeon did hear, and took the time to answer.

"Tell him his mother needs him more. God be with you."

"You too, Simeon," Vincent answered, and found a lump in his throat as another screech of tires came over the phone, and was cut off by the call ending. Oh dear Jesus, let Simeon Lee be safe! Vincent sped up as he reported Simeon's answer to Jon. The young man studied his mother, curled in the front seat sobbing, and quietly nodded.

"Find him soon, okay?" Jon requested. He smiled and shrugged. "He's the only dad I have, and I kind of like him."

"I know what you mean. Simeon will find him," Vincent answered. He sped up again as Pat kept directing him toward Mr. Gibbs safe house, and as the snow began to fall faster he felt a whelming thankfulness that his mom insisted he learn how to drive in all weathers. He didn't know why Simeon wanted him near his plane, but maybe it would help his friend, and he wanted to get back there fast. Vincent desperately wanted to do something to help.

Simeon's little car spun wildly as it sped over yet another patch of icy snow. He grunted in annoyance and fought for control. Again. It seemed like a week he had been striving desperately to stay on the icy road through this snow covered landscape. Cold climes were not among Simeon's favorite things[35]. And demonstrating the meaning of 'breakneck speed' over icy roads had not been on his to do list today. Simeon silently prayed he could stop with his neck still attached.

"Simeon," Vincent's voice broke over his black phone, plugged into the car's speakers.

"Yes!" Simeon almost blurted, very glad to hear his friend's voice. There were at least two cars following him at the same wild speed, and he was out of gimmicks and running out of ideas. Someone outside was what he needed, a friendly smart someone like Vincent Tolliver. But no answer came from his phone. "Vincent, you there?"

"Can't find…" the pilot's voice stuttered through static. "Weather jamming instrum…are you…hear me?"

"No, can't really hear you," Simeon answered in annoyance as he held the wheel steady over a large patch of ice and prayed he would make it safely to the other side.

"Trying to spot…manually…plane…" Vincent's voice came brokenly. "Need visual…"

---

[35] The incident with the horrible Tibetan Chip Monks began his dislike of ice and snow, and it was heightened after he spent two months hunting for a particular emperor penguin and dodging very evil enemy agents in Antarctica's frozen climate.

"Need me to give a visual so you can spot me in your plane?" Simeon asked, in the off chance Vincent could hear it. The police idea must have flopped. Why was it so hard for most people to believe large groups of crazed fanatics with high powered weapons really existed?

"...spot...in plane...visual..." Vincent said through the speakers. A bullet smashed into his side view mirror and another well aimed shot nearly made it through the back window. Simeon glanced behind him. They were pressing in closer, confound their dare devil attitude toward life. He looked ahead again and saw a huge form framed in his headlights. Simeon spun his wheel furiously, trying to dodge it. The tires lost their grip and Simeon found himself spinning off the road toward a pair of large iron gates. He caught a glimpse of giant iron flowers beside the gate as he ducked and covered his head for the impact. A terrific rending sound filled the night. Even with his seatbelt on, Simeon was flung about helplessly with his car as it flipped over twice, then crashed with a grating sound of tearing metal on its side. The noise died, and Simeon moved, assessing the damage. His spine bent painfully, three cracked ribs, a case of whiplash developing, and an indentation in his forehead proving the dashboard was harder than his skull. He was alive, and relatively unharmed for a pretty spectacular crash. Simeon unsnapped his seat belt, snatched his emergency bag out of the passenger window, and squirmed out of his car onto the smashed gate.

"Moo!" the form on the road voiced her annoyance.

"Go home, cow," Simeon told the large animal. The sound of tire's skidding to a halt just out of sight of his headlights drifted through the quiet stillness. His pursuers were stopping to make sure he was finished off. For a brief instant Simeon stood still, unwilling

183

to leave his car in its plight. A loud bang and the sound of something zipping toward him came to Simeon's ears and he dove past the wrecked iron gates, scrambling to get away. His little car rocked with a devastating impact on its carriage, turned toward the road after the cow episode. For half a second Simeon thought it might still make it. Then the grenade exploded. The little car wasn't armored on its underside, and it had been through much in its existence[36]. The vehicle itself added to the explosion, and Simeon watched as his car twisted and writhed in the heat of the flames. He stood helplessly looking on for a moment, remembering when he had first commandeered the beautiful new thing nineteen years ago. But he couldn't stand here grieving over a car. The flames gave off light and Simeon used it. He saw the gates led into a little parking lot with brightly painted old buildings surrounded by very strange iron sculptures. Simeon leaped over the wreckage of the gates, noting the words 'Swetsville Zoo' as he ran over it, and swerved to his left, ducking low. Bullets whizzed past him and he heard at least five people calling instructions to each other back by the road. He slipped his .38 Special out of his pocket and dashed past an old house painted in bright yellows, greens, and reds. An archway of sorts opened up on his left, and it was black enough to offer a fair chance of eluding his attackers for a moment. Two iron shapes stood guarding the archway, but Simeon didn't have time to stop and see what they were. He dashed recklessly along a skinny asphalt pathway, lined with huddled shapes that he couldn't make out in the darkness. As footsteps pounded closer behind him, he remembered there were only three bullets in his gun, and Simeon knew he was in trouble. He spun off the path in an attempt to lose

---

[36] I wish I could tell you some of the things this little car had accomplished under Simeon's deft hands. But unfortunately, the really good stories are very classified and I would have to erase your memory if I let you into the secret. But oh, I wish I could tell the one about the walrus and the gyroscope!

his pursuers.

The ground fell underneath him and Simeon hissed involuntarily as his feet crashed through a thin sheet of ice into a frigid stream. This cold was almost as bad as Siberia's waters, and it hurt. Simeon pulled himself out onto the other side of the little stream and idly calculated how long it took frostbite to make your feet fall off. A flashlight's beam cut into the darkness behind him as his followers tried to pick him out. Simeon found the path again on his side of the little stream and shot along it to his left, passing bigger shadowy shapes as he went. The path curved to his right with several deep patches of black where something stood blocking out the lights of the flashlights from the X box evils searching for him. Simeon crouched down behind the group of dark somethings along the side of the path and watched the lights flickering around him. He was shivering with the cold and knew he couldn't stay out long and live. Especially not after that dip in the freezing stream. He hadn't come prepared for this. Perhaps he could work his way over to the cars on the road and take one. Right now he needed Vincent to know where he was.

Simeon stuck his hand into his bag and dug around with numbed fingers. He pulled out a flare gun and several flares. Vincent had asked for a visual of his position, and this was the best he had right now.

10:20 pm. Feb. 16th; Above northern Colorado

Vincent had obediently called the police of Wyoming and

Colorado and told them of Simeon's danger. It was obvious they thought he was either drunk or a prank caller. After all what did he have to tell them?

"Yes, hello, I have a friend who's being chased down your roads by a group of crazed fanatics. No, I don't really know who they are but we stole this notebook, see... No, I don't know what road they're on. No, I don't really know what their driving, or how many of them there are. No, I don't even know whether they're in Colorado or Wyoming, or which direction they're heading at the moment, but if you'll call the CIA..."

After being firmly turned away by everyone he could think of to call, Vincent tried to contact Simeon. But that was just as much of a failure. As he stood by his plane, the snow swirled around him and the wind blew with chilling heartiness, and that was when Pat ran out of batteries. Nothing he tried could reach Simeon; it was likely he was out on small roads somewhere with no signal. And all his church friend had with him that was traceable was a ridiculous little flip phone. As a last resort, Vincent started up his plane and went air born to try and spot Simeon's car from above. He knew what color car Simeon was driving and he also knew how Simeon drove. If he saw a car zipping around corners, running over curbs, or braking without warning ten to one it was Simeon Lee. But the weather became worse, forcing Vincent to go over the clouds and lose sight of the ground for almost twenty anxious minutes. Finally the clouds blew away, leaving a white landscape, breathtakingly beautiful in the moonlight. But the moonlight only lasted a few minutes before that silvery orb was covered by clouds, leaving only blackness where the houses or towns failed to shine their lights.

But he could see the ground, if he flew a little low. Vincent looked at his compass and realized he must be near the road Simeon had been on at the last reading Pat had managed to get from tracking his phone. He repeated his plea for Simeon to give him some sign of where he was, a message he had been repeating whenever he could see the ground below him. The pilot kept repeating it now, not knowing if Simeon heard him or not. After flying in slow tight circles around the area he guessed Simeon must be in, Vincent realized just how crazy this idea was. All he could see down there were headlights of cars. He couldn't tell what they were, who was driving them, or anything. Vincent turned Perry around to head back to the Cheyenne airport in the hopes that Simeon would find him there, or his instruments pick up a reading.

A brilliant red flare shot up about half a mile away on his right, illuminating trees and a winding river, snowy hills, and pretty farm houses in a brief red glow. Vincent gave a whoop, banked sharply, and headed toward it. Simeon must have heard him after all!

11

Simeon was shocked into dropping his flare gun by what he saw by its light. For a brief moment it brightened the entire landscape around him, and he saw he was kneeling in front of what appeared to be three dinosaur skeletons standing on their hind legs staring over him with sightless eyes, each holding something menacingly over his head. An odd feeling of unreality settled over Simeon as, before the light died, he realized what he was looking at. It was three dinosaur skeletons made out of rusty scrap iron and posed as if they were a rock band. The light from the flare sputtered out, leaving only the black shapes in the darkness above him.

It would have been nice to ponder where he was and why there were dinosaur skeletons made out of rusty bits of iron here, but things started happening so quickly around him that trivial idea was quickly lost. The people who had followed him from Cheyenne could see by the flare too, and the ping of bullets rang off the metal of the dino rock band just beside his head. The moon came out and by its sudden silver light Simeon could see he was hunted by over twenty different hooded figures who wandered haphazardly among more of the scrap iron statues. He pretended to dash away, leading all eyes to the left, and then slunk carefully back, unseen by anyone. His musically inclined dinosaurs were standing as good cover for him, and Simeon stayed perfectly still in the snow. The air was well-below freezing around him and each small breath stung his lungs and throat like hundreds of little pins sticking into him. Hypothermia was already determined to shake his form. Stillness was difficult in this weather. But it was possible he would go unnoticed in this strange place if he didn't move. A bullet suddenly sang off the lead dino singer's ribcage and landed with a soft thud in the snow next to his head. Or, maybe not. Simeon rolled to the right and darted for a tree, glancing behind him as he moved and realizing he was swiftly running out of options.

That bullet had come from behind him, and in that glance back he saw a highway bridge with a river running under it, and four people with M16 rifles standing in the moonlight watching him run and trying to get a bead on him. Simeon spun around a tree and dashed through the snow. He heard a plane buzz the ground, and wondered if it was Vincent or a curious crop duster. A white freezer with the lid partly open and an iron dragon's snout sticking out of it loomed on his right. The moon disappeared again. Simeon jerked his pistol out with uncontrollably shaking hands, ducked behind the iron dragon's home, and froze, hoping he hadn't been noticed. Moving, when you were the mouse in a game of cat and mouse, was a fatal amateur's mistake. Movement always gave your position away. And half the time simply waiting, still and silent in good cover, could win the fight against any number of odds. The bad guys walked around you, getting jumpier at every second, and allowing you to pick them off and still remain hidden. At least in someplace like America, where sooner or later someone would call the police and the bad guys without the gun licenses or CIA badges would be the ones that had to do the explaining. But here he had bad guys from two directions, no extra bullets, and he hadn't come prepared for the cold.

A flashlight's beam from somewhere in the midst of the scrap iron zoo hit his hiding place, and bullets began to whizz around him. Simeon sighed as he realized there was really only one option, and carefully leaned out from behind the freezer. He fired at the lights, watched them go out, and darted from his hiding place. Simeon dodged iron figures as he ran, and reminded himself to Google the Swetsville Zoo when he got out of this. He could see dark figures moving around him, but it was difficult to tell what they were doing, or even precisely where they were. Good, that meant they were just as confused about his shape and he might make it on the first run. Then the moon came out again, shining brilliantly on the snow. Simeon dropped into a crouch immediately, behind an iron pole that curved into a circle and held all sorts of bells and wind chimes designed from more scrap metal. Someone stumbled past him, breathing in nervous gasps, their gun sweeping the whole area in such quick circles there was no chance it could actually hit something. Simeon stayed still beside his pole, watching the man stumble on to his left. A portable searchlight beam from the road spurted to life. The beam of white light was powerful, and whoever held it knew what they were doing. It swept the area directly to Simeon's left in a quick, competent way, and moved on to play over him.

Bullets began to fly around the agent as soon as the beam touched his patch of snow. The people on the road were not the same type as the nervous fellow who had stumbled past a few minutes ago, though they wore the same hoods. As he darted off again, Simeon heard the sounds of bullets hitting the instruments around his head, and felt like laughing. It made such a nice sound. He raised this flare gun and shot a red flare directly at the group gathered on the road, watching half dive away and the others pull their guns up as they blinked in the sudden unbearable glare. Simeon dodged left and right as he moved, hunkered low and sliding his little pistol back into his holster. His heart was pounding in his chest. He hated this idea. Bullets whizzed around him and Simeon put his annoyance at being forced into this firmly away,

190

concentrating on what he was doing. The snow was soft and deep and he half slid down the bank toward the river. The bullets were getting thicker and closer, and Simeon didn't even give himself the second it would take to straighten into a decent dive. He fell into the water like a rock and let it close over his head. The river was as cold as the little stream had been, but this time the glacial liquid closed around all of Simeon. He had been in freezing water before and mastered himself immediately, but it was still extremely distasteful and painful.

Then a bullet creased his scalp. Simeon blanked, every thought of what was happening around him left, and his body automatically tried to breathe. Freezing water poured into his lungs, and a portion of Simeon's consciousness returned to register an agony of frozen fire burning inside him. He fought his way clumsily to the surface of the river, coughing and vomiting as he strove to undo the damage, his mind a mass of pulsating pain. The only thing keeping him cognizant was the sub-conscious knowledge he would die if he blacked out again[37]. The river was swollen with snow and moved in erratic patterns that made it hard to tread water at the best of times. The spy's whole body was numb and unresponsive with cold already, and his vision was blurred and dark from the work of that bullet. The moon disappeared behind a cloud again. Real darkness covered the scene, making the frozen situation even more of a nightmare to the agent striving to survive. He was only half-conscious, and a thousand horrible memories formed in lightless

---

[37] Simeon's instinctively strong self-preservation is only trumped by self-sacrifice, and I would not have it any other way. Self-preservation is one of the strongest ideas running through Simeon Lee, and it combines well with an incredibly active sub-conscious that never seems to rest, and always has at least half an idea what's going on around it. The combined strength of the two are the only way he could possibly have lived through his childhood, the piranha attack in the Bahamas, or the hundreds of similar episodes in his colorful career.

places thundered through his brain, driving his sluggish wits into a panic. The river took a sharp bend, and Simeon instinctively managed to grab onto the bank for a moment as he was flung against it. His frozen fingers bit through the soft snow and found a clump of grass, but it was wet and slippery and his hold was clumsy. For an instant he clung there, coughing and gasping, trying to force the nightmarish memories away, and his mind back into enough consciousness to allow him to make his body drag itself out of the river. The current swirled and tugged at him remorselessly and his weakened, numbed fingers slipped off the grass. Then his mind cleared, of course. Reality swirled back into focus, and a sardonic smile was on Simeon's lips as his head ducked under the water again despite himself. The water's swift passing, the gasping and gagging, all noises were taken over by the enclosed bubbling of the water surrounding him. All these years of living in danger, to have cold get him at last seemed extremely anticlimactic.

But as hope left, his wrist, flailing stubbornly toward the bank, was caught in a strong grip just before he was sucked away. At that moment Simeon didn't even care if it was a hooded fiend, he was too happy to feel himself being dragged from the frigid river, back into the noisy, freezing world. Simeon lay prostrate on the snowy ground, sick and weak, shivering uncontrollably, forcing himself to breathe the freezing air, trying to get his vision back under control, and wondering who was in the darkness beside him. A coat fell over his quaking shoulders and two strong hands pulled him gently out of the snow into a kneeling position.

"Wow, that was kind of a miracle," a cheerful, familiar voice spoke beside him and it kindled a delighted warmth in Simeon, and even quieted some of the debilitating pain sparking through his head.

"Vincent?" he shivered.

"In the flesh!" the inventor answered. "The plane's just a few steps away, let's get you into it and turn on the heater as quick as we can." Simeon didn't reply, but just used Vincent's arm to pull himself to his feet and started moving toward a giant black shape Vincent said was his plane. The black and dizziness receded enough he managed to look at the small snow covered field as he forced his numbed feet to stumble across it.

"How...?" he shivered quizzically, realizing his young friend was a very, very good pilot to have landed safely here.

"Did I land? Well, not too easily, I'll tell you that. It was one of the more hair-raising landings of my life, but I made it down safely," Vincent shivered as he pulled open the plane's door and ducked inside. Simeon slid in and dropped heavily into the co-pilot's seat. Vincent settled in the pilot's seat and began to methodically go through his pre-flight check. Simeon stared at him for a moment, undecided whether he should be amused or frustrated. His remarkable hearing picked out the sounds of a car's motor, coming steadily closer.

"Vincent?"

"Yeah?" the pilot asked, still slowly checking things off on his clipboard.

"Go."

"What?"

"Go!" Simeon ordered, as a dark shape spun into their field. A flash from a gun muzzle spurted into the dark air and Vincent yelped as a bullet pinged off Simeon's door. The pilot grabbed at the yoke and began to edge his plane forward, his eye on the dark line of treetops in front of them. The trim plane picked up speed with impressive swiftness, and though Simeon saw two more spurts of gunfire, none of the bullets came close; the shooters were surprised by the plane's speed. Vince pulled the yoke up smoothly, his face a little strained, and their nose lifted, going into a steep climb. One wingtip slammed into a treetop and sent leaves and twigs cascading onto the white snow, but the pilot corrected the trim easily and they made it. Vincent kept to the steep climb, and didn't straighten out until they were above the snow clouds and out of sight from anyone below. As he trimmed the plane again, Vince blew out a tight breath, glanced to the side at his friend, and gave a little yelp of shock.

"Simeon, your face!" the pilot gasped, punching the autopilot on and grabbing at a roll of paper towels beside his seat[38].

"What?" Simeon blinked, and then felt the gentle pressure of the towel as Vincent pressed them to the side of his head. "Oh. Bullet crease, not as bad as it looks."

"Gosh, it looks awful!" Vincent gulped, grabbing a second roll as the frozen blood thawed enough to flow again and his first roll was soaked with the thick red liquid. His groping hands found the first aid kit and Vincent passed it over quickly. Simeon glanced through it for useful bandages, but paused to hold his hands in front of the vent spitting out warm air.

"Fly the plane, Vincent," Simeon shivered.

---

[38] Vincent always kept a roll of paper towels near him when he flew, as he invariably forgot to secure his drinks before he jubilantly sent his plane into one of his spinning dives. When his instrument panel had begun to turn a sickly puce color he had decided it was probably time to actually try to keep his plane clean.

"I am, don't worry. Can we go back to our New Mexican headquarters now?" Vincent asked as he went back to his instruments, and pretended not to be shocked and appalled by the blood soaked towels now lying on his cockpit floor.

"Please," Simeon nodded, gasping the word out as he forced his body to control its breathing, feeling decidedly pleased he had a headquarters to go to. He finished wrapping an ACE bandage around his scalp, stood up a little unsteadily, and went to find his overnight bag to get out of his soaked, freezing clothes. After ten minutes Simeon was dry and beginning to feel warm again. He sat still and quiet, gratefully leaning back in the comfortable co-pilot's seat. A few more minutes of just sitting with the plane's vents pouring heat into him, watching Vincent taking superb control of the plane, and he felt recovered enough conversation became possible. If he remained perfectly still and didn't move his concussed head or tax his watery lungs too much.

"Well done, taking on so much tonight. Tell me about it?" Simeon said evenly. Vincent felt the simple praise spark inside him, and the aches and bruises acquired suddenly seemed almost pleasurable as they turned into something to be proud of instead of annoyances. He obeyed, narrating his events of the evening with easy honesty as he banked his plane and began the flight back toward New Mexico. Simeon was amused and pleased to find the young man naturally included his emotions and failures in his report, as if that was what everyone did.

"I was very happy to have Smaug with me," Vincent finished up. "Your gift from last night already saved my little heart. (Was that just last night? Sheesh, this has been a busy week.) I was kind of a fool several times, and only what most would call 'fool luck' saved the situation. I certainly didn't act like I know you would

195

have." Simeon heard discouragement in his pupil's voice and decided to answer it.

"Lesson four: never count fortuitous circumstances as marks against your ability. The difference between a decent agent and a good one is usually seen in how they use the opportunities tossed their way. Lesson five; use your own skills, don't try to be someone else. Don't know of anyone else who could have capped that bomb like you did. Glad Jonathan stepped up to help."

"I liked him. Even though he was worried stiff about his dad and stressed out about this evening, he took the effort to say thank you when I dropped them off. And that he missed you. Jon told me to tell 'Uncle Sim' to show up more often and stay longer. I wish I could say I liked his mom too, but she seems kind of...moody. She really didn't like you."

"Schizo."

"What?"

"Michelle Korry is a schizophrenic. Neither one of her like me."

"That...would explain a lot. Why doesn't she like you? Say, does Jon know? He didn't really act like it."

"Knew something was off, warned Saul against her when first introduced, before they were married. Mrs. Korry has never forgotten it. No, Jonathan doesn't know."

"How can you not know your mother is a schizophrenic?" Vincent asked incredulously. Simeon shrugged.

"Gone to daycare and school every day. Has his own friends.

196

Sports. Band. Not home much. Saul's never told him. Even when she's been hospitalized."

"That's just not right."

"No it isn't. But Saul doesn't listen well, the big–" Simeon cut it off as he moved too sharply, a cough racked him, and he spent the next minute expelling the last of the river water from his lungs into a spare Walmart bag he found under the seat. He was weak and giddy again as he managed to lean back, and turned his face to the darkened cockpit window as his thoughts moved in channels almost as dark as the view outside.

"God's still in charge, Simeon," Vincent said quietly, breaking the heavy silence. "We'll find him. Um…shouldn't I land and get you to an ER somewhere?"

"No."

"You sure?" Vincent asked doubtfully, trying to remember if concussion victims knew if they needed to go to the hospital or not.

"Doctor would say rest," Simeon said, a slight smile creeping over his face at the tremble in Vincent's voice. He shot his friend a look that told him clearly it was verging on foolishness to insist, and Vincent changed the subject, realizing he was going to have to learn about a lot more than just guns in this new job.

"Is Mrs. Korry why you haven't visited too much, why you were living in Virginia instead of around here near your almost nephew?"

"I set her off," Simeon nodded. "So try not to be around too much. Saul's wanted me around more. A good man. Stuck it out for almost thirty years now, even though half of her doesn't like him

197

either. Vincent, he's not a Christian. We've got to find him soon. Date?"

"What?" Vincent blinked. "Oh yeah! I did find the date on that black box before we had to race off to this Saul Korry thing. Simeon, those boxes are set to go off on February 20th. We have less than four days to stop this thing. What do we do? Did you find out anything tonight?" Simeon nodded, and explained about the Edward Plant stack he had found in Saul's office, and then allowed a silence to descend as he stared out the cockpit window. Vincent suddenly realized he cared enough about this stocky, serious man that it hurt to see him upset about his old friend's absence. The inventor opened his mouth to try and bring comfort to his new roomy, but a suddenly recalled fact interposed itself instead.

"Oh man, I forgot your car," Vincent blurted out. "Should I turn around, do you think we can get it? I wouldn't mind landing for some dinner anyway. Now that things have calmed down and warmed up, my stomach's waking up."

"My car's gone," Simeon said with audible sorrow. "Hamburgers for dinner."

10:44 a.m. Feb. 17th; Blue Room, PH, NM

Jack stood in the blue room, watching the waterfall make shimmering patterns on the blue rug as the midmorning sun streamed through it. He scowled out the window, composing himself with an effort, and wondering if Mr. Lee would finally talk to him. The agent's studied ignoring of him had finally sent the reporter storming from the kitchen, knowing he would punch the old guy if he stuck around much longer.

Jack took another deep breath, counted to ten, and turned to stalk up the tunnel toward the kitchen again. He kept stopping to look out the window slits; partially to make sure he really was under control and wouldn't blow up on Mr. Lee, but also just to look. It was beautiful up here. Not quite as beautiful as the mountains in Arizona or Colorado, but this had almost a better beauty to it. It felt...more real. It was a wild, half desert beauty that wasn't trying or boasting, but just was. Perhaps the beauty he felt was more of a human perspective on things than a real aesthetic quality. People talked about the glory of the Grand Canyon and the Colorado mountains all the time. But the wild beauty here was unsung. Its surprise made its song more beautiful. Jack stepped into the kitchen and his musings turned into a scowl again. Mr. Lee was still at the breakfast table where he had left him. A laptop was open in front of the spy and several neat piles of silly doodles were stacked around him. Jack sat across from Simeon, his fist balled, and he began to rhythmically tap the wooden table in his annoyance. For two hours he had tried to get a response, a single word, from the infuriating Mr. Lee and was completely ignored. Simeon stood up and Jack half rose from his seat in expectation. Simeon waved him back down and walked to a retro style picture of a teenage girl on the phone, sporting the title 'Call Me.' He swung the picture out revealing a double row of multicolored buttons hiding behind it and pushed the yellow one.

"Good morning. In thirty minutes, it's afternoon. You awake?" Simeon said to the button. An indistinct mumble answered and Jack recognized the billionaire inventor's voice. Simeon reached into a kitchen drawer, pulled out an air horn, and used it by the call button. Vincent's shocked yell drifted around the kitchen before the ex-CIA man cut off the feed from the room. Simeon pushed the picture in place and moved back toward the table. Jack was surprised to see a mischievous twinkle in his soft eyes.

"You enjoyed that!" Jack accused. Simeon jotted a number on one of his pieces of paper and handed it to Jack.

"Number twenty-seven?" Simeon called, obviously enjoying himself. His eye lit on the paper Jack held and he indicated him. "How may I help you?"

"You are in a mood this morning," Jack muttered. "You had better be nice to me because my wife is down in your precious greenhouse helping your prized herbs grow again, and I can make her stop."

"How?" Simeon asked sweetly. Jack had been married long enough to get the joke and despite himself his scowl melted into a smile.

"Nathan Hale has turned into Jack Benny. Look wise-guy, all I want is a little information. I know you found something while you were out and about having fun last night without Judy and me. What's going on? What new leads do you have? And why are you in such a good mood this morning?"

"If that's your good mood Simeon, I think I prefer you somber," Vincent yawned as he stepped out of the elevator.

"Yours?" Simeon asked, indicating the horn sitting on the counter. Vincent grinned and then suddenly looked sad. He slid it back in the drawer.

"I thought I recognized that blare," he answered as he started to mix his morning hot chocolate. "Sort of. Mom used it on Dad a lot, I usually get up without someone horning in."

"Good grief, Phil Harris has made his entrance," Jack complained.

"Did you want me up for a reason?" Vincent asked his prospective boss. He caught sight of the covered dishes on the stove and did a happy hop skip to get a plate.

"Meeting," Simeon answered. "And request. Mind making a flight to El Paso today?"

"Sure thing. What are we doing there?" Vincent asked. Simeon tapped his laptop and Vincent looked at the screen. "That's a nice looking car. An Infiniti Coupe, is that your replacement for your little one that died last night? I notice we're having beef sausage with the eggs."

"You killed a car yesterday?" Judy asked in surprise, stepping out of the glass elevator by the pretty porch doors. "Mr. Lee, the peppermint is growing amazingly, the plantain is still as hardy as ever–"

"I refuse to listen to an inventory of plant life." Jack interrupted irritably. "Besides you'll make Mr. Lee even happier by telling him what's alive down there, and then he'll get giddy and we'll never get anything out of him."

"Why are you happy today, Simeon?" Vincent asked, smothering a yawn. Simeon pressed a button on his flip phone and slid it across to the inventor. A text message was open, showing a picture of a palatial mansion snuck beneath a black hooded guard's arm. *'Having a ball with E. Plant. Pink fish, ha ha. SK'*

"Saul Korry?" Vincent gaped. Simeon nodded and hopped up to get his coffee. "He's alive! And smart. I can't believe he got that through to you!"

"Korry as in Korry Investigative Services?" Jack asked swiftly, grabbing the phone to see what the excitement was about. "They're the Pinkertons of today, is he involved in this? Whoa, that's Edward Plant's place. What do Eddy and Saul Korry have to do with each other?"

"Been there?" Simeon asked from by his special espresso maker he had brought from Virginia yesterday.

"No, I've been to his Florida place, this picture is of his mansion up in Vermont. But every reporter knows about Eddy."

"Eddy?" Judy and Vincent both asked. Simeon held up a hand to stop Jack's reply and pointed to the picture on his phone.

"We have to get in there. Information?"

"Hold on, how do you know this text is really from the person you think and not a trick of some sort?" Jack asked.

"Pink fish," Simeon answered, and that mischievous light was in his eyes again at whatever memory the allusion brought to mind. "Only Saul and one other knows about that. The other's very evil and in Kenya without cell signal."

"Okay. Sure, I have information on Eddy, lots of it. He must be as ancient as you, Mr. Lee," Jack said, leaning back and clasping his hands behind his head. "For those of you who don't know anything about him, Edward Plant is one of the elite upper class which makes him an automatic interest to newspaper people, like the Tollivers, of which there is only one now and I can't tell anyone. Anyway, Edward Plant doesn't like his full name and has everyone call him Eddy. Eddy has grown up as a man of independent means and so has been banging around looking for something to do his whole life. He's latched onto 'the furtherance of mankind' and every few years he finds some other organization to back that he thinks has that goal in mind. I met Eddy once in a brief interview, and I've been to several of his press conferences. (Every year or so he calls together another big meeting of the press to endorse a new cause.) He is a little guy with a lot of presence, a very magnetic and powerful personality. I've always thought of him as a sort of harmless floundering character, who could do big things if he had a purpose. Mr. Lee, are you thinking Eddy is this X character?"

"You read the statement in that notebook. That's a purpose. And this is a big thing," Simeon answered. He leaned against the counter and regarded the three people at the table. "X marks the Plant. We four are the only ones mobilized against this. We are going to bring him down and stop all this killing. Going to eliminate this group calling themselves the PD's by the grace of God and to the best of our ability and we have, possibly, three days to do it. Ready?"

12

2:45 pm, Feb. 18th; 5 Pebble Stone Ct., Orlando, FL

"I further believe, with all my heart," Edward Plant was saying as his closing remarks to the large group of newsmen, "that the Pediatric Development is a very secure and sure way of helping the furtherance of mankind. Thank you all for listening to my plea to help this worthy cause, and I am now open to questions," Edward Plant finished and stood behind his podium waiting for any questions. He was of medium height, with a willowy frame and a handsome, sharp visage. His pinstripe suit was expensively tailored and could not possibly have been a better fit. As Eddy stood quietly waiting, a politely inviting smile spread over his smooth face, you could almost feel a strength coming from him. He was the giant of the room. Everyone else there was a mediocre plebian compared with Eddy Plant. A large tabby cat rubbed against his gray pinstripe suit, and Eddy knelt down to greet the animal as the hundred or so members of the press gathered below him snapped pictures or scribbled busily in their notebooks. A middle-aged woman with dark auburn hair raised her hand.

"I am Lisa Gromit, columnist for the *Evening Star*. Eddy, my readers would like to know why you have waited so long to call a press conference, it's been well over two years. What prompted this one?"

"You may tell your readers," Eddy answered, "I stopped calling press conferences when I thought people had stopped listening to my pleas for support. This conference was prompted by yourselves. Yesterday I began to get calls from various papers

204

telling me their readers wanted to hear what they could do for the world around them, and asking me to make a statement on the subject."

A wispy young man with brilliant blond hair sticking out in all directions grinned as he tapped away, making notes on his iPad. The people standing around him put it down to a private joke, and were right. He was thinking how many hours it had taken Jack and Judy Leason to convince all those papers to call Edward Plant asking for a press conference. A short man standing next to Vincent (as the inventor enjoyed himself being a fake newsman) raised his hand. Eddy stopped petting his happy tabby long enough to wave indulgently at him.

"I'm Thomas Heavington of the *Hampton Gazette*. I was wondering how much you had personally donated to the cause of Pediatric Development?" Eddy gave him a rather long winded answer, saying more about the Pediatric Development than about how much he had donated. Vincent Tolliver slid his iPad in its case strapped on his belt and didn't seem to be listening. He stood gazing around the room, his hands in his pockets. The large tabby cat opened its eyes and looked toward the edge of the stage. The cat leapt up and trotted toward Vincent, tail arched high and his melodious purr very strong. The inventor smiled and began to stroke the cat's back and scratch its ears. A woman on Vincent's right laughed at the loud purr emanating from the tabby, commenting he had quite a way with cats, and the young man just grinned in answer. The conference ended and the newsmen began to file out of Eddy's sea side residence. Vincent walked out the door, switched his dusty brown shoes for roller skates, and worked his way unhurriedly down the street. A few blocks later he stopped beside a sleek, bluish-gray sedan. Vincent slipped his skates off, looked at the ocean rising and falling for a moment, and slid into the car. He pushed a button on the consul and leaned back in the seat with a contended sigh.

"Simeon, are you there?" Vincent asked.

"Yes," answered Simeon immediately. "Transmitter signal coming in well."

"I really like the new car. It's sort of amazing. We're going to have to have a good name for this one. So the transmitter signal is coming in? Has he noticed anything suspicious yet?"

"You bet it's coming in!" Jack's voice broke over the car's speakers. "We've been watching Eddy coo to his cats in his private room. And no one's noticed anything suspicious. I don't think its own mother would notice the few extra patches of hair. Wherever the cat looks we see it. How did you do that?"

"Was it hard to get the cat to come to you?" interposed Judy.

"No, your idea of the catnip worked great, Judy," Vincent answered as he flipped the car on and headed toward the airport. "I broke open the bag in my pocket, and the cat came running."

"Its name is Mr. Tomkins," Jack said. "Address him by his full name; he hates to be called Tom, cat, and especially not puss." Vincent heard Judy laugh and guessed the reporter was mimicking Edward Plant.

"Now we just have to wait for something helpful to happen around Mr. Tomkins," Vincent said. "Simeon, did you get your call through to your friend, do you think you can worry Eddy into heading back to his home base?"

"Plant's readying to fly back to Vermont now," Jack said exultantly. "The whole thing's working just like we planned."

"Well, good for us!" Vincent grinned as he turned into the airport and headed toward Perry to fly back to New Mexico. It was nice to be heading toward friends, especially Simeon Lee. Vincent realized he was silently thanking God for the good man he had chosen as an answer to his desperate plea for companionship, and his smile stayed strong as he started his flight.

10:23 pm, Feb. 18th; Study, P.H., NM

On the third level of the Parabaloni Headquarters is a lovely wood paneled study. It adjoins the bedroom Simeon chose and the agent swiftly decided it was almost as nice a place to work and think as the library. But now it had undergone changes that made it not so comfortable. Vincent had created a hyper sensitive bug and camera that looked and felt like patches of orange tabby cat hair, and it was a brilliant bit of work. But a good deal of equipment and wiring was required to receive anything from the gadget, and so Vincent had changed Simeon's study into a 'War Room' as he dubbed it. In this room, sandwiched in between the wires and boxes, stood a TV broadcasting what Mr. Tomkins saw and heard around him. The cat's experiences were constantly monitored by one of the four people in the large mountain house, in hopes that something useful would happen around Mr. Tomkins. It was Jack's shift now and he was bored with just watching the life of a spoiled cat. The door to the corridor opened behind him and Vincent poked his tousled head in.

"Hi Jack," he said with his habitual smile. "I thought I'd look over the equipment before I went to bed. Learned anything yet?"

"Yes. I've learned that Mr. Tomkins prefers tuna to chicken," answered Jack as he swiveled his chair in a small, bored, semi-circle. "That Edward Plant matches his pajamas as fastidiously as he does his suits. And that he sacks cooks for calling a cat a 'puss' more than twice. Aside from that…no, I haven't learned anything."

"Oh well," said Vincent as he wandered around poking things with his screwdriver. "We'll just have to wait and see what happens."

"I want to see if Eddy can find a cook as crazy as he is about cats," Jack said with a grin as he watched Vincent. "How on earth can you tell if everything's where it's supposed to be? It looks like a hopelessly muddled mass of wires and cables stuck into random spots in black and silver boxes."

"It's not in the least muddled or random," the gadget genius answered defensively. "Each and every cord is where it's supposed to be and doing its particular job. Kind of like a living organism, just not as complex or well designed."

"That sounds like a sentence from these *Creation News Monthly* I found in your library," Jack commented, motioning to a stack of magazines. Jack stuck his hands behind his head and looked at Vincent quizzically. "Do you really believe in the foolscap silliness of creationism?"

"Sure," answered Vincent without bothering to look up from his work. "That's the way the Bible said it happened, so I believe it. It's nice that science backs it up too."

"I guess that's what they call simple faith," said Jack with a sarcastic smile. "So I was wondering, why do some Christians say that God used evolution to create and others stoutly defend the six day creation thing?" Vincent looked up, dropped his tool back into his pocket, and regarded the atheist with solemnity.

"Because some Christians would rather sacrifice their belief, take what the world believes, and try and fit scripture into that. Others correctly take scripture as the truth revealed by God, and interpret the world through it. I believe that God made the world in six days and rested on the seventh like He says in Genesis as firmly as I believe Jesus died for my sins like He says in Matthew. Once that decision is made, I look at science and see it through the eyes of the truth. And yes, the honest to goodness facts of science do fit in with my faith. Why do you ask? Are you coming around to the right view of life?" Jack sat up and pointed excitedly at the TV screen, conveniently dropping the conversation.

"Look, Eddy's doing something!" he said, and Vincent eagerly bounded beside the reporter to watch the screen. Eddy was at his dresser, and he had pulled out a familiar bit of rounded material. Almost familiar that is, this hood was a deep red in color. The philanthropist slid the scarlet hood over his face, leaving only his bright blue eyes to be seen. The two men watched with bated breath as the wiry billionaire leaned down and stroked Mr. Tomkins. For a moment the whole room was filled with the rhythmic sound of the big orange tabby's purr. Eddy leaned over and pressed a button on his night stand. His bed swung outwards revealing a small, well concealed door. He pushed another button and lights shone from inside the door, revealing a starkly empty rectangular stairwell. Mr. Tomkins hopped to his feet and padded after his master, through the door and down a small stair. The stair ended in a very square concrete hall, dimly lit and damp. Eddy stepped out of sight around a corner as Mr. Tomkins paused to scratch his ear. Jack muttered something about the mentality of cats as they waited for the feline to follow his owner, listening to the grunts and claws of the big cat. After a few seconds of scratching he satisfied himself, and bounded around the corner with a happy yowl. A large, shiny metal door stood at the end of the hall, with Eddy standing to the side of it. He took a card out of his pocket, slipped it into a slot, and waited.

"Identify letter," an automated voice from the box demanded.

"X," the scarlet hooded figure in the pin-stripe suit obeyed.

"Sheesh, our villain really is named Eddy," Vincent murmured.

"Enter password," said the box and Jack grabbed at his notebook and pen with delight. That's when Tomkins decided to move to a corner to chase a water beetle. Jack flung down his pen on the table with a disgusted grunt.

"Well, it's an interesting view of a water beetle," Vincent commented. "I never knew their feelers were quite that long." The sound of a door sliding open came over the speaker system, and the cat looked up. The metal door was open and Eddy was in a large cargo elevator. Mr. Tomkins deserted the beetle, darted into the elevator, and lay down contentedly on the floor. The doors closed, and the Parabaloni TV screen was filled with the dull gray of the metal. The elevator gave a lurch, a groan, and then began to hum as it moved steadily downward.

"I'd better get Simeon," Vincent said excitedly. He started moving toward the door to Simeon's bedroom, but Jack called him back almost frantically.

"Hey, something's going wrong with the signal!" the reporter called, his pen pointing at the TV. Vincent turned and saw the screen had black and white lines cutting into it.

"That's not right. Every thing's fine here, I just checked it!" the inventor exclaimed. The lines grew to cover the screen, completely blocking the picture. A dull humming noise came over the speaker system. It began to grow quickly in volume and pitch, until it rang in their ears at an unbearable register. Jack flipped off the speakers as the piercing whine kept rising, and turned to Vincent.

"What was that?"

12:45 am, Feb. 19th; Study, PH, NM

"Well, there goes someone else through the door," Jack commented despondently. The four people were gathered in the War Room, commiserating over a brilliant idea that wasn't working.

"How many does that make tonight?" asked Vincent as he tapped his knee absently.

"It must be the hundredth time we've seen the doors open," Judy answered. "But between Tomkins chasing bugs and the hoods, I don't know how many people have gone in and out."

"It's a good thing there are a lot of beetles in that hallway," Vincent broke in, trying to interject a cheerful note into the conversation. He missed the shudder that passed over Simeon and his sudden pallor at the mention of the skittering bugs[39], and went on brightly. "It makes Tomkins hang out there, and we can see the door."

"A fat lot of good that does us," growled Jack. "Sometime tomorrow is the launch date of this mass murder plot, and we still don't know how to stop it, or have any evidence to send in the authorities to stop it."

"If the cat goes down more often," said Judy hopefully, "maybe one of these times the signal will work."

"No," Vincent answered as he stared glumly at the screen. "The signal goes out because it's blocked by their security system. Probably a system a lot like our own Annette[40] here is programmed to use, actually. Unless that system's turned off or interfered with, any signal will be blocked."

"So there's no hope of finding out what's down there by Mr. Tomkins?" said Judy despondently.

"Not so long as that system is up and Plant stays as firmly resolved not to let the PD's mention business above ground," Jack snorted.

"We have learned some things from Mr. Tomkins though," Vincent said as cheerily as possible. "We've been able to connect a

---

[39] Due to a nasty incident in his past, which I will not go into here for fear of giving you horrendous nightmares, Simeon Lee has a phobia of cockroaches. The beetles in the hallway were not quite the same, but they were close enough they made his skin crawl and a cold sweat start up every time he saw one scamper across the screen.

[40] The automated computer running everything behind the scenes in the Parabaloni Headquarters. She schedules and runs the cleaning bots, keeps a very good lookout, sees the water reservoirs are always clean and filled, knows everything that happens inside the mountain, operates an anti-laser shield that protectively bubbles the entire headquarters, tends to be pouty when corrected and angry when crossed, and the cheesy rolls she makes are superlative.

lot of passwords and letters together. That could be useful!"

"The only way I can think of that being useful," Jack answered, determined not to be cheerful, "is if we're going to try and sneak down there. I don't think any of us are quite depressed enough to be suicidal, so the information really doesn't do us any good."

"I still can't believe no one will move in on the operation before it starts!" Vincent broke out. "I think we have enough on the group to make someone move, but I still haven't budged anyone I can think of to call. How about you, Simeon, have you gotten anyone to listen to you?" Simeon slowly looked up at his friend and his brown eyes focused on him even slower. It was obvious his thoughts had been very far away from the conversation around him.

"No," Simeon answered simply.

"See, no one is going to stop these evil X box villains, and America will have its very own black death to add to the history books," Jack said with morose joy. Simeon sat up and cleared his throat. The others looked at him eagerly.

"Cat's not working," Simeon began in his serious voice. "Except one contact I haven't tried yet (maybe get some FBI involvement late in the game), Vincent, you and I are on our own. We are stopping it."

"Dude, why do you think we've stuck around this long?" Jack broke in with annoyance. "You've got Judy and me too."

"Of course. But how do you think we can do it with just four of us!" Judy burst out. "We only have one day. Less than one day,

213

actually. But…maybe we could all pretend we're butlers and sneak in," Judy suggested, starting to get excited. "Or be a troupe of actors that just happens to wander in–"

"Oh come off it Judy gal, that's hardly going to cut it," Jack interrupted irritably.

"Well I suppose you have a better idea?" Judy said almost as irritably.

"Hey guys, I think Simeon was about to tell us how to win," Vincent cut in. Everyone turned toward their chosen leader.

"Before we go any farther with this discussion, need to stop and pray," Simeon said.

"Oh boy, here comes the mass opium again!" Jack snorted, gave Simeon a baleful look, and swiveled his chair so his back was to the agent. Judy sat still where she was and watched in silence while Simeon and Vincent knelt on the crowded floor. A mixed sensation was going on inside her. Judy had grown up in optimistic atheism. She had always accepted a moral code and relative morality without seeing the opposition they posed to each other. Jack's little comment over Richard the III had troubled her. At the time, it hadn't seemed like much. But when she woke up in the morning, the question had still been there, unanswered. How could you say someone was wrong to murder another person? What was 'right' or 'wrong' about anything? Judy Leason was beginning to realize she had never really thought through life. Now, just as she was realizing that, she found herself watching two men who had thought through things. And they were kneeling on a hard floor in prayer to a deity they had never seen. She felt confused. She knew what Christianity was and understood the hope it held out, if true.

But it was silly. Wasn't it? While on the other side, opposed to Christianity, was...what? Unanswered questions. Judy sat still and watched. The two men offered up praise to their Lord and King for His mercy and love, and asked Him for help and wisdom, unabashedly pouring out their hearts with an ease that showed both were often in contact with their Savior, and that Jack's derogatory snorts and glares had no effect. But Simeon only allowed a quick prayer, and slid to his feet again before five minutes had passed.

"I'm going down there," Simeon Lee said without preamble. Three pairs of eyes widened and stared at him. Jack was the first one to speak.

"If we're going to try it, I'm going down too."

"Jack, don't you dare go down there and die without me!" cried Judy with a determined stamp of her foot. Jack was about to make a rejoinder but Simeon beat him too it.

"You two help outside," he said.

"Why?" Jack demanded.

"Because neither of you are ready to meet your Creator," Simeon answered with bold honesty.

"That's a really dumb reason. I'm going with you," Jack stated with an expression that clearly showed he wasn't going to take no for an answer. "This is my story, and with two of us there will be more of a chance of success."

"Then I'm coming too!" Judy declared.

"No you're not," Jack ordered, and the husband and wife started quarreling animatedly. Vincent leaned toward Simeon to be heard over the Shakespeare-spouting husband and wife.

"I know I'm not very good at this stuff yet, but I would feel a lot better if you weren't alone. You've told me on the job experience is the best way to learn, can't I learn beside you?"

"You're the only one I can rely on to get a signal out," Simeon answered. "Nothing to do with inexperience. Everything to do with your skill. Need you up top, Vincent. Worried?"

"Yeah, about you. Look, Simeon... I've just been getting to know you. And I've been happy for the first time in a year, and while I know it's pretty selfish, I really don't want you dying on me. It would be safer with two, wouldn't it?" Vincent murmured. Simeon nodded at the young man, choosing not to make a comment on the hopeful elation the simple request kindled. Maybe...maybe this young man would actually stick around him for a while. Maybe he might be given at least a year or two of good company before the lonely had to set in again... But it wasn't time to hope for that yet, it hung on the way Vincent reacted at the end of this mission. After it was all over, if Vincent still wanted him, then he would let himself hope. Simeon firmly turned his thoughts back to the business on hand, stepping between the two quarreling people.

"Mr. Leason, you're with me," Simeon said.

"And so am I!" Judy said, turning a glare on Jack as he began to object. Jack's words died in a shrug and he dropped into his chair with a rueful sigh, letting his wife win this one.

"I wish you'd reconsider life first," Simeon said, studying the young couple soberly. "Eternity is a very long time."

"Is it that certain you won't come back up again?" asked

Vincent looking searchingly at his friend.

"Don't really know," Simeon shrugged. "Depends on what's down there, and if we can get a signal out. What do you think, Vincent?"

"Well, from what we've learned from Mr. Tomkins' bugs–" Vincent started.

"Which ones, the beetles or the moths?" said Judy with a giggle.

"I think their system is probably a lot like ours," Vincent went on. "All connected to one main computer that runs all the security things at once. If you guys are going down, we can send down a signal concentration to the brain. That should work fine." Simeon nodded, approving his new roommate's idea. The Leasons stared at Vincent blankly.

"What should work fine?" Judy asked.

"Seeing as how our lives depend on it, could you explain a little please?" asked Jack.

"Look, when you have a bunch of pins scattered all over the table and you bring a magnet to it, what happens?"

"The pins all jump onto the magnet," Judy answered.

"Right. That's what we're going to do with the signal. We send down a gadget that works as a magnet for the computer's brain. It will suck all the signal to that one gadget and leave the rest of the stuff unguarded and free for us to get through."

"Someone needs to carry the gadget to a spot the computer is

217

programmed to consider vital," Simeon put in.

"Right, that's the idea. If it's in a spot the computer feels is important enough to guard, our magnet will weaken the rest of the sections the computer usually focuses on enough to get a signal out. If we can get this magnet working, it will (Lord willing) allow you to get the transmitter devices and stuff you need to send evidence out, down into Eddy the X's headquarters without detection. And let them work down there. It might even do more for us, I don't really know, it depends on what else that main computer is running."

"Here's the plan," Simeon said. "Mr. Leason and I get caught, take the magnet down, set it up. Mrs. Leason comes down after us carrying transmitters to send signal out. Evidence sent to Vincent on top, you relay it, the authorities move in on X and cronies. If fast enough, we down below should live. Let's get to work." Three voices rose in horrified protest, but Simeon held up a hand to stop them. "Watch and see. Let's get to work."

13

"One, you in place?" murmured Simeon into his watch[41]. He resisted the urge to grimace at speaking into a watch. It felt like he was licking his wrist. Simeon, Jack, and Judy stood looking at the high wall around Edward Plant's grounds, a full mile away from the actual house. The couple beside him shivered and shuffled in place as the slight wind cut into their black ski masks. "Cameras?"

"Right, I've got them," Vincent answered from his position in the Parabaloni company car, parked on a road looking over the house and grounds. "I've hacked the security camera's feed already, and I'll blip out Judy, so it looks like there's only two of you breaking in. Are you sure about this, Sim?"

"We get caught," Simeon affirmed. "Keep Mrs. Leason secret."

"I still don't like this, Judy you should stay–" Jack started, but his wife cut him off.

"And just how do you think I feel about you getting yourself deliberately caught by a bunch of lousy murderers?" she hissed at him. "At least I'm going in undercover and with a gun to protect myself!"

"Providing these guards go armed," Jack growled. "Look, Judy–"

---

[41] On the way out to Eddy's house Vincent Tolliver found a box of old ideas he had played with long ago, and among them was a set of watch communicators. Vincent had been so delighted and excited by the idea of using the two instruments in their adventure Simeon finally agreed, just to get him into the plane and on their way to Vermont.

"Don't start again, poltroon. Who else are you going to get to come down after you, we're it, remember?"

"Mind if we get on with this?" Simeon murmured. The Leasons dropped their argument. They were here, it was too late to back out. Simeon lifted his watch again and spoke to Vincent. "Last report you'll receive for a while." He pulled a water pistol out of his black cargo pocket and squirted it at the top of the wall. A hiss sounded and a small curl of smoke drifted into the night sky from the damp puddle he had just created.

"Scan," Simeon ordered. Jack pointed their handheld at the wall, and concentrated on the earbud in his ear.

"Detect no hazards," Pat reported to him. "And you have freezing hands. Wear a pair of mittens for crying out loud!"

"It says it's safe," Jack blinked, deciding not to mention the other part. "Okay, I admit you were right about the acid shorting out the system. But a water pistol? Couldn't you have come up with something cooler than that?" Simeon ignored him and tossed the reporter his pack of spikes. Even without the voltage running on it, the wall would have posed a problem to most men. It was twelve feet high and as smooth and hard as marble. But they had come prepared and the three people swiftly donned spiked black gloves and a small spiked toe on the end of their shoes.

Simeon ordered them over with a sharp wave of his hand as Judy finished strapping on her spike. The spy darted across the road followed by the other two. With their dark clothes, swift action, and the shifting moonlight they looked like the shadows of something real rather than real things themselves. Simeon scaled the wall at the place he had squirted it, being careful to avoid the wet patches of

220

acid that still smoked. It took him two seconds to get over and drop silently onto the other side. There was no one near and no outcry yet. Simeon turned to help the other two alight quietly next to him, removing his spikes with one hand and analyzing the terrain[42]. The snow here was old and packed down by constant guards patrolling the area, and the grounds were thick with Vermont woods, allowed to still look wild. Very good, they wouldn't be tracked easily and there were plenty of places to hide. And not a mongoose in sight. He handed his spikes to Judy as all three crouched on the inside of the wall. She put the three sets of climbing instruments in a prearranged pocket in the very full utility vest she wore, carefully packed by Simeon. The soft thud of booted feet reached the agent, coming from the woods just to the left of them. He darted toward the cover of a large bush, with Judy and Jack scuttling behind him as quickly and quietly as they could. Simeon shoved Jack's head farther down into the bush as two forms stepped out of the trees. By the moon's light Simeon saw the newcomers were supple men in black guard uniforms, with sub-machine guns over their shoulders, and black hoods covering their faces.

"The computer was right, we have a break in," one of the men reported loudly into a walkie-talkie. Another voice barked back over the walkie-talkie immediately, a hard voice with a lilt to it that sounded to Simeon as if the speaker welcomed the diversion.

"A307 and O23, fan out in sections three and one. Alert all you come in contact with. Y, go toward section two, and V40 take

---

[42] The spoiled cat never went out in the grounds, no one had been in Eddy's Vermont place in over ten years, and the security was too good to even get a high aerial shot without arousing the X box people's suspicions. Simeon had no idea what to expect. But at least he was able to prepare for just about anything before being thrown into the situation, which was better than the time in Sri Lanka with the monkeys and the thousands of rabid mongooses.

section four. I'm deploying reinforcements." The two men separated and began to move steadily and stealthily in opposite directions. The man who had spoken into the walkie-talkie walked right toward Simeon and his group. Judy grabbed for their chloroform doused rag and Jack quickly gripped a length of light, strong rope. The man walked slowly past them, looking all around. Jack and Judy tensed to spring, but Simeon held them back. This one was too thin, and spoke in a much deeper voice, Judy could never pass for him. They would have to find another. The couple shivered with more than cold as they stayed still in the silver moonlight, crouching on the icy snow. Every moment they waited increased their danger a hundred times over, and it was just plain scary to be inside the bad guy's territory. Simeon kept waiting till the thin man had passed out of hearing, then he chanced a whisper.

"Night goggles," he said to Judy. She reached into another pocket of the vest and handed out three pairs of night goggles. With those on the world suddenly became alive with eerie green shapes that shone with iridescence all their own. "Single file, stay close," Simeon murmured, and then shot off. Jack and Judy had never used anything like night goggles. In their flurry to follow Simeon, they smacked straight into each other and found themselves sprawled on the ground staring up at eerily glowing green leaves, moving ever so slightly in the wind. Simeon waited till they sorted themselves out, quietly chuckling to himself, and then moved off a little slower toward the left wing of the house. The little group moved in quick, silent dashes from one cover to another. They came across four different guards, a woman among them, but each time Simeon shook his head. The others trusted his judgment as if it was law and waited till he found what he wanted, dashing across more of the icy snow and the few patches of slippery green that occasionally showed through. Tree branches shifted all around them, blown by a gentle wind that brought a sweet woodsy smell with it. At an ordinary time the moonlit scenery would have inspired a dreamy peace and gentle words cooed into a sweetheart's ear. Right now every time a branch moved Jack felt his heart leap and his throat constrict, while Judy fell over twice from slipping on the icy snow as a sudden branch movement caused her to leap unexpectedly. Finally Simeon stopped behind a huge oak tree so abruptly Jack almost ran into him. The spy stood absolutely motionless, pressed against the tree trunk, and the other two did their best to follow suit. When they stood still, Judy and Jack could hear a soft voice coming from in front of them.

"I still think this is another drill," it grumbled. Simeon's lip curled into a half smile when he heard it. Mrs. Leason's voice would fit that range very nicely, and the trim form matched too. Not so willowy in the frame, and a little less in height, but not enough that it would matter if Judy kept her head. His mark was moving straight toward the huge oak tree. Simeon quietly took the rope and gag from Jack's fingers and waited. The guard stepped around the tree and the agent moved like a striking snake, snapping his flattened hand into the black hooded face while his other arm wrapped around the woman's throat and drew her inexorably to the ground. The guard sank into darkness before she even realized she had been attacked. Simeon laid the woman gently on her back and looked up to motion Judy forward. The Leasons stood gaping at him.

"What?" Simeon asked, stepping away to allow Judy to remove the outer clothing layers from the passed out guard.

"That took you, like, zero seconds to bring her down!" Jack murmured. Simeon just moved back to the enormous tree to stand watch while the reporter helped Judy change into the guard's clothes and securely bound and gagged their victim, now in Judy's things. Simeon checked the knots and stashed her in a bush as he inspected Judy through his night goggles. She would do. The utility vest made a few odd bulges here and there but it would work fine. Jack stood up beside the other two, his notebook open with a PD's identification card on it. He handed Judy the card and a slip of paper with F28's password to get through the door.

"Luck is for us, and that cat really likes beetles. I can't believe we had the right password," Judy grinned, her voice only trembling a little. Jack stood up and kissed her hard.

"Good luck!" he murmured into his wife's ear. "Watch yourself, for goodness sake, and get us out of there alive."

"God be with you, Judy," Simeon told the pretty woman, before melting toward the house, Jack following as best he could. Judy silently watched the two of them till they were swallowed up in the darkness. Tingling warmth flooded her and she felt strong, capable, and ready for anything. Simeon Lee had called her Judy. She was accepted as a friend by that good, good man. How did Simeon use the simple act of calling someone by their first name to give such strength? But now wasn't the time to stand around and think, now was the time for action. Judy shoved her night goggles, the card, and paper into one of her pockets and moved off toward section four, F28's machine gun slung over her shoulder and her thoughts with her husband.

9:25 pm, Feb. 19th; Eddy's Grounds

"Stage two complete. All's well," Simeon muttered into his watch. He and Jack crouched underneath a pine tree and stared at the mansion in front of them. The Corinthian columns were laid out in droves at the front of this place, and in combination with the classical style reliefs resting every three feet down the enormous front, Simeon found himself wrinkling his nose in displeasure. It was very poor taste, using that many useless ornaments on the magnificent white stone. He lowered his wrist and watched as another group of guards issued from the doorway of the mansion and trotted down the broad oval steps to the immaculate grassy lawn splayed out directly in front of the building. The snow had been cleared from that area, almost certainly just for aesthetic reasons.

"Sure you want to go through with this, Mr. Leason?" he murmured to his companion. Jack paused before he answered, and for a moment the patch of cold snow trying to seep into his boots, the hard bark of the tree he knelt against, even the softly scented breeze were entirely lost to the reporter. He took the moment to realize how afraid he was. His mouth was dry with his fear and he could feel sweat beginning to trickle down his neck despite the February temperature. And yet Simeon Lee remained so calm, so...peaceful. Even when a single wrong move or a right look from a guard could snuff out their lives in a moment! Curiosity had driven the reporter here and he still desperately wanted to know what was through that door. But it was the quiet longing to solve a problem that answered Simeon's question at that moment. Jack desperately wanted to have Mr. Lee's peace. Something told Jack the quiet man beside him didn't have a void in his life. His heart tugged at him and murmured he had to go down into that hole to lose the emptiness he had begun to realize was around him.

225

"Yes," Jack answered, and wrinkled his nose in disgust to hear the tremble in his voice.

"Then God be with us. Jack, make Him your own," Simeon murmured, and deliberately snapped a dry twig in two before Jack could reply. The reporter felt startled and his fear dropped away to more of a worry. His first name had come from this strange, serious man! Jack wasn't given time to sort his feelings out. The noise of the snapping twig started out from underneath the tree like a gunshot. Six guards moving across the smooth turf looked toward the sound. Simeon and Jack shot from underneath the tree and darted toward a large bush trimmed into a spiral shape, allowing themselves to be seen in the shifting moonlight. A shout went up from the guards, and five of them fanned out toward the bush. As soon as they reached the spiral bush, Simeon took a tight hold on Jack's arm and moved to the cover of a bush cut into a perfect square, being careful not to be seen at all this time. Just as they reached the second bush, Jack heard the fire of a sub-machine gun from one of the guards and spun around to see the spiraled bush splintering into tiny twigs, some flying so high in the air he lost them even with his goggles on. The reporter felt sick, picturing how he would look now if he had still been there. He forced his mind away from that alarming subject and focused on the guards. Five were closing in on the area, while the sixth stood in the open, speaking rapidly into his walkie-talkie. Jack heard movement on the forest side of them and spun around again. He gripped Simeon's arm convulsively as he saw luminous green guards moving toward them. In one quick glance he saw four large rifles trained on him and Simeon. A search light on the mansion's roof picked out their square bush, blinding and pinpointing the suspicious ones, and immediately the triumphant shout of their enemies rose around the two men. Simeon slowly lifted his hands and placed them on his head, removing his goggles

226

as he went. In one slow, fluid movement he rose to his feet and faced the man who still stood talking into the walkie-talkie. Jack followed Simeon's example. He was surprised to find that he was still alive as he stood next to the short, stocky Simeon. A sudden stillness enfolded the scene, the breeze and the occasional shifting foot of a guard the only noise.

"J, I want to know who they are," Eddy's voice shattered the silence, drifting out of the walkie-talkie. The man slapped the walkie-talkie on his belt and regarded the two men with interest.

"Now I just have to decide whether I should shoot you here and then find your papers, or find a better spot," the hooded J said in a cultured sneer. The voice fit his tall form and supple carriage very well, the reporter decided as he watched this J, and wondered what his face looked like under the loose black hood draped over his head and sweeping his broad shoulders. "We just wrecked one bush it; would be a shame to ruin another." Jack saw his eyes crinkle in a smile behind the almond shaped eye holes as this J character began to play with his automatic rifle slung over his shoulder. The reporter felt his fear being replaced with a quiet fury against this man who could stand and joke about the lives of fellow humans. J's gun snapped up and sent a shower of bullets spraying between the two men standing by the bush and Jack dodged involuntarily. J burst out laughing, a cold, heartless sound that made Jack even madder than the bullets had scared him. Simeon didn't even glance to the side at the sudden spray of lead. The stranger stopped laughing to glare at the spy.

"What, old man," J sneered at Simeon. "Aren't you worried about dying?"

"No," Simeon said with easy calm, and flicked a finger at him,

227

indicating a change in subject. "Want to talk to the man in charge."

"How do you know I'm not in charge?" J said. Simeon smiled and raised an eyebrow in answer, with an expression that held mystery and disdain and meant clearly he knew who was really in charge, and wouldn't they like to know how he knew. It raised the curiosity about these two trespassers to almost a fever pitch, as it was supposed to.

"Bring them inside," J commanded. "X wants to speak with you. When X is done, I think you'll wish I had finished you out here."

9:31 pm, Feb. 19th; Eddy's Grounds

"All second group agents report to the front of the house," a voice broke over Judy's walkie-talkie, making her ram her head into a tree branch as she leapt in surprise. "Intruders have been pinpointed. Repeat, all second group agents report to the front of the house immediately." The walkie-talkie went silent, and Judy was enveloped once more in the eerie silence of the woods. She turned to look behind her at the mansion. Sounds of a rapid fire gun going off shattered the silence and brought Judy's heart into her mouth with fear for Jack and Simeon Lee. A search light sprang to life suddenly on the roof and pointed at something on the ground. Judy started trotting toward the commotion, hoping F28 was in the second group of agents. As she neared the area she heard another burst of bullets, and her mouth pursed in worry. She trotted out of the trees and bushes, and relief washed over her as she saw all was well. Simeon and Jack, hands tied behind them and surrounded by guards, were being led through the mansion's massive wooden doors.

Stage three was complete then. But she would have to give them a few minutes before she followed them down. Wait, she didn't know where to go to get down. Judy walked slowly over the immaculate grass, up the steps, and on through the door into a vaulted entryway with checkered marble tile. There was only one door, on the far side of the palatial room, and she stepped toward it over the grey and white tile, holding her rifle with a studious competence that showed she knew how to use it.

"One," she murmured as she walked, "can you hear me?" Vincent's voice came through her hidden Bluetooth immediately in the affirmative. He sounded high-strung and uneasy. Judy wondered if she sounded that worried.

"They're being taken down now. I'm following," she said in a whisper.

"Right," Vincent said through the Bluetooth, trying to sound as if he knew what he was doing[43]. "When stage four is complete, I'll let you know and you can follow them down. Tell me when to start working the feed from you and sending it to the folks Simeon's superior has standing by."

"Okay," Judy murmured under her hood. She heard footsteps behind her and didn't say anything else. A glance behind showed a man in a black guard outfit like her own striding toward her

---

[43] Simeon had informed the others Vincent was in charge of the above ground operations, and Judy was to stay in constant contact with him. Vincent was doing his best to remain confident and steady; but his mind kept drifting to some of his more spectacular mistakes, such as the flamingo and cream puff catastrophe.

quickly.

"What are you doing here?" the newcomer demanded suspiciously. Judy gulped and hoped she would be able to follow Simeon and Jack down when Vincent gave the all clear.

9:39 pm; Elevator, VM

The elevator seemed to drop forever. Wherever they were going must be a very long way down. Despite his best efforts Jack found himself wondering if he would make it back up to the surface alive. Would he ever see Judy again? Jack glanced to the side at Simeon and felt a little safer. He had a friend down here. And what a friend. How many times had this unexplained old guy done this before? Jack's agile mind drifted off to speculation on the ex-CIA agent's past, entirely forgetting his worry about the situation. Simeon's mind was more on the task at hand, as he got himself refocused and un-panicked after having to face all those beetles in the hallway, and flexing his muscles to test his bonds. There was little hope of breaking them off without help, these people knew what they were doing. But as the elevator hummed and vibrated slowly downward, in the back of Simeon's mind the thought of Saul Korry kept rushing forward. Was he still alive? He was in the midst of another passionate prayer for his old friend's safety when the elevator came to a stop and the thick gray doors slid open. Whatever Simeon and Jack had been expecting, they didn't expect what they saw.

A vast white walled room, domed and spacious, stretched

away into other large white rooms. Hallways and doors opened up everywhere they looked, and people were coming and going through it all. Men and women in everything from sloppy jeans and t-shirts to full business dress walked in and out, up and down stairs, each hurrying to their own specific job. It looked more like a mall or airport than an underground hideout for murderers and conspirators. But unlike a mall or airport, every figure that moved in that room wore the dark hood of a PD.

J stepped out and the other guards pushed Simeon and Jack after him. Their leader sauntered across the busy white room, into an unadorned rectangular corridor on their left. The two prisoners were shoved down a flight of metal steps, through a steel door, down another white walled corridor, and pulled to a stop before another steel door, this one with all the latest in security locks. Simeon even saw one he didn't recognize[44]. J went through the numerous scans, questions, and keys with a swift ease that proved he was often here. When the heavy door swung open, the two prisoners were pushed into a wide hallway lined with two inch wide iron bars, intersecting each other to make up cells. There were guards everywhere here and all of them leapt to attention when J came in. One of the guards, apparently the one in charge, stepped forward to receive orders. J obliged.

"Search them. Make it thorough P2, I think at least the old man's a sly character," he said, and stood aside to watch as Simeon and Jack submitted meekly to the search. Everything on them, from their wallets (with everything important carefully taken out of them beforehand) to every fold of their clothes was looked through. As he submitted quietly, Jack's heart was pounding. Every moment he expected to have the guard searching him give a triumphant cry

---

[44] After all, he had been out of the business for two years.

and feel his half of Vincent's security stopper wrenched from where it was strapped onto the side of his leg. But apparently the skin-like quality of Simeon's concealment tape[45] was good enough to pass the test. Everything was scanned, with every scanner imaginable. Simeon's opinion of Vincent's watches went up considerably as it passed scan after scan and remained strapped on his wrist. One last scanner was pulled out by P2, and it beeped over Simeon's jacket.

"Nuts," Simeon silently complained. He had hoped Judy would be able to find them by that tracker. The jacket was taken from him and tossed over a guard's arm. As he watched it being sent off toward the labs with an outwardly uninterested look, inwardly he was anxiously wondering how on earth Judy was to find them, or anything else, in this huge underground headquarters. But J was finally satisfied the two men were clean. He left the room without a comment, and P2 motioned them toward the line of cells. Jack started moving toward them but stopped when he saw Simeon hesitate.

"Why do you wait?" P2 asked.

"Could I have my New Testament back?" Simeon asked. P2 cocked his head in interest at the request. He took the scanner again and ran it over the little book. He turned a knob and tried a different test.

"Why?" he challenged.

"To read[46]," Simeon said simply. P2 picked up the Bible and

---

[45] The ex-CIA agent stoutly refused to tell where he had gotten an entire roll of the stuff.

[46] This was quite a truthful answer, but there was also a bit of sentimentality attached to that particular little book that led Simeon to request it back. He had been given it two years ago by the man who had led him to Christ, thirty seconds after Simeon's first real prayer and ten seconds before he had to leap over three airplane seats to tackle a particularly evil high-jacker headed toward the cockpit with a jar of deadly raspberry jelly.

flipped through it carefully.

"I'll consider your request. Now move," P2 ordered, pointing toward the cells. They obeyed, heading quietly down the jail hall. Each cell was open to the others, it was simply a line of bars with different lines of bars intersecting them to make individual cells. Simple and effective, Simeon admitted. A guard went ahead and opened up two of the cell doors. As they approached Simeon saw two big, black, leathery hands grip the bars of an adjoining cell. A thrill of relief and joy coursed through him as a familiar voice boomed at the foremost guard.

"So you finally brought me someone to talk with?"

"Depends what you mean," Simeon answered.

"Sim?" Saul Korry cried in delight, then quickly forced his tone to a disappointed growl. "Your conversation is a bit lacking, yeah. It's about time you came to get me out of here!" Simeon was shoved into the cell next to Saul as Jack was pushed into one on Simeon's other side. The doors slammed shut and the sound reverberated around the hallway.

"Okay, so you aren't down here leading an invading force of partially trained chimps to get me out, like Cambodia. You're losing your touch," Saul rumbled, his large face tightening despite himself. Simeon shrugged apologetically as the guards wandered back down the hallway.

"Good grief, you still have your hands tied and everything. And I thought I was getting rusty in my old age," Saul muttered. Simeon didn't answer, only stuck his hands through the bars and let his friend remove the ropes. Then he crossed his cell and untied Jack's hands.

233

"You first. Camera watching, be discreet," Simeon whispered in the reporter's ear as the last rope came off. Jack had trouble hearing him through Saul Korry's lecture, but he got the message. Saul hadn't stopped talking, mostly upbraiding Simeon for falling into the hands of the enemy. His conversation was peppered with fascinating allusions to the past and Jack burned to know what they meant. Simeon remained quiet, but a small smile played on his lips as he listened to the barrage, and it was obvious he didn't mind his friend's complaints. Jack managed to remove his half of Vincent's gadget and get it working under the cover of looking for an elusive thorn in his shoe as he listened.

"Well, do you have anything to say for yourself?" Saul finally wound up, glaring at Simeon.

"It's good to see you, old friend," Simeon said. The wrathful look died from Saul Korry's eyes and he smiled back at Simeon.

"You too, Sim," he said. "I didn't ask about Michelle and Jon because you said you would take care of that. You always do. Does a friend have them stashed somewhere?"

"Uncle," Simeon answered. Saul started up again, this time about mutual acquaintances and places, mostly using a sort of best friend/CIA code that was entirely unintelligible to the unenlightened. Jack leaned back on the metal cot in his cell and amused himself by comparing the two men. They were quite a pair. Simeon was short, quiet, with an air of a cat. Not the housecat like Mr. Tomkins but the watchful, powerful, incredibly efficient panther. The type you don't even know is near you until it's too late. And then Saul; huge, boisterous, reminding one of a bull, eager to charge through anything and able to trample over whatever got in his way. It must have been an interesting set of circumstances

234

that had made these two men such fast friends[47]. Simeon listened to Saul's monologue with obvious pleasure, nodding every once in a while. He surreptitiously removed the other half of Vincent's gadget, placed it in the shadows underneath his cot, and got it working. Jack was honestly amazed. He knew what Simeon was up to and he still had a hard time believing he was doing anything but adjusting his shoelaces after the guards had pulled them apart in their search. As Simeon activated the second half of the gadget, the blowing air from the ceiling vent suddenly stopped. The lights flickered and a noise like a rush of power in a big machine came to their ears through the wall. The floors trembled, and shook dust from the ceiling. Two seconds later, all was back to normal.

"What was that?" asked Saul in a subdued voice. Simeon only shrugged in answer.

"How's your stay been?" Simeon asked. Jack looked a little closer and noticed the big man's cheeks were sunken and his dark face was a series of vicious cuts and swollen bruises.

"Oh, all right I guess," Saul answered wearily. "The food's not bad. The service is pretty rotten. Nothing like Cambodia. I got a little banged up at the beginning and not exactly gentle treatment since, but not too bad." Simeon was about to press further but P2 suddenly stepped up to the door of his cell.

"It's clean, old man," he said waving Simeon's New Testament at the bars. Simeon moved toward the guard to take his book and

---

[47] Nothing could break the brotherhood that had come about by almost strangling each other in a filthy tent in Yemen's Empty Quarter shortly after they had first met. Boy, I wish I could tell you about some of the circumstances those two went through! The Donald Duck fiasco, now that was a frightening bit of work on their part, and they only survived it by a furious determination to make certain the other made it out and the surprise interposition of an English ally.

Saul's mouth snapped closed. Jack saw a new look come over his face, one of almost disgust. P2 hesitated before he handed it over. "Why do you want it? It's been proven false through science."

"No proof against it. If science did claim a proof, I would believe the Bible," Simeon answered.

"Why?" said P2.

"Scientists are fallible. God isn't," Simeon said seriously. P2 handed him the New Testament and walked away without another word. Simeon noticed a thoughtful tilt to the hooded head though, and offered a quick prayer for the man's soul as he turned toward his cot.

"'Scientists are fallible and God isn't,'" Saul scoffed. "So you're still into all that Christian stuff?"

"You would be wise to 'get into it' too," Simeon answered without hesitation. Saul snorted harshly.

"I don't need that kind of a crutch," the big man boomed. Jack wondered if he sounded that conceited when he said that. "And you didn't used to either, Sim."

"Not a crutch," Simeon answered with quiet firmness. "And I always needed it, still do. You do too you just won't admit it, you big gorilla."

"You used to be strong, Sim. Now you decided you're not as strong as some dead guy from the Middle East," Saul jeered, working his way into an argument[48]. Simeon didn't move. The big

---

[48] In their younger days Simeon and Saul's arguments were a bit...explosive. During one they wrecked a London opera hall that had stood through three wars and two centuries. It

man turned away from his friend and lay down on his cot, the metal creaking with his weight and his face turned to the back wall. Jack winced at Saul's words and nasty attitude. That was exactly what he would have said. That is what he thought. And yet to hear someone else say them, to Simeon who was…was what? A good man? Yes. A man who did his best to live what he believed. That was admirable in anyone, according to Jack's standards. And he suddenly found it hurt to hear that belief ridiculed for no particular reason. But there was a reason! There had to be.

"So, are you going to introduce me to your friend or what?" Saul interrupted Jack's disturbing thoughts. Simeon looked up from where he had flipped open his New Testament to the Psalms.

"Jack Leason, investigative reporter. Jack, Saul Korry, private eye, sometimes ferryman."

"I'd forgotten about that," Saul chuckled at Simeon's reference, shifting his weight to lay comfortably on his back. "Nice to meet you, Jack." The reporter smiled at the way Saul raised his foghorn-like voice to get across Simeon's open cell to him, and opened his mouth to return the greeting. A large metal door clanging farther up the hall interrupted. J sauntered back. He stopped outside the cells with P2 and nine well-armed guards, and stood still surveying the prisoners in disturbing silence. Saul and Jack swallowed nervously and glanced at the cell between them. Simeon closed his New Testament and stood up.

"X?" he asked J. The sharp eyes behind the mask crinkled into a humorless smile, and the black hooded head nodded with a sense of relish in what was coming.

---

turned out all right though because the exploding bats came in right after them, and of course that took the blame for the damage.

14

"Are you supposed to be here? Let me see your card," the guard said impatiently. Judy fumbled for F28's wallet with an annoyed grunt as close to the complaining voice she had heard in the garden as she could get. There were at least fifty cards stuffed in the wallet. "Well?" the guard asked, suspicion in his voice.

"Hold on a minute," said Judy as she slowly flipped through the cards and wondered frantically which one she was supposed to be looking for.

"Judy, the gadget's working and you can go down whenever," Vincent's voice broke into her ear, and Judy's hand leapt up to the hidden Bluetooth in shock. She quickly scratched at the hood there, murmuring something about lice. The guard in front of her stepped back, one hand straying to his rifle. To Judy's infinite relief, two more guards suddenly came into the room, and the one asking for identification turned to them. Each held up a white card with a little red stripe across the top. The first guard waved them past, so Judy grabbed a similar card in F28's wallet and handed it over. He glanced at it and handed it back to her.

"Next time have it ready," the guard complained. Judy nodded, shoved the wallet into her pocket, and walked quickly after the other two guards. She followed them through several huge rooms, carefully walking slow enough to not overtake the two. They wandered into the cellar, stacked with wines in amazing bottles. Judy was impressed by the color variety as she stepped carefully down the wooden stairs. One of the guards shoved a particularly

239

green bottle toward the corner. A rack slid open to show a secret door leading into a long hallway, sloping down. Judy waited for a few minutes for the two guards to get ahead of her, then repeated their maneuvers. She found herself walking into the same hallway she had watched Mr. Tomkins play in for the past two days. It was cold concrete, dimly lit, damp, and crawling with bugs. The hallway abruptly ended, and Judy was confronted with a large shiny metal door and a small shiny metal box.

"Identification card," an automated voice demanded. Judy had heard that same voice dozens of times through Mr. Tomkins' bugs, and she thought it sounded a little different this time. Sluggish maybe? But she didn't stop to ponder it. She pulled out F28's wallet, found the one labeled 'identification,' and inserted it into the appropriate slot. She had the little slip of paper Jack had given her and was ready when the automated voice required it.

"Password?" the voice definitely sounded deeper, it was almost a growl now. Like a game does when it is running out of batteries, Judy thought as she typed in the password. The door slid open and she saw the empty metal interior of the freight elevator, just as she had seen it again and again from the cat's perspective. But from here on out it would be unexplored territory. What was down there? Judy took a deep breath, grabbed her card, and stepped into the elevator.

"Here I go!" she muttered into her Bluetooth as she felt herself dropping toward the PD's headquarters.

9:54 pm; Cell Block, VT

P2 opened the cell doors, a length of rope held in one hand. Saul stepped forward quickly, his hands closing into fists and the light of battle in his eyes.

"Don't," Simeon ordered. He knew he and Saul could knock these few guards out till next week, with relatively marginal danger of getting shot, but that wasn't what he wanted. They weren't down here to escape. They were down here to stop X. To do that they had to find him, and since this J was taking them there anyway, they might as well comply for now. He slipped his New Testament into his front pocket and stepped out, hands held out quietly to be bound. P2 did so quickly and thoroughly. But not roughly, Simeon noted. And P2 allowed him to keep his hands forward this time, definitely more comfortable. And useful, Simeon considered as he surreptitiously brushed his right hand over a button on his watch. Saul shrugged and moved out of his cell beside Simeon. Jack stepped out on Simeon's other side and held up his hands to be bound as Simeon had done. P2 took two other lengths of ropes to bind the two men, but J interrupted.

"No. X said only the short old man needs restraining. Now let's go."

"Why?" Jack asked.

"X doesn't view you as a threat," J shrugged. "Why he doesn't, you can ask him yourself. If you behave yourself and don't give us a reason to shoot you. Now shut up and move." Jack did as he was told. The group was led through the headquarters, passing through white room after white room till the reporter was amazed by the size of the headquarters created underground, and half forgot he was underground at all. It felt much more like some sort of large business corporation than an evil bad guy's hangout. There was

241

laughter and the buzz of conversation all around them, and if it hadn't been for the hoods and the heavy weaponry pointing at his back, Jack would have been tempted to disbelieve his own memory of where he was. There must be five hundred people down here. The reporter realized that was just in this enormous domed room and there were innumerable smaller rooms opening off of it, and even a second story winding around the wall with more rooms. Eddy Plant had been able to bring a remarkable number of people into his PDs, and the reporter's fear came back as he walked. J came to a stop in front of him, and Jack looked ahead again. There was a large, oak door in front of the group, the first one not painted the habitual white of the rest of this headquarters.

"Listen up all," J drawled to Jack, Saul, and Simeon as they stood outside the door of X's office. The man smothered a bored yawn, and Jack's fist itched to punch him. "Even though only P2 and I are going in with you, these other guards are staying right here by the door and if any of you come out without me, P2, or X you won't make it very far." J turned his back on his three prisoners and knocked on the door.

"Come in," Eddy Plant answered. J opened the door and slipped in. P2 nudged Simeon forward with the muzzle of his gun. Simeon pushed Saul, and Saul pushed Jack, and with a deep breath the reporter followed J into the office.

9:55 pm; PD Headquarters, VT

The doors of the elevator opened and Judy stood staring at the

242

scene in front of her with open mouthed surprise. Where did all these people come from? And what were they all doing? She stepped out of the elevator onto the black and white swirled tile and mingled with the people hurrying back and forth. Her feet seemed heavy and her eyes darted around desperately as she moved through the crowd. Where on earth was she supposed to go?

"Vincent?" she murmured into her Bluetooth, under cover of an explosive sneeze.

"Yeah, are you down? Can I start up the camera and bug?" Judy gave a quiet acquiescence. There was a short pause, during which Judy tried to take in how spacious this domed white room was, and how brilliantly lit. Her eyes were a little dazzled by the artificial lights on all this whiteness, and she felt almost lightheaded when combined with the steady, loud hum of the mass of busy humanity down here. She noted the second story running around the edge of the dome and her jaw involuntarily dropped open. A gasp came from Vincent, reminding Judy of what she was doing, and she snapped her mouth closed. She couldn't look like a tourist here.

"All that is under Eddy's house?" Vincent said in surprise. Judy was passing through a small group of people and didn't dare answer out loud. "Where's our two fellows, have you seen them?" Judy shook her head no as quietly as she could and walked on slowly, hoping Vincent would get the picture. "I'll get a tag on Simeon's coat, hold on a minute…" came Vincent's voice. Good he had understood. "Right, got it. Okay, keep going the way you're going, head toward the wall. There's a left turn coming up."

Judy followed Vincent's precise instructions with ease, stepping through hallways and vaulted white rooms and crowds of busy people. In six minutes she found herself standing in front of a metal door. This one was labeled, unlike the others she had come across so far: *"Lab, only Grey and Red Passes May Enter."* There was a wide window stretching down the hallway and showing the activity going on inside this room, and Judy glanced in it before she took out F28's wallet and began to look it over to see if she had either of the color cards demanded.

"Judy, look in the window again, I think I saw something," Vincent ordered excitedly. She did as asked. "There, it's little red tubes being loaded into black boxes. I played with those boxes enough to know what they look like, those are the same type I carried out of my church."

"You mean we're looking at people putting together a mass murder tool?" Judy murmured incredulously.

"Yeah, I'm thinking so. Judy, stick around for a little while if you can without getting caught. I'm going to start sending your feed to the folks waiting for evidence," Vincent ordered. Judy slipped out of the main hallway into a small doorway a few steps down and held her rifle as if she was guarding the door, waiting for Vincent's next order. As she stood looking in the window and watching little tube after little tube being placed in its own metal contraption, Judy felt her heart beginning to beat wilder and wilder. Here she was, watching these X box people work on their first big offensive...and she stood here. And where were Jack and Simeon?

9:59 pm; Outside Eddy's Grounds, VT

Vincent Tolliver was getting worried. He had brought Judy to Simeon's signal, but it was obvious the Parabaloni leader wasn't in that room. So how on earth were they to find out where he was?

"Tolliver?" a gruff voice broke over one of the numerous speakers crowded in Simeon's new car. That was the leader of the group waiting for evidence, Agent Tom Tyler of the FBI, the man they had met briefly back in Washington.

"Yes sir," answered Vincent, his mind elsewhere.

"Look, I'm only here because that Lee character knows all the right people and strings to pull, and I was ordered here. And then I find I'm in charge of a whole passel of local law enforcement, FBI agents, and the Vermont National Guard, all waiting in the dark of a cold winter night."

"Yes sir…" Vincent murmured, and only his natural politeness kept it from being an annoyed, 'So what?' Vincent was trying to think and this guy didn't seem to have anything new to say, just the same gripes he had been complaining about for the past hour.

"I admit, when you started sending us a feed with a whole underground hideout with hooded people wandering around, I got suspicious. But that's all they seem to be doing, wandering around."

"But what about now, Judy's found a lab–"

"Yeah, all the test tubes they're filling are suspicious certainly, but here's the deal; we can't go barging in on such a well known do-gooder as Edward Plant with just the knowledge that he has an underground cavity where lots of people walk around with hoods on and put tubes filled with red stuff into boxes. For all we know that red stuff may be raspberry jam, not this andorsonii-whatever. I

245

haven't heard, or seen, any evidence of this massive wave of death you and Lee called me about. And if I don't get some solid proof in the next twenty minutes, I'm leaving." Vincent opened his mouth to reply, but a thought interposed itself into his mind instead.

"The watch!" the inventor yelped.

"What?" Tyler asked in some confusion. But Vincent wasn't paying him any attention, he had remembered another tracking device Simeon had taken down with him. It didn't have the best of signals and didn't stay activated all the time like the jacket, but if Simeon knew he needed to be found he might have managed to turn it on. Vincent began to flip switches, looking for the signal. There it was. And it was in quite a different part of the PD headquarters. Vincent flipped on his link to Judy's Bluetooth.

"Judy, I think I know where Simeon is. Let's go find him."

10:00 pm; Eddy's Underground Study, VT

"Ah, right on time, J," Eddy Plant said graciously, from where he was settled comfortably behind a large mahogany desk. Unlike all the other PDs, this man's hood was red, not black. And unlike the other PDs his hood was not on, but lay on the desk in front of him. He spun his chair to face the three men who had come in behind his guard, but his eyes and welcoming smile were turned wholly on Jack. "Welcome to my study, gentlemen." Simeon's eyes ran around the room in his habitual manner. It was very tastefully done up, and seemed to match this dignified man in the immaculate

246

suit sitting behind the big desk. It was decorated with dark furniture that blended in with the oak bookcases and scarlet rug, and lit by lamplight. While the lamps emitted quite enough light to read comfortably by, they created a subdued, peaceful atmosphere. It reminded Simeon of his favorite espresso shop in London.

"We are all known here, men," Eddy said, abruptly turning his attention to P2 and J, "you may remove your hoods if you like." J whipped his hood off his face gratefully and ran his hands through his dark hair to make it smooth. He was a sharp character of ruddy hew. He draped himself on a wooden chair in the right hand corner of the room. Simeon already knew as much as he wanted to about J, he was much more interested in P2. When the guard removed his hood, Simeon was happily surprised. He had expected at least a little of the hard killer in the man's face. Instead he found himself looking into a handsome, pale, middle-aged face that was at once sorrowful, intelligent, questioning, and worried. Simeon felt immediately that this man was at a crossroad in his life. With God's help he would help him through it onto the right road.

"Please be seated, gentlemen; you here, Mr. Korry," Edward Plant motioned to a chair a little to the left of his desk, "and Jack Leason here, if you will," and he motioned to a deep, comfortable armchair directly facing the desk. Saul sat down without a word, a distrustful scowl on his face. Jack remained standing.

"Why do you know my name? And why do you want me here? And what are you people? What are you trying to do? Why do you have tubes of that andorsonii stuff, and why all the hoods and secrecy?" he demanded. Eddy raised his eyebrows in surprise and chuckled quietly. The sound was musical and winning. Jack found himself relaxing despite himself in the presence of this man he had always considered smart and tasteful.

247

"Those are quite a lot of questions for one paragraph, Jack," Eddy answered, perfectly at his ease. "But, I should have expected it. A man of your intelligence and quick perception would have many questions for me. Have a seat and we'll start working on an answering them." Eddy motioned again to the armchair and flashed a smile at the reporter. Jack gave in. He sank down in the chair and waited to hear what was coming. His intuition told him it was going to be remarkable, but it didn't prepare him for just how remarkable and world shaking the next few hours talk was going to be.

10:04 pm; PD Headquarters, VT

"Quick work Judy! The signal is coming from that door in front of you. Now, let's get you through the door," Vincent said over Judy's Bluetooth. She would have given a lot to be able to give a smart answer back at that point. There were eight guards all standing in front of that door, leaning on automatic rifles, and all Vincent had to say was, "let's get you through." The guards looked at Judy. She looked back, giving her best smile and wondering if they even noticed it under her hood. *Come on, Vincent, think of something fast!* she thought furiously.

"Call for Mr. Tomkins," Vincent ordered. What? "Come on, just look behind you and call the cat!" Judy felt like an idiot, but she turned to the corner she had just come around.

"Mr. Tomkins?" she called.

"Mrrow?" a distinctly feline answer sounded out, and the big

248

tabby cat came bounding around the corner.

"There's your in," Vincent said excitedly over the Bluetooth. "I have a strong hunch the cat's master is behind that door, and he always welcomes his cats. Take him in." Judy leaned down and stroked the cat. It began to purr its deep, happy purr. She picked it up and the cat rubbed happily against her chest, shedding all over the black shirt, and purred even louder. Judy took a deep breath and moved toward the door. The guards outside hesitated for a moment, but then looked at the cat and made way. Edward Plant must definitely be in there. Judy stepped to the door, the big tom cat still purring in her arms. *"Well, here goes,"* she thought, and knocked on the dark wood.

10:05 pm, Feb. 19th; Eddy's Office, VT

"Now, who's that?" said Eddy in annoyance. He had just finished getting Jack, J, and Saul tall glasses of sparkling water and another interruption annoyed him. After the initial meeting, he completely ignored P2 and Simeon, and in the presence of this dynamic man, everyone seemed to forget of their existence.

"Come in," he called. The door was opened a little timidly by a trim guard with a purring cat in her arms. As soon as he saw the cat, Eddy's annoyance faded away. "Ah, Mr. Tomkins, I was wondering when you would join us." The cat hopped out of the guard's arms and trotted toward his master. Eddy sat him on his lap, and stroked him happily. No one (except perhaps the forgotten Simeon and P2) noticed that the guard stayed in the room when she shut the door.

"Now where were we?" asked Edward Plant, though he remembered precisely where they had been.

"You were telling me," spoke up Jack, "that you remembered our interview eight years ago. Instead of being flattered to get me in the right mood for the kill, I would love to have some questions answered."

"I suppose you would," Eddy said, flashing an encouraging smile at the reporter. "Well, to answer your questions, I suppose I had better start with the first one; what are we. I know you know our initials, PD, and our logo." Plant waved his hand at a magnificently framed picture of the silver tree insignia. "The PD stands, quite simply, for the Practicing Darwinists. That is what we are. We, along with all intelligent people in this age, have agreed wholeheartedly with Darwin's evolutionary explanation of the way of the universe. It's easy to understand why so many have accepted it, I happen to know you agree that the world was fashioned through evolution, Jack, and you too, Saul Korry. As I say, all people of intelligence accept the truth of evolution today."

"If all intelligent men accept the theory," broke in Jack, "why all the hoods and secrecy?"

"I have only explained one of the parts of our name," Eddy said patiently, "the Darwinists. Now we move on to the other word. Unlike most of those who say they accept Darwinist teachings, we have decided to do something. We are trying to practice what Darwin laid out." Edward Plant stood up suddenly, moved to where he was in front of Jack, and leaned on the desk with a thoughtful look, as if he were trying to put into words something

250

that ran deeper than words could express. Finally he spoke again.

"Have you ever looked around you, Jack, at the members of mankind, and thought that something was missing? As if there was an emptiness, or hole that needed filled?"

"Sure, I've thought that before," Jack answered guardedly. He felt a little uncomfortable at the penetration of this man.

"I thought you would have. That's because you are an especially perceptive man. I thought that the first time I met you. I've felt that for years, that incompleteness. And I finally pinpointed it. We are incomplete, Jack. Mankind isn't done growing yet. Mankind is the highest of the animals right now, by right of evolution, but that doesn't mean we should be content with it. We are still incomplete, there are still higher evolutionary things to achieve! Can't you see it? A higher man, a man of such superior qualities and talents we can't even imagine what he would be like. Would he continue to have a body like we do now, or would that gradually change?" Eddy went on, painting a picture that was at once beautiful and exciting about the new mankind that could emerge if man now would only rise up to the challenge and make it happen. It was a world without war, without sickness, without all kinds of horrors. Mankind would rise above baseness, above all that was superstitious or stupid. They would rise as a body toward completing themselves and the world around them. If someone without Edward Plant's charisma, intelligence, charm, or way with words had voiced these thoughts to Jack, he would have put them down as silly utopian ideas that had no relation to real life. But here, in the lamp lit room, with the world's ideal do-gooder voicing them, Jack felt himself swept into the vision.

"But how," he interrupted, "how does mankind now, rise to

251

being mankind then?"

"By education, selective breeding, and strong wills," Eddy answered immediately. "I see no reason why these things, with a little help from chance of course, shouldn't be able to achieve the very things we're talking about. If intelligent, well-built people produce offspring with other intelligent well-built people, it is obvious that in a few generations their offspring will be more intelligent and better built then their producers were before them. It's very simple." Edward Plant went on to explain the genetics of the thing, and why it would work, how long it would take for mankind to begin to rise, and how long it might take for them to reach the levels they had discussed. He had charts of many of the things he talked about, and he pulled them out of drawers in his desk for Jack's perusal. The reporter offered opinions on some of them, and even corrected Eddy on a mistake he had made in his math calculations. Mostly, however, he remained quiet and kept his thoughts to himself. But Simeon, watching from the back of the room, where he comfortably sat on his heels on the thick scarlet rug with the watchful P2 beside him, saw he was growing more animated as Plant talked. And his eyes were getting an excited look in them. Saul too, though he said nothing and moved very little, was gradually becoming less and less suspicious and more and more interested as the talk went on into the night.

"Now I expect you understand our insignia," Plant said finally, beaming at Jack.

"Sure," answered the reporter without hesitation, "it's a picture of mankind's family tree. A new, healthier mankind growing out of an old, sickly mankind." Plant gave a pleased chuckle, then he turned to J for the first time in well over an hour.

252

"You see J, I told you he was a smart one to have on our side." Jack looked up in surprise. It was true he had become interested, even a little captivated by the vision Eddy laid before him. But he hadn't come nearly far enough to consider himself on the side of these PDs. "That's right, Jack Leason," said Eddy noticing his surprise, "the reason I brought you into my office and have spent all this time explaining to you what we are trying to do, is because I want you to work with us. You have a wonderful talent with that pen of yours, Jack. I know if you once put your mind to it, you could win over hundreds, maybe even thousands to our side just with your stories. It doesn't take much, really. Just dropping a hint here, and throwing out a comment there. A really intelligent man can do it so well that his readers don't even realize they're being influenced until they are under his spell. We have a good number of PDs in the media, all quietly working away to carve America into the beautiful vision I've showed you. We have almost as many there as we have in the schools. That's the really important place, Jack, that's where these future generations we've been talking about get their ideas from. I don't mean their schooling, that can come from anywhere for all I care. I mean their ideas, the things that will shape their lives and bend their hearts. If we can get the children now (the adults of the next generations) to embrace our vision, the war will be won." Simeon saw Saul beginning to nod his head in silent assent to the idea and Jack looked only a little less accepting. He felt his stomach turn in disgust. Eddy was still going on about how marvelous the new man was going to be, and how many problems it would solve in the long run, when suddenly he was stopped by a question from the back of the room.

"Where do we come from, Mr. Plant?" asked Simeon in his quiet, commanding voice. Everyone in the room looked at him in surprise. For two hours they had been encouraged to forget he was there, and they had done so very easily and completely. To hear him speak so suddenly now reminded, at least Jack and Saul, that there was a real world out there. A world that said different things than Plant had been saying in his office deep underground his house.

"What do you mean?" said Eddy, and Jack heard just a hint of annoyance in his voice that didn't fit with the gentle, friendly way he had been speaking earlier.

"Can you tell me where we all started?" Simeon clarified.

"We evolved, of course," Eddy snapped. There was no doubt about the annoyance now.

"What from? Where did it all start?" insisted Simeon.

"It all started from cosmic dust–" said Edward Plant, but Simeon interrupted him.

"Where did the dust come from?" he asked. Eddy glared at him and said nothing. "Had to come from somewhere. Didn't it?"

"It must have come from a neighboring planet," barked Eddy in a mean, harsh voice, so unlike the tones Jack had always heard him use, the reporter leaned back in surprise.

"Where did the neighboring planet come from?" Simeon Lee prodded. Eddy said nothing, but only glared at the stocky man crouched on his rug, his thick back leaning comfortably against the wood paneled walls.

"Admit it, Mr. Plant," said Simeon, sliding to his feet and facing him. "You don't know how it all started. You just believe it did." Jack, Saul, and even J and P2 looked at Eddy for an answer. Under their searching looks, Eddy knew he couldn't show the

254

dislike he felt toward this man who insisted on showing the weakness of his beloved belief. Edward Plant shrugged carelessly and answered.

"All right, I don't know. I suppose that's something those future generations we are going to bring into being will have to find out. I wonder what else they will be able to–"

"So you just believe it happened as Darwin says it did," Simeon interrupted.

"What are you trying to prove?" Eddy asked with disgust. The left corner of Simeon's mouth moved up slightly in satisfaction. That made it easier. He shifted his weight and looked Plant straight in the eyes. Saul recognized the stance, and knew his friend was getting ready for a fight.

"I'm trying to prove you believe in evolution just the way I believe in Christ, the creator and savior of my soul. But my belief is true and yours isn't. There's no real scientific proof to back either belief, we just believe. And while some call Christian's conceited and wrong for forcing their morals on people who don't believe in their God," (for a single second Simeon met Jack's eyes, and the reporter knew he was thinking of several discussions he had gotten Vincent into) "you PDs murdering people you consider unfit for your new mankind is incredibly more conceited and wrong. That is what you're doing, isn't it?" Silence greeted the question. Simeon answered it himself. "That's what it comes down to; eliminating those who don't fit, or refuse to fit the standards of evolution. Remember Tom Smith? Mr. Madani? Jenny Rhen? How many more, Mr. Plant?" Eddy looked at Simeon. He had been planning on bringing up that part of the plan a little more delicately, but as long as it was out...

255

"You know, you really are an admirable fellow," he said, a smile curving over his face as he studied Simeon Lee. "If you would only give up your silly superstitions and idiotic moral beliefs, you could go far. But to answer your question, yes. That's obvious. Those who are sickly or stupid, or..." he in turn fixed Simeon with his eyes and a sneer, very like J's, cut across his mouth, "those who refuse to give up their superstitions and would hamper the furtherance of mankind, must be…well, done away with. To answer another of your questions, Jack, that is the reason for the hoods and secrecy. The hoods are to protect ourselves from spies in our midst. No matter how much a person finds out they will never see any real faces or learn any full names here.

"The reason for the secrecy is obvious. America (and even the world) is not yet ready to accept this elimination as a needful thing, and if we came out into the open with it now, not only would we be hounded and persecuted for our ideals, but the cause of man's furtherance would be hindered. Now, with man still so caught up in the webs of religious 'rights' and 'wrongs,' mankind would be disgusted by our ways, and would fall deeper into the slum of helping the weaker and encouraging those of lower intelligence. In a few generations (chance and evolution willing) through the schools, books, media, movies, we will be able to get mankind to the point of accepting this elimination. And after that point, mankind will begin to do the elimination and the selecting on their own, from our guidance. But before that glorious point can be reached, we have a whole slew of men and women who are still holding mankind back." Eddy turned suddenly on Simeon, pointing an accusing finger at his head.

"It's men like him, men who carry their superstitious works around with them in their pockets, men who tell the children it is 'wrong' to oppress those weaker than themselves, these are the men who are holding mankind back from the vision I have shown you. Eliminating people like him has become one of the Practicing Darwinist first concerns. Once they are out of the way (or at least thinned out so that there are not enough of them to do anything substantial) there will be no one to stand in the way. The future generations will be educated and molded into those who will work toward the furtherance of mankind, like we've talked about. That is what Operation Weed is about; that is what we have named my brilliant maneuver with the black boxes. It is our first big step in the direction of thinning out the objectors to mankind's furtherance. Jack, did you happen to find out any of the details of our plan, during your investigations?" Jack nodded automatically, his head spinning with two opposite ideas. "I thought you would have. My boxes are designed to spray the strain of deadly virus into the air at the touch of a button. We have placed our black boxes strategically all over the country, where the most troublesome people will catch the virus strain. Mostly in churches, actually. Most of the people dedicated enough to actually be a nuisance attend church weekly. I don't know why it follows, but it usually does. So when we release the bacteria in churches, everyone that attends that church in the next two or three weeks catches it. That way we eliminate thousands, maybe millions, of those who would stand in mankind's way in one fell swoop. It's ingenious, isn't it?"

Jack thought of all the people, people like Simeon and Vincent, good people who had never done the PDs any wrong except to disagree with their philosophy, dying violent deaths from a sickness caught at their own churches. The places they felt safest in this world, probably. He felt ill. How could he have listened so calmly and cheerfully to this man? Of course! To get to the point Edward Plant had been talking about so hopefully, members of that same

257

mankind the PDs were supposedly trying to further would have to die. Jack shuddered as he heard Eddy going on about how all traces of the bacteria would be gone by the time investigations happened, and of course the contraptions were designed to self-destruct, so there would be no evidence of any foul play to be found. Edward Plant sounded so excited, so happy about this Operation Weed. He sounded as happy talking about the destruction of certain mankind as he had talking about his vision for the whole of mankind. Jack wondered for a moment if he was insane. He realized with a horrid feeling that instead Eddy Plant was incredibly sane. Saner then most men in this world. He was only taking a belief to its logical end. Jack felt sicker still when he realized he had believed in that same belief his entire life. He sank into the arm chair, his world collapsing around him.

"And you've actually gotten people to go along with this elimination?" said Saul in a voice as revolted as Jack felt.

"Of course it takes a little work," Eddy answered. "Most people need a little help over the hump religion has put in their path. I've found that this book," Plant leaned over and picked up H. G. Wells' *War of the Worlds* off his desk, "has been very useful in that. I issue it to all those who join our group. Have you read it, Saul?"

"Yes," Saul answered, looking a little perplexed. "It was an exciting read."

"Yes, it is exciting. But it is also useful. It strips away all the preconceptions imbedded by the idea of a God creating man on purpose, and shows man as only the animal he is. It shows again and again that there is no difference between a man and a lower animal, like an ant, or a cat. In fact I have met cats that are more

258

intelligent than some people. Then it only takes a few well-placed words to link the book to the modern world, and you have overcome the silly drawbacks of men about things like 'the sanctity of life.' I usually liken the Martians in Well's book, marching around the countryside in their iron machines, to humans nowadays in their cars. After all, it is a shock sometimes to see a human form emerge out of these iron machines that seemingly move on their own volition. You see? It isn't really very hard to overcome a man's hesitation to eliminate. All you have to do is keep pointing out that the man he is eliminating is no more than a lower animal. Eureka! You have one less person standing in the way of the furtherance of mankind. But I have been talking too long, I see it is already the 20th of February. This is the date we picked to launch our Operation Weed, and it must be done early this morning, before people begin to go about their normal daily activities." Eddy reached into his desk and pulled out a silver wand with one single red button on it.

"Here it is, gentlemen," Eddy almost cooed. "The signal to operate the contraptions must be sent from a good height. A helicopter is programmed to fly up, above this house, and send the signal launching Operation Weed. This button turns the helicopter on and begins its flight. It will do the rest itself." Eddy looked around the room, a triumphant smile on his face. "A new man is going to take the place of this old, pathetic one, gentlemen! But I would like very much, if you, Jack would be a part of this new era." Jack looked up to find Eddy standing over him, his remote in hand.

"Why do you want me?" Jack asked a little huskily.

"You are a perfect paradigm of who we need to start this new man. Handsome, intelligent, talented, healthy– and I hear your wife is as desirable as you. In fact, I want to see you join us so much I'm going to give you the greatest honor of the age. Will you, Jack Lewis

Leason, push this button to launch the new age of man?" Jack suddenly found himself holding the remote that controlled the lives of thousands in his hands and J's machine pistol pointing warningly at his stomach.

15

"America (and even the world) is not yet ready to accept this elimination as a needful thing, and if we came out into the open with it now, not only would we be hounded and persecuted for our ideals, but the cause of man's furtherance would be hindered." Eddy's cultured voice sounded distorted and a little out of place as it flowed from the surveillance cameras in the crowded FBI van.

"You bet it's going to be hindered," Tom Tyler growled, and he headed for the door, touching his earpiece that connected him with the various team leaders out here waiting on the snowy road. "I think we've heard enough. Let's go get them. Tolliver! What's their security looking like?"

"Non-existent, sir," Vincent's bright voice drifted over his earpiece. Tyler's boots scrunched as he landed on the snowy road, but he hardly noticed the sound as he began to trot toward the dark woods. "I knocked it all out."

"When?" Tyler barked. That idiot, if their surveillance was offline, they would know something was up and all attempts at a surprise attack were destroyed!

"About three hours ago," Vincent answered easily. "But don't worry, they haven't noticed yet. I've got an old feed, from three days ago, cycling through their stuff. Apparently February the 17th was a pretty quiet night, only a barn owl has disturbed the scene for the past two hours."

"You're not bad, Tolliver," Tyler commented. "See if you can get their guards called back to the house."

"On it. Oh, and the gate's unlocked for you, head a little west to catch the driveway," Vincent said, and Tyler was grinning as he switched feeds.

"Ryely and Hannson, did you hear that?" he asked. Bob Ryely, in charge of the hundred members of the National Guard out here answered immediately in a firm, military bark. He was well ahead of the FBI, the Guard was going in first. Hannson's feed crackled a little as he answered, but the police chief's voice was steady enough.

"Yes. And we've got your back, sir," Myles Hannson commented. This was hardly a normal night for a state trooper, sneaking through a dark wood with high-powered rifles and bulky bullet-proof vests...but then it wasn't exactly an everyday occurrence for any of them to find a passel of hooded murderers busy under a philanthropist's mansion. A siren sounded distantly, behind the high wall separating Eddy's place from the rest of the woods. Tyler's mini army must have been noticed finally, and armed resistance would be pouring out to meet them. The bloodbath that would follow flew into Tyler's mind, and he began to run, his gloved fingers clammy as they clutched his pistol.

"It's ok, Agent Tyler, it's just me," Vincent's cheerful voice spilled into his ear. It was a little muffled, as if the inventor was eating something. An audible swallow came over his feed, and the young man went on in a clearer voice. "You asked for the security to be recalled to the house, I just activated an alarm down in their tunnel system, and have it running around from alarm to alarm down there, as if it's the invisible man, stuck in their maze. All of Plant's security should be headed that way to make sure Mr.

Invisible's caught." Tyler was about to answer when the trees in front of him broke and he stepped out into the moonlight pouring onto a snowy drive. Various agents moved quietly out around him, and Tyler controlled his breathing, looking for the first wave of their people. The National Guard could be seen as a dark clump of well drilled men gathered in front of the enormous iron gate. Tyler saw a bulky form spin on his heel and look his way, and recognized Ryely.

"Do we go in, sir?" Ryely demanded of him.

A vast, deep boom sounded in the still night. The ground under Tyler's feet shivered, and the trees canopying the mansion's drive suddenly dropped piles of snow as they were shaken at the roots.

"Uh…" Vincent muttered over the feed. Tyler motioned Ryely on, beginning to run over the snowy ground. "Uh, the, um, the computer exploded."

"What computer?" Tyler demanded as he darted into Plant's grounds and deftly began to direct agents and state troopers into the trees, starting to surround the place.

"The main computer, the thing that runs everything in Plant's vast network," Vincent answered. He sounded shocked…no he sounded scared. "It must have been the added stress of trying to track my Mr. Invisible, oops. Things are about to get bad, Tyler. Well, not for us necessarily, we're above ground, but–"

"Tolliver!" Tyler barked, and the inventor forced his thoughts in order and stopped rambling.

"Everything underground is at a standstill at best. At the

worst, the computer's explosion starts a chain reaction and everything down there begins blowing up. And yeah, that second scenario is what I'm seeing. The elevator's not going to work anymore, send your people towards the south section of the mansion, you're about to start getting a flood of smoky, panicked folks pouring out of the underground hideout into the Vermont night. They should be pretty confused and easy for you guys to scoop up, at least. Be careful sending people inside, the mansion is built a little off centered from the PD headquarters, to hopefully avoid caving the roof of the underground section, but it's still probably going to be a little wobbly. The tunnel system is already caving in, Mr. Invisible is caught in a jumble of concrete."

"I'm a little more worried about your real people than about the invisible Mr. Invisible," Tyler stated. "I'm sending the state trooper's back to get the paddy wagons so we can start hauling these panicked people away, you concentrate on getting Lee and the others in your little team out of there." Back in Bertram's solid interior, Vincent's face tightened.

"I would just love to do that," the inventor murmured to no one in particular. "But Judy's feed died when that computer exploded, and so did every other means of communication I have, except a silly little watch that Simeon will only notice if he deliberately thinks of it. Come on guys, realize something's wrong!"

1:23 am, Feb. 20th; Eddy's Study, VT

What do I do? Jack's mind screamed at him. He had always believed in the further evolution of man, it had been a lovely thought. But in solid reality, he would be condemning hundreds of thousands of people to death whose only crime was that they objected to Eddy's vision. But if he destroyed this remote in his trembling hands he would almost certainly die himself, die slowly in agony, a bullet through his stomach. Was he ready for that? The memory of that horrible moment in the truck shot across Jack's mind. Oh heaven, was that endless, helpless nothing the only other choice? A cool, calm voice rose from the back of the room, broke into his panic, and spoke comfort and peace to his soul. Simeon decided it was time to set these people right.

"Before this goes any farther, I would like to say a few things. I've listened to your view on life, Edward Plant, and I've said nothing to negate it. Now I will. Unless you think your view can't hold up to a little criticism," Simeon added as he saw Plant stirring to cut him off; now the philanthropist couldn't without letting everyone in the room think he was afraid the spy could tear his evolution apart. "I could give lots of contrary scientific evidence to the view of evolution, but in the end it all comes down to faith. You choose to believe that your view of life is correct because you don't want to believe in a God of the universe. I know there is a God of the universe (true fact, whether you believe it or not). He is the one who created this world. He created everything, and He called it good. Then He created man and woman and called it very good. But mankind, with everything for him and with a God that walked with him and loved him, chose to shake their fists at the One who had given them life, and broke the only law set down by God. The perfect world broke that day. The world isn't getting better, it's getting worse. Open your eyes, for crying out loud! Mankind isn't evolving into a better state. It's falling into a worse one. And yes, there is an incompleteness, a hole, in man, like was brought up in this conversation a while ago. But it doesn't come from man having higher things to evolve to; it comes from man rejecting his purpose.

265

Every man, woman, and child was created (literally) to serve and honor the God who created them. Any who lives without doing so is an incomplete man, woman, or child.

"I heard you talking about your vision, and I heard my vision too. I heard heaven in your words. It's a land without war, without sickness, without evil, without sorrow, without the stupidest of men, the atheists. I can say that because I used to be as strong an atheist as any in this room, ask Saul Korry. Know what changed me? Wasn't a string of arguments, though those can be useful. It was Jesus Christ, my Lord, who found me in my deepest hurt and met my deepest longings. It was my Father God who, instead of leaving mankind to his own devices, sent His only Son down from heaven to die for the rebellious race. While they were still rebelling. Talk about love. And what a purpose, eh? To serve the one Being in all of creation who is at once all loving, all knowing, all powerful, all justice, the greatest good. And here's what my philosophy looks like practically. I can stand up like this, with P2's gun pointed at my back knowing it will go off at the touch of a finger if he decides I've said too much, and you know what? I'm not in the least worried about it. If I die, I go into that vision of heaven. I go to meet my Savior who has met my needs and loves me more than His own life. And I'm telling you now, Edward Plant, that I will die rather than stand by and watch you kill thousands of those my Savior loves and gave His own life for. I have nothing to lose. I stand here a complete man. Made new, made whole, and I will be made perfect. Will you ever be able to say that of your evolving mankind? Will they ever be perfect? All those God claims will be. Will your evolving humanity ever get rid of death? Even the death of a bug, or a flower? I'm going where there is no pain and death is wholly defeated. Will they ever be happy, killing each other off? God wipes away all the tears of His saints, and sorrow is no more. With evolution as god will there ever be a completeness, or just a steady, empty longing for higher things? I am already complete, even though I still stand in this broken old world. Mr. Plant...your vision's pitiful."

Silence dropped on the room. It was interrupted by the sound of moving water, the clink of a glass, then a sort of 'Pft!' noise. Everyone looked toward the sound. Eddy's wonderful remote stuck up out of Jack's glass of water. A little trail of white smoke drifted off it. No one said anything for a moment. Then J slid slowly to his feet, keeping the muzzle of his gun trained on Jack.

"That wasn't very smart," Eddy said. He sounded disappointed, but not disappointed enough Simeon realized. "I had hoped to make use of you, Jack. But I suppose it can't be helped if you've chosen to stay in the shadow with the other ignorant people. J, will you please see to getting these people out of the way?" A cruel smile flitted over J's face, as he motioned Jack out of the chair to the wall. But Jack didn't move, he sat frozen with panic, watching J's finger begin to tighten on the trigger. Suddenly the gun wasn't in J's hands, it was in Saul's. Jack blinked, how on earth had he managed that? J looked as confused as Jack felt.

"Okay you little weasel," Saul boomed at J, "move to the wall yourself."

"Saul, you too?" Eddy said mournfully.

"If you think I'm going to stand by and watch two innocent men be killed," Saul growled, "you've got another think coming. I ain't that rusty."

"Well, I have a gun too," Eddy said with a long suffering sigh, and brandished a nasty looking pistol at Saul. "Give J back his gun, Saul." Saul studied Eddy for a moment, and did as he was told. J pulled the gun back furiously to strike the big man with the butt, but Eddy clicked his tongue distastefully. The guard lowered the weapon, but remained in a fine temper and the three captives knew it was not going to be pleasant when this J got them out of the dim office and into his own territory. Saul and Jack decided not to tamper with him farther and moved meekly to the wall next to Simeon. The philanthropist reached into his desk drawer. The three men watched in helpless horror as Eddy took out another little remote, just like the one Jack had destroyed.

"I always have two of something important," Eddy explained simply, his finger traveling quickly toward the red button.

"Push that button and I'll shoot!" a new voice interrupted from the shadows by the door and Jack nearly fainted in relief. Judy was there! Plant looked up in shocked surprise as Judy stepped from the shadows, still wearing her hood and holding F28's submachine gun competently[49]. She didn't know why murder was wrong, but after helping foil a massive murder plot, her heart told her it was very wrong and they were very right to have stopped this plot. So far only Christianity explained that feeling to her. And she was proud enough of her husband for making the right choice, something deeper inside her than her reason told her it really was the right choice.

"Well, I think I learned something about dimly lit rooms today," murmured Eddy as he moved his finger away from the button.

"Don't any of you try anything funny," Judy said. "For an

---

[49]Judy's grandfather was an old army veteran who had routinely taken his granddaughter out to practice at the local shooting range, and she was a deadly shot. No one ever bothered her during her college years after she had used her marksmanship to part the hair of a particularly annoying chap who had an orangutan for a pet.

hour now, US agents have been infiltrating this area and beginning to move in and arrest your PDs. If you try to run, you won't get anywhere." Judy spoke with such certainty that no one there doubted her. It didn't hurt that she had just sprung from nowhere like a trap door spider popping out to grab its prey. "You," Judy waved her gun at P2, "over there with the other two. And you," here she waved her gun at J, "drop your gun." J scowled horribly, but he slowly let his machine pistol drop to the ground. He certainly wasn't ready to die. Jack let his breath out in a long sigh of relief. He was beginning to think they might stop Operation Weed and make it out alive when Simeon gave a shout and leapt forward. Before he had crossed half the room, Edward Plant had pushed the button.

"Operation Weed is on its way!" cried the philanthropist joyfully. "I may not live to see the end of it, but there's nothing you can do to stop its beginning."

"Vincent! He pressed the button, the copter's going up! Vincent?" Judy yelled into her Bluetooth. She whipped her hood off, a horrified look on her lovely face. "I can't get through, it's just static." Saul and Jack leapt toward her to try and help find a way through with her walkie-talkie, all three of them furiously hammering out ideas. Simeon swept up Eddy's pistol and kept the three forgotten bad guys covered. He carefully pressed a button on his wrist watch.

"Vince, get your watch," he told the instrument, searching for something on the contraption. He pulled a tiny earbud out of the side and put it in his ear, then snapped a finger for silence and got it. Everyone in the room stood stock still and silent as the short spy listened to a wristwatch. Simeon slipped the earbud back into the watch and pointed at the door. Judy crossed to it in one bound and jerked the heavy oak open. A great wave of heat swept in, seemingly born on a dark cloud of smoke that washed in and began to shift and undulate along the ceiling of the underground office, poking into corners, looking for a way out.

"Computer overloaded and exploded," Simeon stated quietly. "The second lab area is on fire, and the whole underground is collapsing in on itself."

"Oh, and now they tell us?" Jack gasped as he looked over his wife's shoulder to see the PD headquarters going to ruin.

"Vincent couldn't get through on anything but the watch, and I didn't hear him," Simeon answered from by Eddy's desk, using a paper knife to slice his ropes off. No one really heard him. A wall on their left crumbled in on itself, revealing another wall in ruins on the other side.

"I don't suppose the elevator will work now?" asked Jack nervously.

"No," Eddy answered mechanically, watching his underground headquarters collapsing around him. "If the computer's down, the elevator won't work. But there is a stairway, just in case of emergencies. To the left of the elevator."

"What are you all standing there for?" a big voice boomed at the group by the door. They turned to see Saul Korry, his hands full of books and documents from Eddy's desk. "You can stand around and watch the fun of a collapsing building if you want, but I need to get home to my wife. Move over and let me out." Saul barreled through the startled group and started running down the corridor toward the stairway out. Simeon followed, handing more documents and books to Jack and Judy as he passed.

"Move," he said simply, but it was enough. The whole party broke into a run, following the wide back of Saul. It was a long way to go, and everywhere they looked was desolation and ruin. But as he raced along with the others Simeon noted no bodies or survivors mixed up in the piles[50], everyone else must have gotten out. Or be buried too deep to see. They were almost there when a wall collapsed right behind them, showering the group with rubble, and drawing shrieks and shouts from the little band. But the stairway was in sight, and the few burns and bruises acquired were ignored. The lower part had already collapsed on itself, but that didn't seem to worry Saul. He dropped his armful of books and papers, made a gigantic leap, and caught hold of the lowest stair with his fingertips. By the time J had reached him, Saul was already on the stairs, kneeling down to help the others join him. J leapt, grabbed his hand, vaulted onto the stairs and bounded up them without a glance back.

"Up!" Simeon ordered his old co-worker, only just in time. Saul desperately scrambled up the stairway as the bit he had been standing on crumbled into a dusty heap on the blackened ground. The gap between the floor and the stairway was now huge. The rest of the group stopped underneath it and looked up in dismay at the only way out.

"Where's X?" P2 asked suddenly. They looked around and saw that Eddy wasn't with them.

"Forget him, this is his own making anyway," Saul boomed. "Sim, help them up." Simeon quickly dropped his handful of stuff, held his hands into a step, and motioned Judy up with a jerk of his head. She leapt onto Simeon's shoulders, caught Saul's hands, and

---

[50] He had been through enough war-torn scenes to know what to look for. And I will leave it at that, it not being a cheerful subject.

271

was quickly beside him on the stairway, doing her best to help the others. Twenty seconds later only Simeon was left on the ground. He stood still and looked back at the way they had come. Simeon could hear the philanthropist shouting, though he couldn't hear the words through the crackle of the flames, growing higher and lapping closer.

"I know you can make this jump, little bro," Saul broke the silence. "Don't you dare throw your life away running after that evil idiot! Sim, you're not that dumb, we're this close to getting out!" A huge crack broke across the ground fifteen feet from where Simeon stood. The floor on the far side of the room suddenly sank down, leaving a ten foot drop where it had once been even and leaving Eddy on the other side of the drop. The rumble of the collapse died and quiet fell for an instant. Even the ones on the stairs could hear him now. Simeon looked up at the others and they all knew he was going back for him.

"Simeon, leave him!" Judy cried.

"Get up here, Simeon Lee!" Saul bellowed.

"He's a mass murderer!" Jack argued.

"Also a man made in the image of God, a man who still has life," Simeon answered. He grabbed two books, threw them up to Saul, and motioned to Jack and Judy. "Get them out. Saul, there's a young man up there, Vincent Tolliver. Watch out for him for me. Judy, vest."

"Simeon," yelled Jack in horror, "look at those flames on the other side, you can't survive over there!"

"Neither can Plant," answered Simeon with his usual

simplicity.

"Get both of you out, Simeon Lee," Judy called down, her voice a little thick, and threw the vest with the words. Simeon caught his carefully packed utility vest, waved it at the others, and ran toward the drop off. He heard screaming coming from behind him and turned to see Saul and the others scrambling upward desperately as the stairs crumbled below them. An instant later only a heap of rubble was left where the stair used to be, filled so tightly not even a water beetle could have gotten through the pile. Simeon prayed the others had made it up all right, pulled a slender rope out of a pocket, and trotted toward the jagged break. He hooked the rope on a sharp piece of wall that still stood, slid the rope around him, and dropped out of sight on his way to save a murderer.

1:40 am; Outside Eddy's Grounds, VT

Vincent sat in the car surrounded by his heaps of instruments. He felt stunned. The helicopter had been launched, thousands would die, maybe millions, if it wasn't stopped…and Agent Tyler had ditched his earpiece[51], there was no quick way to get a message to him. Vincent was the only one up top who knew, through listening in on that silly little watch he had strapped on Simeon's arm in fun. He saw something stirring on Eddy's grounds

---

[51] Agent Tom Tyler was all right at multitasking, but he wasn't great at it. And as he was trying to direct the multitudinous people under his command and get them to snap up the hundreds of hooded PDs that poured from Plant's headquarters, Vincent Tolliver kept butting in with little silly comments that didn't require an answer, like, "Oh there comes another one out the door, do you see them?" or most frequently, "Thought of any way to get a message through to Simeon yet?" Tyler had cut his feed to the inventor.

(something more than the crowd of PDs pouring from Edward Plant's mansion and being scooped up by the waiting agents). In the left corner of the yard, the one nearest him, something was definitely happening. Vincent grabbed his night goggles and zoomed in on the area. Good night, the ground was splitting in half! That must be where the copter was coming from. And he was the only one who saw it.

"Jeepers!" Vincent shouted to no one in particular as he grabbed some tools and his skates from the back. He vaulted out of the car and strapped on his skates, trying to decide the best way to stop this thing. He couldn't just blow up the helicopter and be done with it, all the boxes would still self-destruct, letting the stuff lose anyway. The only way to stop the contamination was to get into that copter and reprogram those boxes. And Eddy probably had it on a timer, and if he was destroying the evidence the helicopter would be blowing up on its own soon. Vincent stood up and began to zoom down the hill toward the wall around Eddy's grounds. He could see the blades of the helicopter now, it was beginning to rise. The cold wind whipped around his head and his blond hair began to sting his face. Vincent found himself praying desperately that the machine wouldn't blow up while he was in it as he whizzed toward it. *"Well, if I die I go to heaven and there's nothing frightening about that,"* Vincent thought. The wind became frenzied as the sharp blades of the copter whirled it through the night air, getting stronger the higher it rose. It was out of the ground now and moving quick. Too quick, Vincent thought frantically as the inventor watched it already beginning to rise over the wall. The helicopter was a small one, obviously not designed to carry people. Well, that was about to change. Just before he rammed into the wall, Vincent slapped one skate against the other. A slight 'poof' sounded out into the cold Vermont air, and Vincent soared above the gate, shot upward by a high pressure jet of CO2 stored in the bottom of his skates. Vincent threw up his hands and managed to catch hold of one of the runners on the helicopter. He hung there, as the copter rose further into the air.

"Now what, genius?" he muttered to himself.

1:42 am; PD Headquarters, VT

Edward Plant lay among the wreckage of his headquarters, his ankle trapped under a large beam. But even if he had been able to move, his way was now barred by a ten foot, jagged wall. Eddy felt the first waves of real panic creep over him. It was hot down here and getting hotter. The fires must be getting closer. He looked around, his panic growing swiftly into hysteria as he saw no one near, only heat and ruin, and knew this was how he was going to die. Edward Plant felt a scream beginning to rise in his throat as helplessness and panic overwhelmed him. That was when he saw the miracle.

Over a pile of rubble in front of him, the stocky form of Simeon Lee came into view. His face was smudged with dirt and the black grime left behind by the flames. He had ripped off the sleeves of his shirt in this heat, and his bare, muscular arms were crisscrossed with strange frightening scars. An ugly vest covered in bulging pockets hung over his ruined shirt and made him look like a geeky trout fisherman. Right then, Edward Plant had never seen a more beautiful sight.

"Hi," Simeon nodded.

"What are you doing here?" Eddy croaked in amazement.

"Came after you," Simeon answered, moving over to the beam. He reached into a pocket and pulled out a round metallic object that just fit in his palm. He slapped it on the beam right on top of the fallen man and stepped back.

"Cover your head," he ordered Eddy. The philanthropist did, and so missed seeing the small bomb explode. But he felt it. There came a hot searing pain near his ankle, along with a tremendous pressure; but only for a moment, replaced by the delightful knowledge his leg was free. He staggered to his feet and faced his rescuer. Simeon didn't give him the chance to say anything.

"Stairs are gone. Know another way out?" the agent asked. Eddy shook his head miserably and Simeon shrugged. "Guess we'll find one." A dull boom sounded from their left, and the heat rose a little higher. Simeon motioned Eddy to follow him and started to look for a way out. Eight minutes later they were still looking. As they passed by a hallway, a new wave of heat and noise spun out to hit the two men with the physical force of a searing punch, as something else exploded. Simeon and Edward Plant crouched down and covered their faces, waiting to make sure that was all. Again. This was the third time something had blown up near them. This was ridiculous! And every time something exploded, it left another pile of burning rubbish, and every fire added to the heat and the smoke. It was becoming almost unbearable. Simeon reached into a pocket of his vest and pulled out two little masks. He put one on and handed the other to Eddy. That made it a little better. It filtered

276

out the good air from the bad, and kept out most of the smoke. It should last as long as they did in this heat. Simeon moved forward again, searching for a way out. There had to be something! It was maddening, only a little above their heads the cold, February air stirred the trees and brought life and refreshment to those who were up there. But when he looked up all he could see was the blackened dome, crumbled in places to reveal the bare rock above it, dancing in the heat waves that covered everything. Simeon stopped walking for a moment and leaned against a wall that used to be white and was now blackened with soot and smoke.

"Lord," he wheezed through the smoky air, "help." He had been going to say more, but an unexpected sound split the air above his head. For one wild moment, Simeon thought it was the wall above him crying out in pain as it caught on fire. Then the sound came again and he recognized it for what it was; the frightened yowl of a cat. Plant seized his arm and pointed upward. Simeon's smoke reddened eyes followed his finger and saw their way out.

Mr. Tomkins stood above their heads, yowling at them from a hole in the ceiling. And what a hole. An air vent, large enough for a man to crawl through comfortably. If the cat had stayed silent, they would have passed this by, this glorious pathway that led up to the top, to those fresh, cold breezes. Simeon quickly reached into his vest and pulled out a length of rope attached to a slender grapple gun. It looked like a pistol but instead of a normal barrel, it had a long metal tube with a delicate four pronged grapple poking out of the tube. Simeon tied one end of the rope around his waist and handed the other to Eddy, motioning him to do the same. Then he pointed the tube up through the hole and pulled the trigger. The grapple shot up and Edward Plant heard a metallic 'clunk' sound high up in the vent where it landed. Simeon reached into yet another pocket of the vest and pulled out two pairs of the climbing spikes. He tossed Eddy a pair and quickly had the other one on. The philanthropist slid the tools over his shoes a little awkwardly. They felt strange and uncomfortable. He watched as Simeon grabbed the rope in both his hands, placed his feet on the wall, and began to walk up it. Eddy took a deep breath, and did the same. It was much easier than he had thought it would be.

"Hello Tomkins," Eddy murmured as he passed his cat. He grabbed the big, orange tabby and held him with one arm while he climbed with the other. The two men climbed in silence for several minutes, the vent growing darker at every step. The only light came from the fires burning below them and everything above was in total darkness, enhanced by the intense smoke. Simeon abruptly stopped, and Edward Plant felt his stomach churn with fear as he realized why. They had reached the top of their rope. And they still had far to go. If they removed the grapple gadget to shoot it higher, there would be nothing to hold them in the tunnel. They would plunge back down into that fiery horror below them, or they would stay here till the smoke and weariness killed them.

1:50 am; Above Eddy's Mansion, VT

Vincent struggled to get his feet onto the runner of the helicopter and wished he had worked on his chin ups this year. There, he was up. The helicopter was listing dangerously to one side with Vincent on it, but it was still rising. The pilot quickly took a flathead screwdriver out of his pocket and pried the door open. He squeezed inside, and found himself surrounded by so many wires, buttons, instruments, and gadgets that he hardly fit in the midst of it all.

"Feels like home," Vincent muttered to himself. "Pat, are you around?"

"I'm in your pocket, dopey!" Pat's muffled voice came. Vince pulled the machine out of his pocket and grinned at her.

"Sorry, I already forgot I picked you up from where Jack left you by the wall."

"Just tell me what you want me to do, I was having a lovely dream about a place where I was left alone while I napped and I want to go back to it," Pat huffed. Vincent just checked the fascinating urge to find out if his handheld was joshing him or really had the ability to dream, and began to wield her with all the skill gunfighters in the old west used with their pistols. Pat fully and quickly related the findings, and soon Vincent knew all he needed to stop Operation Weed. But he seriously wondered if he would have the time to do it. The helicopter was rising steadily, slower than originally planned with the extra weight Vincent gave it, but still steadily. As soon as it got high enough the signal would go out, and all those boxes would release their bacteria into the air.

"Lord Jesus, help me be in time!" Vincent prayed desperately as he flipped his screwdriver out of his pocket and got to work.

2:08 am; Air vent, VT

279

"What do we do now?" Edward Plant asked. Simeon looked down at the man below him. Bother, Mr. Plant was nearly exhausted. He probably stayed in his study and managed things, leaving the exercise to people like J. Simeon looked up into the blackness above them and tried to estimate the distance they still had to travel. He needed the length of rope and grapple. He had one more gun that worked with this grapple, and he could use it again if he hurried, before the grapple's battery charge ran out completely. He began to work, talking to Eddy as he did so.

"Next step tricky, do just as you're told." Another length of rope, shorter and thin and spidery, swung down from above. "Tie it around you–"

"Mr. Tomkins?"

"Okay, and your cat," Simeon assented, finishing fastening the other end of the spidery rope to his chest in a firm harness. "Tie it, untie the other rope, and let go of the wall." A protesting cry came from Eddy. "Won't fall unless I do." Simeon answered the cry confidently. Edward Plant tried to imagine the competent Simeon Lee making a miscalculation and falling. He couldn't. He did as he was told. As soon as he untied the first rope, he felt himself swing out from the wall, powerless to stop it. He hung there, Tomkins protesting loudly as the cat crouched tied to the little man's chest.

"The first rope is untied," Eddy said, as firmly as he could manage.

"I know," Simeon grunted from above him. For a skinny gent, Plant was heavy. Now came the tricky part. Simeon clung to the grapple with one hand as he untied the rope from around him with the other, and retracted the rope and grapple into a different gun.

Now there was nothing holding either of the men up but some flimsy spikes and Simeon's grip on the grapple. Simeon refused to think about that uncomfortable fact as he quickly fished into another of his pockets. He brought out a round, white object. It looked like a candle, but it wasn't. It was a self-adhesive stick of dynamite, designed to light the moment it adhered to something. For a moment, Simeon considered how crazy he was to use dynamite to hold onto a wall, but it was the only thing he had that would suffice to keep him from falling back down the vent. He squared his jaw, and stuck the stick on the wall.

A hiss started up in the quiet air vent, and with it a light sprung up from the fuse of the dynamite. Eddy watched in amazement as Simeon moved in such a rush there was no way to follow it in the dim light. He grabbed the dynamite and let go of the grapple. The grapple gun came off the wall, Simeon pointed it up into the shaft, and fired it. Plant heard the same 'clunk' of metal on metal from somewhere up the vent, and at the same time he felt himself jerked upward, drawn swiftly by whatever wonderful gadget Simeon had just fired into the darkness. A sense of exhilaration came over the philanthropist as he rose swiftly into the air, farther from the burning mass below him. But before he rose more than a few yards, a huge noise rent the quiet air. A painfully bright light lit the vent, and a piercing roar enclosed the two men and the cat. Plant felt a wave of furiously hot and powerful air hit him from below, and he was pushed upward by it, more forcefully then he was drawn by the rope tied around him. Half a second later, the noise was gone, the light had died, and only a burning heat remained. Simeon saw the grapple as he rose above it, and just managed to grab it before the light died. The two men and the cat hung suspended in a dark, stifling hot air vent.

"Where's that heat coming from?" Eddy coughed shakily. Simeon looked below them and didn't answer. His charge was better off without knowing. A glow had started underneath them from where the dynamite had gone off, and it was creeping toward them. The small fires below had joined and become a raging inferno. The blast from the dynamite had added to it, and now the flames were licking up the side of the vent, greedy for the bit of air it felt through it. Eddy made the mistake of looking down. Both men stared at the rising flames.

"Quick, shoot the grapple again!" Eddy cried at Simeon.

"Can't," answered Simeon. "Has to recharge."

"So we're stuck here?" Eddy almost shrieked, sweat pouring from his brow as the flames came closer, looking for air. Simeon took a firmer grip on the grapple gun and dug his spikes fiercely into the side of the vent. Plant's rope was cutting into him, and his strength was ebbing fast. His fight with the river a few days ago hadn't been forgotten by his body. And he wasn't as young as he once was. Simeon looked down at the flames, then he looked up. A dim square of silver moonlight marked the end of the vent, and as he stared at it a waft of air stirred his hair. But it was too far. He couldn't climb that length quickly enough to get away from the growing flames. They would be cooked while only halfway up. But it was so close... A wild idea came into the head of the ex-CIA man as he looked at that exit. The grapple gun had pulled them up, but the force from the dynamite had pushed them farther. And that had only been one stick. Simeon reached into a pocket of his vest and pulled out three more of the self-adhesive sticks of dynamite.

"What are you thinking?" Eddy asked, and he didn't bother to try and hide the fear in his voice. "If you set off more dynamite, the

282

flames will follow faster, and we'll die that much faster!" Simeon weighed the three sticks in his hand, considering. He looked down at the man hanging below him.

"If we're going to die anyway, Edward Plant, let's at least have a wild ride on the way out." Simeon pulled two silvery blankets from one of his copious pockets and tossed one to Eddy. "Wrap around you and your cat. Heat resistant. Might help." Simeon wrapped the other one around himself, breathed a prayer for protection, and flung the three sticks of dynamite down into the rising flames below. A huge sound enfolded them. Simeon swung his feet from the wall and let go of the grapple gun. He found himself enveloped in something so noisy, hot, and powerful, it was too much to register. It made him feel like chaff thrown in the fire he had read about. He felt himself hit something large and metal, and his senses began to darken. As he dropped into unconsciousness, Simeon realized he had just been flung against the outer covering on the vent. His body dropped and hit something very hard, and he knew he was out in the Vermont air. But...why did he still feel so hot? His last fleeting thought was a sad certainty that death wasn't going to be cheated out of its prey tonight. Vincent came to mind, and Simeon realized he was very sad to be leaving the messy young inventor alone again as he dropped into complete unconsciousness.

16

A deep, rolling rumble came from Eddy's gardens and Vincent glanced out the tiny window of the little helicopter.

"What was that?" the handheld asked out loud.

"Pat, I think I've got it," Vincent said instead of answering. "It's one of two wires here, if I cut the right one it disarms the boxes."

"What about the other one?"

"That will set off the boxes and explode the helicopter."

"Well, which is it, idiot?"

"I haven't the faintest idea. Do you like black or green better, Pat?"

"Vincent, be serious! There has to be some way to know, think of it."

"Not that I know of. I've been praying over it for a while, but I'm out of time. I pick... green," Vincent held the wire gingerly and snipped it in half, cringing in the tight interior of the little copter. Nothing happened. He blew out a pent up sigh of relief and felt his whole body sag with the sudden knowledge it was over, and he was still alive.

"Thank you Jesus!" he murmured earnestly. Pat cheered with very unladylike volume as she rested in Vincent's hand. The inventor held her carefully and squirmed out of the little helicopter door to drop onto the roof of Eddy's mansion. He landed feet foremost, blond hair flying wildly in the wind, a Texas cheer breaking from him. Vincent glanced down at the front of the mansion as he landed and his delight rose higher. Jack and Judy were stumbling out, along with a scholarly looking guy and a hulking fellow that must be Saul Korry. They had made it! But before the delight had a chance to settle in, Vincent glanced back at the door and realized no one else was coming. His new roommate wasn't with them.

Simeon hadn't come out. Vincent's first thought was a denial that flooded him. No! He had just been getting to know the gentle, mighty Simeon. Life had been going back to sweet and interesting and good with Simeon Lee in his life. He couldn't be gone already. Not already! Simeon Lee was going to come home tonight, be a friend who would stick up for him, and tell him if he was wrong, and just be there to laugh and cry with. Vincent's breath seemed to choke him suddenly, and he forced himself to calm down, willing himself not to give up hope yet. And promising himself if Simeon rose from out of that collapsing underground hideout he would ask him flat out to stick around, and pray he said yes. What had happened down there?

He jerked a little yellow block out of a cargo pocket, along with a little circular disc. The disc went snapped on the block, he shoved his earphones into the jack, pointed the disc at the group at the front of the mansion, and flipped his gadget on. One of the FBI agents had come up to them and Jack was explaining what had happened. Jack's strong, descriptive words filled the inventor's ear as he told what they had left behind. Vincent felt his throat begin to constrict as he listened to his friend relate Simeon Lee going back

285

for Edward Plant, the man who had tried to kill him and thousands of others, just as the stairs began to collapse. He opened his mouth to try and turn his sorrow into a prayer, but the words never came out.

A great noise rent the air, a larger version of the rumble he had heard earlier. The ground shook underneath him and Vincent fell flat on the roof from the trembling of the mansion. Down on the grounds he saw a large metal grate shoot into the air, followed by two silver somethings and a host of flames licking out of a hole in the ground. Vincent whipped his goggles on and zoomed in on the area. One of the silver somethings flung off the silver and was revealed as Edward Plant. But instead of running away from the flames, as Vincent had assumed, he ran toward them. Of course, the other silver thing! Yes, that was it, Plant was dragging it away from the flames now onto a round circle of concrete, and Vincent could see it was Simeon. They were out! But those flames were too high. They were licking at the grass and shrubs around the two men faster than they could move. Good heavens, they were going to be surrounded by flames before they could get out. They'd be cooked like smoked chickens! Vincent leaned heedlessly out over the edge of the mansion's roof, yelling and bellowing to try and get someone to notice him, and gesticulating wildly at the wall of flame. Someone had to be able to help them!

2:24 am; Eddy's Grounds, VT

"Simeon Lee, please wake up!" Edward Plant cried. He was kneeling beside the still Simeon with Mr. Tomkins crouching beside him. They were out in the open air now, but not much better off. The flames had followed them out, rushed on by the added explosives and the longing for oxygen. They were all around them now, leaving only the little round patch of concrete Eddy had poured as a gazebo foundation. What were they to do now? The flames were growing higher, not lower. Between the heat and smoke they couldn't live for long here. Their masks were even gone.

Simeon stirred and coughed. Edward Plant helped him sit up, but there was nothing else to do. Simeon blinked and tried to get himself to work. His head was roaring and the world around him spun and tipped in a truly sickening manner. He must have banged into that heavy vent headfirst, and it had only been a few days since that bullet had creased his scalp. The flames licked out at them, and the scent of singed hair and skin merged with the incessant smoke that sapped their life. Simeon tried to stand, but the asphyxiation and concussion were too strong for him. Flames roared around them, reaching eight feet into the air, and higher in many places. The way they danced and crackled suddenly looked to Simeon like evil natives laughing manically over a heathen sacrifice. He had been through that in Brazil ten years ago, and the memory made him shudder. But it also made him remember he had made it out of that situation only by trying the ridiculous and hoping for a break. He opened his eyes again and forced them to focus on the dancing fire. These flames might be high, but it was possible they were still a thin wall. He staggered to his feet, his strong hand wrapped around Plant's collar, dragging the philanthropist with him. The terrified X still clutched his petrified cat and the animal yowled and screamed in horror. Simeon dimly heard Plant screaming and felt him struggling to get out of his grasp as he lunged for the wall of flames, but the agent held him fast and ran.

287

The heat was incredibly intense as it engulfed him, and Simeon knew he was burning. His clothes were on fire, his hair crackled, and he could feel his skin blistering and blackening. The stench was horrible, and the pain almost too high to register. But then it was over. He was out of the flames, onto a gravel path and able to feel the cool Vermont breeze. Simeon gave a final heave, flinging the slight Edward Plant farther away from the licking flames, and rolled toward him to put out the fires eating up his clothes. Simeon came to a dizzying rest under a perfectly trimmed pine tree, and let himself lay there. He felt feet pounding toward him, and was vaguely glad of it as he let his blistered, bruised body drop into darkness again. Oh, his head hurt.

3:12 am; Eddy's front porch, VT

"I'm fine, Vincent," Simeon said again. He kept having to say that to one or another of his friends. He had been looked over by a paramedic, his head was bandaged, and his burns tended to. But he must look awful because the four people around him kept insisting he was on his death bed and refusing to let him get up and leave. And so Simeon, Vincent, Saul, and the Leasons sat on the steps of Eddy Plant's mansion, watching the PDs being packed off to jail to await their sentence. The five people on the steps were being systematically ignored by all the state troopers and FBI agents. Obviously orders had gone out that these ones were not to be noticed. But one tall, well-built, older man (older then Simeon and Saul by at least fifteen years, Jack decided) approached the group and stood in front of Simeon.

"You look awful," he said.

"Thank you, Mr. Gibbs," Simeon said.

"A lot better than when you came back from that last fiasco of the Carmichael life," his superior shrugged. Saul snorted and Mr. Gibbs grinned at the two men. "But I guess that doesn't take much effort, does it Saul? Anyway, well done Parabaloni. I knew I had a good idea when I enlisted you and Mr. Tolliver in my wild idea. And you, Saul, that was a brilliant stroke bringing out those books, only you and Lee would think of that in the midst of an exploding, burning underground hideout. They'll convict every one of these people of attempted murder, probably some of full blown murder. But you missed the list of who was in this group."

"What?" Saul rumbled. "Are you saying you don't know who out there in this big old world is a Practicing Darwinist?"

"That's about the size of it," Mr. Gibbs answered as he sat down next to his two retired agents.

"But you won't be able to prosecute them," Judy put in, smothering a yawn.

"It's a lot worse than that, sweetheart," Jack murmured worriedly. "That means they'll still be out there, doing their old jobs with their old ideas."

"You guessed it," Mr. Gibbs sighed. "The hoods and letters were actually very clever even if they looked ridiculous. No one in the group knew anyone else in the group by anything but a letter, and most of them never even saw a face. We can't get a list of names by asking those we've captured. But cheer up. Most of the PDs were down there, helping launch their first big operation. The number

289

still at large shouldn't be big enough to make much of a difference."

"I disagree," Vincent said, settled close to Simeon's bruised form. "It only takes one man with an idea to make a difference." As if on cue with this comment, Edward Plant was led past toward a police car parked on the left of the group. He still held his petrified cat, and carried himself with a puzzled air, as if he was trying hard to grasp what had happened. Simeon watched them go by, studying the philanthropist. They had managed to save each other from that inferno, but Mr. Plant was hardly out of trouble. Simeon stood up and walked toward Edward Plant and his escort, his feet scrunching heavily on the gravel walkway. He reached them just as they stopped by the police car. The two men stood in the cold February air and looked at each other in silence for a moment. The thin Eddy looked miserable and lost. Simeon pulled out his new testament and exchanged it for the big, orange cat. Edward Plant looked at the cat beginning to relax and purr in Simeon's burnt, scarred arms, then down at the little Bible in his hands. He nodded slowly, and slipped into the back of the patrol car. Simeon stood in the driveway holding Mr. Tomkins and watching the patrol car slide out the gates with its lone passenger in the back. He felt suddenly cold, tired, alone, and very old. A warm hand dropped gently on his shoulder and Simeon looked up to see Vincent, his blond hair and attire wilder than ever.

"It's his own choices Simeon, and what happens to him now isn't our worry. You made the right decision going back for him. Oh, incidentally, I don't think I've ever felt quite so relieved as when you came back out of that burning hole. Always come back, okay?" Vincent's tone was an urgent plea, and Simeon knew the young man meant it. He nodded, hope and joy at being asked for such a promise flooding in, pushing out the cold, and making his eyes wet.

"As much as is in my power, I promise I will always come back for you," Simeon answered steadily, not allowing how moved he was to show. He was rewarded by a happy smile from the inventor.

"Thanks. Let's go home," Vincent said. A wide smile spread over his friend's face. "What's with the grin?"

"Nice to have one to go to. It's been a while."

"Yeah," Vincent smiled down at him. "It's nice to have someone to go home with." Simeon just nodded and walked toward his car, stroking the big, singed cat as he moved.

Jack stood up stiffly to follow, as he saw their ride readying to leave, but then he noted how still Saul and Mr. Gibbs were as they watched the newly formed Parabaloni. Mr. Gibbs stood grinning, his hands in his pockets and a very pleased, rather paternal look on his face. Saul's expression was a bit harder to read, being a little mixed. Jack saw excited hope and pleasure fighting with a distinct worry on the big man's face.

"What's up?" the reporter asked.

"That Vincent Tolliver had better be a good man," Saul growled, more to Mr. Gibbs than in answer to Jack's query. "I might just kill him if he breaks Sim's heart again."

"He is a good man, Saul," Mr. Gibbs smiled, rocking happily on his heels. "I knew I had a good idea teeming those two up."

11:23 am, Feb. 22nd; Crossview Church, Mayhill, NM

"How firm a foundation, ye saints of the Lord,

"Is laid for your faith in His excellent word!

"What more can He say then to you He has said,

"To you who to Jesus for refuge have fled?"

Jack's voice faltered at the words, even with Vincent singing so happily and firmly in his ear, and Judy holding his hand on his other side. How firm a foundation! What a beautiful thought. A foundation. Jack had something to stand on now, something to base his life on. Or what was left of it. All those years he had wasted on trivial things that wouldn't last more than his lifetime. But no more! He had Jesus as his refuge now, and he was going to serve Him as wholeheartedly as a fallen man could. There was more than enough of his Savior to fill any void, no matter how large. God was there wherever the reporter looked, and he couldn't understand how he had missed it his whole life. Jack sent his voice intertwining beautifully with his wife's light soprano[52]. He gripped Judy's hand tighter, and felt a little squeeze in answer. She was here, ready to help him up when he fell and search the scriptures with him. Jack saw a beautiful life laid out before him, and stood a little taller

---

[52] He had first met Judy in a college choir class, though Jack wasn't actually there as a part of the class, but had ducked in to get away from the mob of furious gangsters hunting for his blood after he had been seen snooping on their illegal snail-racing activities for the college paper. He had come back as an official member of the choir next week and bribed the baritone who stood next to Judy with free football tickets, in order to take his place. Judy let him stay, and things had developed nicely after that.

because of it.

"When through fiery trials your pathway shall lie,

"My grace, all sufficient, shall be your supply;"

Judy sang the words and thought immediately of the wall of flames she had seen when she jerked Eddy's office door open, only two days ago. She had been terrified, and had prayed a prayer for safety and strength in that instant. Judy had decided she liked a world where people were brave and good and could explain why, liked it much better than the questions the alternative left open. It had been her very first prayer, and it had been answered. Judy thought how wonderfully comforting and happy it was to trust in this God who had finally claimed her soul. She glanced at Jack and saw him studying the words in the hymnal with a thoughtful look and smiled, singing louder than ever.

Saul sang the words beside his life-long friend and also thought of the flames. But they were the flames he had watched Simeon Lee running toward to save a murderer.

"The flames shall not hurt you; I only design

"Your dross to consume and your gold to refine."

Saul thought of past days; the last time he had sung beside Simeon had been about twenty-eight years ago in London. In those days Simeon would have acted very differently than he had two days ago. Saul sighed, and prayed the Lord would refine him as he had his friend.

"E'en down to old age all my people shall prove

"My sovereign, eternal, unchangeable love;

293

"And when hoary hairs shall their temples adorn

"Like lambs they shall still in my bosom be borne."

"Old age, and hoary hairs," Simeon thought to himself as he sang, *"that's me."* But by the grace of God and faith in His sovereign will, he had still been able to stop a group of crazed murderers and save thousands of lives. And yes, even a few souls had been saved from eternal damnation. His life had been awfully lifeless before he had trusted God enough to take the plunge back into spy work. And how hopelessly lonely he had been without that never-leaving love of his Jesus. No matter what came and went, he knew he would always be loved now, carried gently like a lamb in the bosom of ceaseless Goodness. Simeon bowed his head and thanked his Savior for waking him up and driving him into His service. And for the young, cheerful man he got to drive home with this afternoon and who would fill the extra chair at dinner.

Vincent Tolliver sang the old hymn with more relish than usual, and that was saying something for this young man. He was thinking of how lonely and useless, and almost desperate, he had felt only a few weeks before. And now he stood here, next to a good man who would drive home with him today and be around to talk to, and was as much in love with his Savior as he was. And he had just helped foil an evil murderer and save hundreds of thousands of lives. He was actually making a difference in God's world. Vincent smiled as he came to his favorite verse, and he sang the promise of God with a full heart. Saul, Jack, and Judy were even included in the promise now, and it even held true for his parents and would for all eternity. God was so good!

"The soul that on Jesus has leaned for repose,

"I will not, I will not desert to his foes;

"That soul, though all hell should endeavor to shake,

"I'll never, no never, no never forsake[53]."

11:23 am, Feb. 22nd; Vermont Correctional Facility, VT

The cell was dark, but there was still enough light to read. Edward Plant was making use of it. Simeon Lee's little New Testament was open on his lap. It had been open more than closed since it had reached Eddy's hands, and he was beginning to understand why a man would go back to almost certain death to save another. Even another who had insulted and tried to kill him.

Edward Plant laid the New Testament on his cot, slipped to his knees on the hard floor and folded his hands in prayer, giving his soul to the One he had fought against all his life.

A guard passing by his cell a few moments later was surprised to hear tears of remorse and joy coming out of the cell of a mass murderer.

5:34 pm, March 1st; 57a Y Street, Fairfax VA

---

[53] "How Firm A Foundation," by R. Keene (probably). We do know it's from Rippon's *Selection of Hymns* from the year 1787.

Vincent sat on Simeon's couch petting Mr. Tomkins as the cat purred and shed on his lap. Doing nothing for a moment felt very nice. Simeon slid his favorite copy of Mrs. Browning's poetry into one of his moving boxes and shot a glance at his young friend. Vincent looked happy. So was he. Life was very good right now.

"How's the bruises?" Simeon asked.

"That's a funny question," Vincent grinned. "They were purple last time I checked. Are all judo lessons that rough?"

"Um...yes," Simeon answered with sarcastic thoughtfulness at a foolish question. Vincent chuckled and stood up to follow Simeon down the hall to pack up the last room.

"Judy's quit her lawyer job now," Vincent commented.

"Really?" Simeon asked, flipping on the light to the only room in the duplex he had bothered to personalize and getting another box ready.

"Yup. Jack says she's been making him favorite dishes all week, and even trying her hand at bread. They sounded really happy. But guess what, he couldn't sell his story."

"Why?" Simeon asked, pointing at the eight pictures on the wall in a silent request.

"Too pro-Christian and anti-evolution apparently," Vincent answered, handing down the pictures. "Jack was pretty mad. He's still looking for someone else to buy it, but he says he's probably going to have to start his own newspaper to get it published."

"Should."

"Yeah, that's what I told him," Vincent said. He paused at the two pictures with dogs. "They were both very pretty. And very different." Simeon glanced at Vincent, then motioned to the grinning corgi.

"Molly was brilliant and sweet. Played nurse when I got sick, even trained herself to hand me the aspirin bottle when I dropped it. I used to drop it just to watch her pick it up." He motioned to the other picture, with a basset hound staring moodily out. "Tried it on Diogenes once. Ate the whole bottle, lid and all. I had to rush him to the emergency clinic to have his stomach pumped." Vince laughed and handed over the pictures. The two men went back to packing up the armory, and the inventor suddenly realized what had just happened. The request not to pry into Simeon's past had been lifted, he was accepted a little farther into this good man's life. The inventor was grinning as he grabbed more ammo boxes and tossed them to his boss, but he wisely chose not to comment on his realization.

"Saul's back working," Simeon said. "Called yesterday to say he had picked up a Bible at a bookstore."

"Good," Vincent said. Simeon grunted in acquiescence. "Is Mrs. Korry any better? And how is Jon holding up, now that he knows about it all?"

"She's okay now Saul's home. Jon chewed his dad out for keeping him in the dark, and is helping now."

"Good for him, I like him better for it. Well, I guess he shouldn't really chew his dad out, but that would have been my first reaction too," Vincent said, and Simeon nodded contentedly. The two friends finished packing up what could be boxed in the

297

room, and Simeon stood surveying it for a moment. Vincent pointed at a tall pillar of black metal with wires drifting off it.

"What's that?" he asked, expecting to hear it was the latest in ground to air missile launchers.

"Looper. For music," Simeon said.

"You play music? Keen. Your voice is certainly good enough for it, it reminds me of a guy named Aimeri Carmichael Mom and Dad used to listen to a lot." A smile twitched over Simeon's face and Vincent had the idea there was more behind it then the compliment[54]. "I enjoy the piano, we should jam when we get the chance." Simeon nodded happily and flipped out the light with his elbow as he carried the last box to stack in the living room. That was it. Everything he wanted to keep was in the four small boxes by the front door or large enough to wait for the little truck he had ordered for next weekend.

"So what now?" Vincent asked, a little tentatively. "Did I qualify? Have I driven you nuts yet? You've promised you'll stick around and I'm holding you to it you know, whether I get to work with you or not. Do I? And are you satisfied with New Mexico, or sad you're leaving this home?"

"Never was home, Vincent. I just lived here. Like I've just lived hundreds of other places on this globe." Simeon stroked the big cat shedding on his couch and dropped a hand on the eccentric

---

[54] He was right. Aimeri Carmichael was a former alias of Simeon Lee. He had grown very famous and stinking rich under that name before giving it up to save the millions of people in London from being bombed out of existence, having been given a very hard ultimatum by a very nasty man – But there isn't time here to go into Simeon Lee's quiet sacrifice of turning himself in. The resulting next six months of his life had been hard enough to take two years to recover physically from, and even sent him to a mental institution for a brief time.

young man's shoulder. "Now this is home. New Mexico's a fine place to keep it." The Parabaloni leader picked up the cat and headed to the door. "Qualify isn't the right word. Superb, better."

"Dude, I've failed every test you've given me so far!" Vincent laughed incredulously.

"Tests are for learning, not passing. Character is what counts. If you want the job... lots more bruises, heartache, no sleep, stress levels you can't even imagine yet... Well, yours if you want it."

"Hot dog, yes!" Vincent grinned, slipping out the door so Simeon could lock up. "Thanks, Simeon. Let's stay in dry old New Mexico then and wait for another mission, and you can give me more bruises and watch me fumble more lessons, especially the juggling ones you're making me do. Just two slices of lunchmeat, waiting to change the world for Jesus Christ!"

"Two slices of...?" inquired Simeon, unlocking his car door and slipping into the driver's seat.

"Sure. We are the Pair-a-baloni, aren't we?" the inventor laughed. Simeon groaned and tossed the purring Mr. Tomkins at Vincent's head.

Author Bio

I'm so excited you read my book! I love to hear feedback, please leave me an Amazon review and tell me what you think. Don't forget to check out my website, catherinegrubensmith.com, for news on my latest books! You never know when the writing itch will hit and a new story will shoot from my laptop to your hands.

I know you could be reading a good story instead of a long explanation of myself, so let me keep this brief. I live in the middle of Texas, and grew up mostly in a dusty town in the southern New Mexican desert. (Yes, New Mexico is a part of the United States, and no, I am not a missionary, and yes, you can drink the water.) It is my delight and privilege to be a housewife to a wonderful man, mother to our little boy, an editor at Seasoned Words Editing, and an Earl Gray connoisseur. Another of my constant activities is trying to keep our dogs, Beatrice, Lynette, Buddy, and Biscuit, from terrorizing the house and neighborhood with their determination to be always underfoot and hungry. (The work of a dog lover is never done.) When not writing, reading, chasing children or dogs, I can be found baking, hiking, or possibly broad sword fighting with my older brother. If you want a fuller explanation of me, go and read Psalm 30. The heart and purpose of my life can be found there, especially in the last two verses.

Series by Catherine Gruben Smith:

Parabaloni Series

Dreaded King Saga

Fairytales of Deweot

Made in the USA
Middletown, DE
29 April 2019